A Nate to Remember

(A Poppy Cove Mystery)

by

Barbara Jean Coast

For information, email **Cozy Cat Press**, cozycatpress@aol.com or visit our website at: www.cozycatpress.com

COZY CAT
P R E S S

ISBN:1939816653

Printed in the United States of America

Cover design by Paula Ellenberger
http://www.paulaellenberger.com/

1 2 3 4 5 6 7 8 9 10

Acknowledgements

Living the writer's life is such an adventure. Many days are spent living in one's head, and, especially for us, in a different time. There are so many muses that help us get in the mood for telling the Poppy Cove tales, and we give special thanks to Rita Cagle and her Living Fifties Fashion website which inspires such glamour, Dave Smith and his Retro Rumpus Room group that gives us goofy chuckles, and John Pizzarelli and Jessica Molaskey's Radio Deluxe which gives the perfect musical touch of class from all eras.

We feel so honored to have the love of our friends and families, the warm support of the cozy mystery readers and bloggers, and the encouragement of the Cozy Cat Press gang—Editor and Publisher Patricia Rockwell and our fellow writers.

Warm Regards to All,

Andrea Taylor and Heather Shkuratoff
(AKA Barbara Jean Coast)

You are cordially invited
to the Inaugural
Santa Lucia
Fine Art Exhibition

Waterfront Beach
Santa Lucia, California

Sunday, April 20, 1958
10 am to 4 pm
All are Welcome

CHAPTER ONE

"Ooh, I like that!" Daphne Huntington-Smythe exclaimed. She, as well as most of the Santa Lucia social set, had turned out for the inaugural art show on the beach.

Margot Williams took a look at the painting that her friend and Poppy Cove business partner was analyzing from an arm's length away. She tilted her head in the opposite direction of her companion. "Hmm."

"What?" Daphne questioned.

"It's different," Margot replied, diplomatically.

"It's bold."

"That's true." Margot pursed her lips, thinking about the work of art in front of them. It was an oil abstract with large, interlocking shapes in different hues and colors, ranging from blue to red to green and layering and floating upon each other, a very new style. She wasn't sure what she made of it and was a little surprised to see Daphne so enthralled with it. "I didn't think this was your style."

Daphne laughed. "Me neither. It actually reminds me of my dress!" She looked down at herself. She was wearing a new spring frock done in an atomic print fabric. Margot had created it for their shared design atelier, Poppy Cove, which was now three years old. The dress was sleeveless with a fitted V-necked bodice and a slim silhouette that just skimmed above the knee. It was in a bright turquoise cotton that had a white hash-marked overall detail, and red, blue and black satellites throughout the fabric. The new fun prints, of which they had a great selection, had proven to be very popular that spring.

Daphne played with her turquoise bauble necklace while musing out loud. "Hmm, I never really thought about what kind of art I liked until the show. I mean, we have some family portraits and nice landscapes that mother picked out to go with the furniture. They were always just sort of there." She tossed her blonde curly locks, biting on the arm end of her sunglasses, studying the painting from a different angle. "What do you think?"

"More importantly, what does it make *you* think?" Daphne was startled to hear a new voice in the crowd. She turned around to see a man, middle-aged, balding, but with longish hair, tied in a ponytail. He was dressed in a loose-fitting, paint-stained smock, blue denim jeans and leather sandals. He was not like anyone she'd ever seen in her fair Santa Lucia.

Before answering his question, she looked over to Margot, who shrugged with a bemused expression. Nervously, Daphne licked her lips, cleared her throat, and looked around before giving her reply. She relaxed her eyes, then widened into a full-face grin. "I see the ocean! Our harbor, to be exact."

"Ah, exactly." The man stepped back with a sense of satisfaction.

"Really? Where?" Daniel Henshaw, Daphne's latest steady beau, stepped closer to the picture, squinting and tilting his head.

"Here." She pointed out all the shapes, narrating her newfound recognition. "That's the water. The green triangle? That's a sailboat; the red's the sun."

Daniel scratched his head, running his fingers through his wavy blonde hair. "What's this yellow rectangle then?"

"That's the beach!" she exclaimed.

The stranger stepped between them and put his arm around her shoulder. "Someone who appreciates my work."

"You're the painter?" Daphne asked.

He nodded. "Adonis."

Daniel could not hold back his smirk at the man's name. Adonis looked Daniel over, top to bottom before carrying on. "I am Greek. It is a good Greek name."

Daniel took the friendly approach and extended his hand. "Don, I'm Daniel. Dan to my friends."

The artist took a closer step towards Daphne and folded his arms. "Adonis," he repeated his own full name firmly.

"Right. Well, good to meet you, Adonis. Detective Tom Malone, Santa Lucia Police Department." The strikingly handsome friend of Dan's, and Margot's main squeeze, stepped in to remind everyone that he had the power to keep it all friendly. Even in his plaid madras shirt and chinos, he cut a commanding figure.

Adonis sniffed and turned his head to Daphne. "So you like my work, do you?"

She nodded, wanting to make the mood light again. "Yes, especially this one." She indicated the one right in front of her.

He took it off of its display easel. "It's yours," he said as he gave it to her.

"Oh, no. I couldn't possibly take it." Daphne looked around at her companions and blushed. "It's your hard earned work, I'd be happy to pay for it."

"No." He shook his head. "My gift."

Daniel's jealousy was getting the better of him. He was looking steamed. Tom held him back by his arm, and indicated to his friend he needed to keep his cool.

Daphne put her arm on Adonis's and insisted, for many reasons. "No really, I couldn't."

"Oh, why not?"

She smiled and shrugged, wanting for the moment to be over.

"Well, if you're sure." He set the painting back on the easel. He slipped his hand in his pocket and pulled out a card. "If you change your mind, you can come by my studio."

She moved closer to take his card and as she did, he leaned in and whispered in her ear. "You could model for me, too. Your shape is a classic beauty."

"Yes, well," she stammered.

Dan and Tom both decided it was time to steer their girls into a new direction. As the two couples walked away, Adonis kept eyeing Daphne as they moved on to other artists. "What did he say to you?" Dan asked as he glared at Adonis.

"Oh, I don't know; I really didn't hear him," Daphne demurred. She wasn't sure why she'd focused in on the paintings by that particular artist. She felt they stood out like a sore thumb, if she was honest with her thoughts. And to further her honesty, she privately wondered what it would be like to be an artist's model. She, as many members of her family had sat for portraits, but she was pretty sure that's not what he'd meant. Daphne decided to shrug it off and just enjoy the company of her friends. She wouldn't call him anyway, or would she? The more she tried not to consider calling him, the more she felt curious.

All around them were people they knew—friends, including Poppy Cove clientele, and the general social set of their town, Santa Lucia, California. There were exhibits of all kinds—statues, other paintings, photographs, sculpture, pottery, to name a few. The art show had been organized by the mayor's wife, Elaine Stinson, who was an accomplished watercolorist in her own right. Her work was much more traditional and very popular among their crowd.

Not only was Elaine's exhibit populated with spectators and buyers, but as usual, Loretta Simpson, the *Santa Lucia Times* Society Editor and her photographer, Jake Moore, were on the job, getting the scoop on the events and causing a human traffic jam. "Did you get a shot of that one? How about this one? Make sure you get that, too. I want lots to choose from. And don't forget the crowd shots, either. Get plenty of pictures and some close ups, too." As Loretta darted about in her usual bird-like manner, Jake calmly followed with his camera lens, capturing everything in his vision. She chased down the woman of the hour and proceeded to ask her questions about the event and her artwork.

As the Mayor's wife, Mrs. Stinson was involved in many community events and charities, such as the Santa Lucia General Hospital Auxiliary Committee. The more she learned about the people and how they lived in her town, the more she wanted to help. The group listened to Elaine being interviewed by Loretta, who was writing furiously on her steno pad while pushing her cat-eye glasses up her nose intermittently. Elaine explained to her reporter friend how she had the idea to host such an event, with all the artists donating a modest percentage of their sales to the Children's Charity Fund run by the hospital committee. From the looks of it, the first annual event was a great success with a long future ahead of it.

"Well, that'll keep Mom busy for a while." A younger version of Elaine stepped forward to Daphne and the rest of her group as they came closer to the exhibition. Marlene Stinson, the daughter of the Mayor and Mayoress, smiled and gave Daphne a quick hug. "Good thing I came to help her."

"I'll say. How are things in the south?" Daphne had known the Stinsons all of her life. After attending college in Santa Lucia, Marlene had moved to Laguna Beach and was currently working in an art gallery.

"I love it! You've heard my news?" The ash blonde beamed and held out her left hand. On it was a sparkling new diamond ring.

"Yes, I read the engagement announcement in the paper. I was so happy to read your news." Daphne looked down at her friend's hand and gestured to her companions to have a look as well. They all made the appropriate well-wishing comments, although there was a brief flitting eye contact between Margot and Tom that caused a negligible tension that only they picked up on.

"Yes, we're just working out the date now," Marlene continued. "By the way, David said to say hello to you if I saw you." David was Marlene's older brother, and had been a high school sweetheart of Daphne's briefly, many years ago.

"Great, sure. Tell him I said hello as well." Their companionship had been pleasant but short, and romantic as far as high school infatuations go, but in Daphne's mind it was ancient history. Daniel, however, was unsure and the mention of a former beau after the Adonis experience was enough to set her current's teeth on edge. She immediately gripped his arm a little tighter to reassure him and made sure to include Dan in their conversation, letting Marlene know very clearly that Daniel was the man who was important to her now.

Marlene was quick and picked up on the implication, changing the subject back to the art show. "We've had such a great turn out. There are so many people. Even the weather worked in our favor." All week had been foggy, damp and gloomy, with some concern on how a *plein aire* show might affect some of the materials. Today, as it turned out, was a bright and sunny day with very little humidity and just a light breeze to keep the bright sun heat temperate. Marlene looked around at her mother's displayed artwork and saw many red dots on the listings. "I don't think I'll have any to take back with me." Any remaining works of Elaine's were going down to

Marlene's gallery where they would fetch a pretty penny for the popular award-winning artist. Elaine had won many local and statewide competitions for her dreamy landscapes of their local scenery, as well as a loyal collector following.

Margot, Daphne, and their dates continued their art show stroll along Waterfront Beach. The location was so picturesque as it ran along the ocean side surf with the town and hills in the background on the opposite side. The promenade was shaded with flowering shrubs and palm trees, adding to the aesthetic appeal. The next grouping they came across was large with a hand-lettered banner announcing that it was for the works of art by the Stearns Academy for Girls Fine Arts Department. There were six young ladies, from the senior class by their look of maturity—four painters and two sculptors—exhibiting their work, some of it appearing quite accomplished. Supervising the artists was Headmistress Katherine Larsen. She was a slim, dowdy, middle-aged woman towering in height over everyone, in sensible shoes and a dull shapeless tweed suit. She had an assistant supervisor, whom Daphne did not recognize. She glanced at Margot, silently asking her if she recognized the woman. Margot shook her head. Tom glanced around the crowd. Even though he was off duty, as one of Santa Lucia's finest, he was always on alert for potential trouble.

Daniel, on the other hand, perked up noticeably when he saw Headmistress Larsen's helper. How couldn't he? She was a gorgeous, full-figured woman in a tight black satin wiggle skirt, a striped red and white bateau jersey sweater, with red lips and glossy black hair and long cigarette holder to match. "Ooh, Daniel, you came! I am so 'appy to see you." She walked up to Daniel's free arm and latched on, planting a large lip print on his cheek.

He blustered and moved infinitesimally closer to Daphne. Daphne in turn glared at the woman, then regained her composure and radiated her golden California smile. "Why, hello, I don't believe we've met. I'm Daphne Huntington-Smythe, Daniel's girlfriend. Who are you?" Her wide grin extended so high it almost hurt her face.

"I am Sophie! I teach with Daniel. 'E is my favorite." She gave him a playful slap on the arm and would not let go. "Come now, you naughty, naughty man. Who is your leetle friend? You 'ave not told me of 'er." Sophie playfully wagged a finger from her free hand while giving him a saucy grin. She had a strong and seemingly affected accent that sounded to Daphne like the woman's attempt at exaggerated French.

Daniel carefully extricated his arm from the possessive woman and replied, "Yes, Miss Dubois, I have told you of my girlfriend Daphne on many occasions."

"Oh, phoo. I do not listen to matters like zat." She blankly tried to dismiss the very presence of Daniel's choice of companion.

Daphne was not one to be ignored. "Well, he's certainly never mentioned you. Why don't you tell me all about yourself, Sophie?"

"Eh, moi? I am just Sophie." She touched her chest with her hand, attempting to blush with false modesty and moved even closer to Daniel, regaining her grasp on him.

Daniel unsuccessfully tried to remove himself from her clutches again and nervously cleared his throat, while Daphne kept her eyes on him. He decided the best thing he could do would be to focus on his girlfriend and answer her questions. "Sophie is the art instructor at the Academy."

Daphne's lip curled, "Have you been there long?"

"Since zee school opened," Sophie replied lightly.

"Funny, I haven't seen you around."

Sophie laughed. "Oh, all zose men at zee Academy keep me so well, zere is no need to leave."

"Is that so?"

"Zey meet my desires, bring me everything—food, flowers, take me away on zee weekends. I 'ave no need to leeft a feenger."

"All of them?"

"Oui—tout." Sophie patted her hair, smoothing her curls in place.

Daphne realized her eyebrows and the rest of her face were frozen in a tense expression. She consciously forced herself to look carefree. Daniel said nothing. She glanced around and looked at the exhibition. There was some nice work—landscape paintings, sculptures, still lifes and abstracts. The artist pupils were in their Stearns Academy uniforms—plaid skirts and art smocks, looking sharp and eager to share their work. She saw Margot and Tom had been talking with the headmistress and students. Daphne poked Daniel in the ribs with her elbow and motioned to him that they should walk away from the French tart and join their friends. Sophie shrugged indifferently and slipped her arm away from Daniel as he began to pull away. Another handsome man approached the art display and she briskly wiggled over and poured her charms onto her new prey.

In contrast, Headmistress Katherine Larsen was no nonsense. There was no mistaking she was the one in charge. Her brown hounds-tooth suit was shapeless on her tall, lean frame. Her hair was short and close to her face, and her glasses were precisely in place. She was chatting formally, yet politely, about the exhibit and introducing a couple of the girls to Margot. Every so often, she would take a strong look in Sophie's direction, making mental notes of what she would need to discuss with the art teacher Monday morning, regarding her behavior.

The foursome moved on to some rather bizarre and misshapen plaster of Paris objects, for lack of a better term. Some had obvious handprints and unbalanced proportions, others had wire showing. No one else was looking at the eyesores. Towards the back of the display, Margot saw a dejected looking mousy girl slouching in a canvas chair with her head down, not meeting anyone's gaze. She wondered if she could find something nice to say to cheer the girl up. "Hi, Barbara. So, is this your work?"

"No," she sighed. "It's mother's." 'Mother' was Nancy Lewis, the banker's wife and a top society maven in Santa Lucia. Also a bossy pain in the neck, but one of Poppy Cove's best clients. Barbara or 'Babs' was Nancy's eldest daughter. She'd just finished high school and was showing no inclination for college. She was dragged along by her mother to all of Nancy's society functions, and was also set up on dates with any eligible young man who couldn't come up with an excuse to decline in time before Nancy could confirm dinner arrangements. In Babs' defense, she wasn't an ugly or awful girl, just awkward and unable to get out from under Mommy's control of her life.

"Oh." Margot and her friends tried not to laugh or smirk as they studied the pieces around them. Tom caught a statue in his grasp that almost fell on him and attempted to right and balance it.

"Mother says if you break it, you buy it," Babs flatly stated.

Determined to keep conversation with Babs, Margot asked, "Has that happened?"

"Yeah, once. That's how she managed to sell one today."

"How could you tell if it *was* broken?" Tom muttered under his breath. "I could use a hand here. How about it, Dan?"

Between the two men, they managed to break off what appeared to be an appendage (arm?) from the piece. Dan tried to stick it back on, to no avail.

"That'll be $50." An enthusiastic voice came from behind. Nancy Lewis greeted them, carrying two cups of coffee.

"What?" Tom remarked.

"You heard me—that statue costs $50." She turned her attention to her daughter. "Barbara," she snapped, "you told them, right? That if they broke it..."

"Yes, mother."

"Well, you heard my daughter. Will that be cash or cheque?"

"Isn't that a little high? Some might call it robbery or extortion, Mrs. Lewis." Tom went into policeman manner.

"Well." She gave the coffee cups to her daughter and walked up to Tom, pulling down her grey suit jacket hem with an officious tug. "It's all for charity. A children's charity, I might add. Besides, it's a Nancy Lewis original. I've been told my style is unique. I have no doubt that one day it will be very valuable. Think of it as an investment, or an improvement to your home décor."

"I saw that, Henshaw. If I'm paying, so are you." Tom said as he saw Daniel trying to discreetly pocket the broken off piece he still had in his hand.

"Oh, all right. Let's just take care of it. It is for charity." Dan grabbed his wallet, as he was willing to pay half. After all, a healthy share of the proceeds from the sales today was going to a good cause.

Margot wanted to keep things pleasant while the men settled up. "Have you sold many pieces today?"

"Some." Nancy vaguely dismissed the question.

"That's the second," Barbara informed them. "Dad was the one who broke one earlier. He had to buy it, too."

"Barbara!" Nancy hissed. She grabbed the money from the men. "I've had many spectators, some who've wanted to buy the collection as a whole, so I'm just holding out for a generous offer for whatever the men in this town don't manage to break." Babs sniffled at her mother's remarks.

"Right. Fine. Good for you, Nancy." Margot replied. After an awkward silence, the girls and their dates decided to move on.

It was late in the day, around 4 p. m., and the art show was winding down. The two couples decided that it was too early to go for dinner and thought they'd take a walk along the beach, past all the people and crowds to the quieter end. As they walked, they came across a trashcan. Dan and Tom looked at each other, gave a mutual shrug and buried their new art acquisition discreetly where no one would find it. No harm done—Nancy would never know, the charity got their money and no home would ever have to display such a work of art.

The group paired off. Daniel and Daphne strolled ahead, arm in arm, laughing and talking about nothing, just enjoying each other's company in a relaxed and romantic fashion. Margot and Tom were paced a few feet behind. Although Margot's ankle had healed well from an unfortunate spill six months earlier, she still found she did not walk as briskly as she would like, getting fatigued easily. They were close, but not holding hands, a little distance between them.

With the other couple just out of earshot ahead of them, Tom decided to bring up what was now a familiar topic between them. "Margot," he started.

She recognized the tone in his voice. It was *that* conversation again. She sighed and sat down wearily on a nearby driftwood log. "Yes, Tom."

He sat down beside her. "Have you thought more about what I've asked you?"

She hesitated. "Yes, it's almost the only thing on my mind these days."

They sat in silence for a while, saying nothing. "Do you have an answer?"

"It's not that simple."

"You keep saying that, but you don't say why." He stopped, turned to face her, grasping her gently, but firmly on the shoulders, meeting her eyes. "Listen, I've done my time on the San Francisco streets as a beat cop before I was here. Believe me, with what I've seen there's nothing you could tell me that would shock me or change my mind about wanting to marry you." He paused. "I'm not a saint, either. I've done my share of things that were on the wild side, I've known a few women in my time and don't regret it, or expect you to be perfect. I've been patient with you, knowing you've had something to say, but not wanting to, and I could have run background checks on you through my legal connections, but I haven't. I trust you and know whatever you've done, well, it can't be all that bad and if it were, you would have had good reason. So what's it going to be? Will you marry me?"

It was the longest speech she'd ever heard from him, and when she looked into his eyes, she knew he meant it. She opened her mouth, paused and closed it again. She was distracted as she saw a familiar figure past Tom's shoulder running towards them from a deserted area of the beach.

"Malone, is that you?" A uniformed officer huffed as he slowed down towards them.

Tom turned and acknowledged him with a nod of his head. "Jenkins? What's going on?"

"They said you were here." Jenkins motioned to Daniel and Daphne who had stopped a few feet ahead and were now walking back to them. "Good thing. Chief's looking for you. There's a body washed up."

"Where?"

"Down the way, 'bout a hundred yards."

Tom stood up, brushed off his pants, shaking sand off of the cuffs. "What do you have so far?"

Jenkins scratched his head, reciting the particulars. "Male, Caucasian, late twenties, early thirties. Medium build, around six feet. Dressed in a dark suit, white shirt. Been in the water a very short while."

"Anyone recognize him?"

Jenkins shook his head. "Not from what we could tell, but hard to say. Looks like he was roughed up, but could have been from being tossed around in the water, rocks, waves. Minor bloating, too."

"Anything else?"

"Yeah. Don't think he died from drowning or being beat up. There's a bullet hole. Shot clean through the heart."

CHAPTER TWO

"Right, I'm on my way." Tom turned to address his friends. "Mar, I'd still like an answer. If I'm not too late, I'll come by your house tonight. I've got to go."

He took off with Jenkins, not giving her a kiss good-bye, pre-occupied with the impending murder scene. The gesture did not go unnoticed by Daphne, who looked at Margot's rather sheepish expression. "What?" Margot asked her.

Daphne shrugged. "I don't know. Is it just me, or is something amiss with you and Tom?" She was standing there holding hands with Daniel, who was busy craning his neck to check out the murder scene.

Margot reached for Daphne's free hand to get assistance to stand up. Daphne obliged, still waiting for her friend's answer. Margot wanted to brush it off, not wanting to discuss it further with anyone. "Nothing, Tom's just busy." She got up and smoothed down her skirt, thinking to change tack. "Looks like he's now tied up for the evening. Let's go to Antonio's, I'm famished." She actually didn't look it; she looked a little pale and shaken.

Daphne switched her attention, sharing Daniel's curiosity, wanting to find out more about what was happening down the beach. So far, there hadn't been much of a crowd forming, mainly just the police and a couple of other bystanders. "Sure, but let's go have a look. I'm dying to see what's going on there."

Margot gave Daphne a funny face, who giggled when she realized her turn of phrase. "Oh, you know what I mean. Let's go and see if they know who it is yet." Daniel was all for it, but Margot hesitated.

"No, let's not."

"Oh, why not? You never know, maybe we can help."

"You mean like the last time we came across a dead body?" Margot said flatly and shook her head. "No. Tom wouldn't like that. He's already warned me about not getting involved.

"Aren't you the least bit curious?" Daphne egged on.

"No."

"Jenkins said he was shot clean, once through the heart. That must be a crime of passion, don't you think?"

"Or a hit man. Wouldn't it take some skill to be able to do that?" Daniel interjected.

Margot said nothing. Daphne thought in the silence about the possibility of a hired gun, a killer on the loose, even watching them. She gave an involuntary shiver. Maybe it was time to go. "Okay, dinner it is. Let's go."

Margot was relieved, but surprised her friend gave up so easily. "That's it?"

"What?"

"You're not going to try any further?"

Daphne smiled. "No, you're right. The cops don't know him, so chances are we don't either. If Daniel's idea is right, there could be a killer watching the scene and the last thing I want is to be involved in another murder." She continued to look in the direction of the scene of the corpse. "Besides, Weathers has just shown up. He'll have the story in the *Times* tomorrow." She looked at Daniel, who had a neutral look on his face and took his hand again. "Let's go eat."

With that, the trio made their way off the beach to Antonio's, the favorite little Italian place in Santa Lucia.

****

Monday morning started off as business as usual at Poppy Cove. The storefront was closed to the public with the back room ready to hum all day. Daphne picked up the *Santa Lucia Times* off the doorstep as she arrived at nine a. m. sharp. The front page had a picture of the body on the beach from a distance. The headline and article were written by their crack crime reporter Michael Weathers. It was vague, as it seemed that by press time there wasn't much information to go on. She turned to the society pages and saw Loretta's write-up and photos about the art show. There was a great image of Elaine, but unfortunately, Nancy was jockeying in the same frame in an unflattering pose, foisting one of her atrocious works into the shot at an awkward angle. Daphne laughed to herself, wondering if Loretta had decided to include it on purpose.

Daphne was set for a busy day after her restful evening. They'd had an early night after dinner at the Italian restaurant, but she couldn't help but notice that Margot was very preoccupied and jittery. She knew that her friend and Tom were having a serious and obviously private discussion that was prematurely interrupted. Margot never said a word about it, remaining quiet and withdrawn throughout the evening. After knowing her friend for a few years, she knew when Margot would talk and when she wouldn't. And last night was the latter. Hopefully, she'd unzip her lip and let it fly today. Daphne loved her friend, but she had to admit, curiosity was also gnawing at her.

She fussed around, waiting for Margot to arrive. Everyone else showed up promptly—Marjorie, the head seamstress and Margot's right hand, as well as the rest of the girls from the sewing room staff. 1958 was turning out to be an extremely lucrative year. Recently Poppy Cove's business had greatly increased, in large part due to the patronage of Joyce Jones, an up and coming movie star whose visit the previous year had brought great attention to Margot's design aesthetic and Daphne's knack for picking the right, 'just-so' accessories. Joyce began making frequent trips to the shop, bringing along her movie star friends who were equally as enamoured with the ladies' work. Their biggest moment was a couple of months ago in February, at the Spring Fashion Show that had been held in the neighboring Poppy Lane Tearoom. It had always drawn a big crowd, due in part to the fact that part of the proceeds went to the March of Dimes. The movie star and her friends, attended this year's event, where they bought up one of each design and wore them out and about for their social happenings in Hollywood. At the fashion show, Jake had snapped a picture of Joyce flanked on either side by Margot and Daphne, all of the ladies at their glamorous best, which he sold for a pretty penny to the Associated Press. The picture went nationwide at the end of March—into *Look* and *PhotoPlay* magazines, as well as various news, gossip and fashion rags around the country.

Poppy Cove's business had doubled, with no sign of slowing down. The girls bought another industrial machine and hired extra help for garment construction—another sewer, in the form of Kaye, long-term client Mrs. Marshall's eldest daughter, and Jeannette Fox, a new girl in town, as a cutter. Although Kaye's experience was from home sewing, she was quick and steady, so her skills transferred well to the higher speed industrial machines. Jeannette, on the other hand, had come from cutting men's suits in the New York garment district and had a smooth glide with both the shears and cutting blades. Both new employees had only been with the shop for a couple of weeks, but they were proving to be valuable resources, both very accurate in a speedy fashion, and able to keep working while contributing to the gossipy banter of the back room girls.

Daphne sighed and drummed her fingers on the counter, then looked at her watch. It was going on fifteen minutes past the hour. Almost everyone was in their place, ready and working, save a couple of exceptions. Marjorie appeared thrown off and somewhat stressed, as both Jeannette and Margot had not arrived yet. She came out to find out where they were as they were late for their production meeting. Being that Miss Fox was new to the job, it was not good form, but not alarming for a young girl to be late to work, but it wasn't like Margot. Daphne lifted up the telephone receiver to give her a call and set it back down when she heard the rattle of a key in the front door and saw Margot through the glass. Daphne gave a momentary sigh of relief until she had a good look at her friend.

Margot appeared weary, unsettled, and rumpled. She had trouble getting her key out of the lock. "Sorry I'm late; I overslept."

Marjorie and Daphne gave each other a quick glance. That wasn't in Margot's nature. Daphne spoke first. "Really?"

Margot managed a nod and primped her pageboy waves, which were flatter than usual. "Didn't get much sleep," she mumbled. Again, not a usual Margot trait.

Daphne looked over at Marjorie, who nodded and picked up her clipboard. "I'll just go to the back, dear, until you're ready. The girls have started up on the stock orders. We'll keep going, but you should be aware that Jeannette has not shown up yet either. Lord knows we have plenty to keep us busy until you're ready." She patted Margot on the arm and gave a brief sigh, leaving the shop owners alone to talk.

Margot kept her head down, pretending to look at the appointment book on the counter. Daphne gave her friend a moment, but just a fleeting pass. Daphne was more known for her impulsiveness than patience. She gave a huge sigh, giving her lilac shift dress a tug at the waist and inquired, "Mar, what's going on?"

At first, Margot said nothing, face burning. Finally she looked up at her friend. "Tom asked me to marry him," she expressed flatly.

Daphne's face lit up. "Well, that's wonderful news—how exciting! To be honest, I have to admit I'm not surprised. I mean it's about time, really..." she continued to babble on. "Have you set a date? Ooh, you can make your own dress! I know just the right handbag, and that pin over there would be darling." She stopped and looked at Margot, who wasn't responding in the manner she was expecting. "You did say yes, didn't you?"

"No."

"You said no?"

"No, I didn't say no."

"Then you said yes?"

"No. I haven't said anything. I haven't given my answer yet."

Daphne was shocked. Isn't that what every girl wanted? A man she loved to propose to her? She knew what her answer would be when Daniel asked. Well, if he asked. They were getting along swimmingly, but that hadn't come up quite yet, but she was mentally lining up her approach of not so subtle hints. She knew that Margot was devoted to her work and said that she wasn't interested in marriage, but Daphne thought that when it was serious, that Margot and Tom would naturally fall into matrimony, as they were so perfectly suited for each other. Maybe she was wrong. "Why not? Don't you want to marry him?" she asked gently, in almost a whisper, even though they were the only ones in the room.

Margot's response was an exhalation bigger than the moon. "It's a bit more complicated than that."

Daphne waved her hand in a dismissive gesture. She realized it must Margot's reticence to marriage. "Oh, don't worry so. Sometimes I think you think too much."

She paused, contemplating how to approach the subject without hurting her friend's feelings. "Look, I know you said you didn't want to get married to anyone, but Tom's not just anyone. It's Tom." Margot did not respond, so she carried on. "I know you love your independence and your design work. Do you really think that would change? He's not going to want you to give up Poppy Cove. He's not like that, he knows what your business means to you."

Margot looked at her friend, studying her expression. Daphne looked pleased with herself, as if she had all the answers Margot needed. Margot decided to let her think so. The faster she could acquiesce, the faster Daphne would drop the subject. She touched Daphne on the arm as she replied, "You know, you're right. I'll, I'll give him an answer soon."

Daphne was relieved, believing she had truly solved a romantic crisis. "That's better. And I'm sure both of you will be very 'happily ever after.' I just know it!"

Margot picked up the newspaper lying on the desk. "As soon as Tom has a break. He's busy now again and you know how he is when he gets on a case. I'll bet he wouldn't even hear a word I'd say." *Maybe that would be better,* Margot silently thought to herself. *He might not want to know what I need to tell him.*

Daphne followed her friend's gaze to the headlines again. "Looks like this one's a real mystery. No one seems to know who he is."

Margot glanced at the photo. "No, the police are saying he's probably not from Santa Lucia." She scanned the article briefly and moved on to Loretta's section where she featured Sunday's event. "Nancy's busy making waves again," she chuckled.

Things settled down into more of the usual Monday routine and the girls focused in on the tasks in front of them. Besides the influx in regular business, they were heading into another busy season. The town's Founders'

Day was coming up in May, and along with it was the Miss Santa Lucia pageant, which included the contestants modeling the latest Poppy Cove summer fashions and accessories, with this year's collection named 'Making Waves.' It would be great fun and quite whimsical, featuring flirty backless sundresses, romper playsuits, shorts, capris and midi tops. They also would debut a new line of swimwear called 'Swan Dive' out of Los Angeles, which inspired Margot to create some glamorous cover-ups and Daphne found some darling swim caps in matching bright colors with floral appliqués and details that hugged the scalp, not letting any water in, but without mussing and squishing the hair too much. She also found some roomy, colorful beach totes and fabulous sunglasses in a daring new wider, rounder shape, giving more mystique to the face.

Daphne had her list of items she needed for the upcoming show and went upstairs to their shared private office to work on them. Margot went to the back room to confer with Marjorie regarding the sewing schedule for the week, even though Jeannette still had not shown up.

The production crew broke for lunch after a busy morning. As usual, Margot and Daphne went over to the Poppy Lane Tearoom for lunch. Their good friend and hostess with the mostest, Lana, greeted them as they took their usual table by the bay window. She brought them coffee and took their lunch order expressing a huge, exhausted sigh.

"What's up, Lana? You don't seem like your usually perky self." Daphne remarked.

"Oh, me? Sorry, I'm just run off my feet." The tearoom had also had an influx of business over the past year. "We were open on Sunday. We had so many of our regulars asking if we'd be open during the art show, we decided to do it. Turned out to be really busy." She looked around and saw that it was crowded, but only with familiar customers, so she decided to sit down and join her friends for a moment. "It'll get better though. We've hired a new girl and she's doing well. She picked up on the routine really fast. Hard worker, quick to train. She should do well on tips, too. Really pleasant."

They sat quietly, letting Lana catch her breath while they watched the new girl work her way around the tables. She was young; in her early twenties, fair, and slim. She was a nondescript kind of pretty, not exactly plain, but wouldn't stand out in a crowd, either. She was efficient and suitably chatty with the clientele, but kept a good pace. Lana's forehead creased in slight concern. "I just hope we can keep her. She's new in town and looking for a place to stay. Right now, she's in a Mrs. Coleman's Boarding House, but she needs somewhere permanent. She says if she can't find somewhere, she's going to move on." She caught her new employee's eye, who flickered a slight look in their direction, colored a titch and kept working.

"Mar, didn't Jeannette say she was staying at Mrs. Coleman's?" Daphne remarked.

Margot thought for a moment. "Yes, that's right." She turned in her seat to face Lana. "She's our new cutter and didn't show up for her shift today. Can we speak to your new waitress? What's her name?"

"Diane. Diane Phillips." Lana signaled for her to come over to the table.

The waitress greeted the ladies with a smile. "Yes?" She asked expectantly.

Daphne and Margot introduced themselves and then inquired of Diane if she knew of Jeannette and if she'd seen her that morning.

Diane thought for a moment before replying. "Yes, I know her. Her room's just down the hall from me. But no, I didn't see her today. I leave early, around 6:30 to help here with the morning rush. I don't usually see anyone."

Margot continued the gentle interrogation. "Do you remember the last time you saw her? Did you see her yesterday?"

"No, I don't think so." She thought for a moment and focussed her green eyes on Margot. "I'm not sure when I saw her last, but she's pretty quiet, keeps to herself, except for going to work and mealtimes. Don't get me wrong, she's nice and all that, but we've not been that chummy. I've been so busy now that I've taken this job." She glanced around, seeing that there were plenty of tables to clear.

"Oh, right. Did you work an extra shift yesterday?" Daphne asked.

Diane nodded. "Then I didn't get home until late last night."

"Oh, did you attend the art show after work?"

"No, I went down the coast to Ventura, surfing."

Daphne grinned. "There are some great spots just down the way. You didn't go alone did, you?" she remarked with some concern.

"No, I was with some friends," she replied lightly, tucking back a lock of auburn hair behind her ear.

"It's been nice chatting with you all, but it looks like Diane and I have to get back to work." Lana stood up with a sense of urgency as she looked around the tearoom.

After the café staff departed, Margot and Daphne sat in companionable silence briefly, until Daphne asked, "Well, are you thinking what I'm thinking?"

Margot grinned. "That we should pay a visit to the boarding house?"

"Exactly. It's not far from here and we can make it a quick visit. I'm sure Marjorie can keep everything running smoothly without us. We won't be long. Maybe Jeannette's sick or something. If she keeps to herself like Diane says, and doesn't know that many people here, I'd hate to think she was all alone and thinking no one cares."

"True," Margot affirmed. "And, if she's not there either, maybe Mrs. Coleman will know where she is."

With that, the girls decided to take the short walk to the house, just a couple of blocks away at Laurel Avenue and Bay Street. It was a big, old, two-story traditional craftsman with a handsome front porch and well-manicured lawn. The girls noticed that the hand carved, wooden sign announcing, 'Mrs. Coleman's Boarding House—A Respectable Establishment' had a 'No Soliciting' placard attached at the bottom, under a 'No Vacancy' sign. "Well, doesn't look like Jeannette's checked out," Daphne remarked.

The girls rapped on the front door with its sturdy, original brass knocker. While they waited, they took in the detail of the porch. The warm oak floor was polished to a sheen, and not one spider's web could be seen among the intricate cutwork molding. Flower baskets hung full of geraniums and impatiens, carefully tended without a straggler or dead plant among them. Beside the door was a plaque with a list of rules engraved in brass. No unauthorized guests in private rooms, adhere to meal times, curfew is strictly maintained at 11 p. m., male and female guests must only fraternize in publicly designated meeting areas unless legally married to each other—the list went on. The girls looked at each other with open mouths, just imagining what it must be like to live as an adult under such strict conditions.

The prim and proper Mrs. Coleman opened the door briskly and peered at the girls sharply over her small wire-rimmed round glasses. "Yes?"

The girls began to introduce themselves when Mrs. Coleman put up her bony hand. "Stop right there, girls. I've got no vacancies. I'm not interested in what you're selling, and I've read the good book. So if you don't mind, I've had a hectic morning." She started to shut the door on Daphne and Margot before they had a chance to let her know of their purpose. Margot put a firm hand up to stop the door, while Daphne stuck her foot in the frame.

"Please, Mrs. Coleman. We're only inquiring about the welfare of one of your paying guests. She's an employee of ours and hasn't shown up for work today." Margot managed to get out with some authority.

Mildred Coleman stopped and squinted at the girls. "Who?"

"Jeannette Fox," Margot stated. The girls elaborated about their concern and Mrs. Coleman reluctantly let them in.

Mildred Coleman listened with folded arms and pursed lips as Margot and Daphne explained who they were and why they'd come to see her. "Hmm, odd. She's not been much trouble. Come to think of it, I haven't seen her around, not since Saturday morning."

With all the order and rules that Mrs. Coleman had, it seemed strange to Daphne that a guest could be gone that long without the landlady being aware of it, so she asked, "Didn't you think that it was worrisome that you have not seen her since then?"

Mrs. Coleman shook her head. "She's paid up till the end of the month, and as long as she doesn't drag any miscreants in my home, disturb me outside of the curfew, or demand to be cooked for besides the meal times, I don't care. Her room was tidy, her manners quiet. I don't ask anything else. Besides, she mentioned she was looking for a permanent apartment for herself by the end of the month. Maybe she found one."

Daphne ventured further. "Would you mind letting us in her room to have a look around? Just to see if she had left any notes or anything that may tell us where she is."

The diminutive Mrs. Coleman folded her arms tighter, and pursed her lips until the rims were white. "No, now that's not right. I like my privacy. I tell my guests to keep out of my living quarters and I give them my word I won't go in theirs."

Daphne tried to appease her, while still pursuing the request. "Oh, we perfectly understand and see that you have only the utmost respect for your residents, absolutely. We wouldn't ask, of course, but we're just concerned. She doesn't seem like the flighty type and we're worried for her safety and well-being, that's all."

Mrs. Coleman thought about it further and relented. "Fine, but don't be long. I've already had enough disruptions around here today and I've got a great deal to keep up with, so let's just make this brief, all right? And I'm standing right at the door, so no digging around or taking anything out, do you understand?"

The girls nodded and hurried up the stairs behind her, keeping their heads down and staying in line. The place was immaculate, with warm wood trim everywhere, stained glass windows and gleaming brass accents. The doors all had numbers on them and the details appeared to have been cleaned and polished with a fine brush. The scent of wood oil hung in the air. They reached the top floor and a bank of doors ran on either side of the staircase. There were plaques that indicated women were on the left, men on the right, and another warning about fraternizing being prohibited in the private rooms. There appeared to be three bedrooms per side, with a washroom at either end, also clearly marked for the appropriate sex.

Mildred walked up to the last bedroom door, knocked, and called out Jeannette's name. "Just in case," she mentioned to the girls. There was no answer so she let them in with the master key.

The room was neat and tidy, with everything seeming to be in their proper places. Mrs. Coleman stood in the doorway, watching Margot and Daphne go over everything, clearing her throat, snuffling her nose, or making other noises of disapproval if she saw them picking something up or lingering on an object for what she considered to be too long. There appeared to be nothing out of order; clothing was hung properly in the closet, the bed was made, and there was no sign of a struggle or evidence that someone had left in a hurry. There was no handbag and the light coat they had seen Jeannette wearing to and from work wasn't there, so it appeared that she'd left with somewhere in mind and dressed for the day. There were also many garments and items in the dresser and closet, giving the impression that she'd be back shortly.

"Ladies, have you seen enough?" demanded Mildred Coleman. "I have to get this place spic and span before I start preparing dinner."

The girls looked at each other, trying to imagine what exactly was left to be cleaned in the place. They also understood their welcome was worn out and started to leave, no wiser on the whereabouts of their employee than when they'd shown up. As they reached the landing, Margot recalled an earlier remark and turned to Mrs. Coleman, mentioning, "You said that you had another disruption today?"

Mildred narrowed her eyes suspiciously at her. "Why are you asking?"

"Um, well no reason, but you brought it up, so I was just curious," Margot tried to keep it light, but was intrigued.

"It was nothing. It had nothing to do with Miss Fox, I'm sure," Mildred snarled.

"Excuse me, but are you talking about the police visit this morning?"

Daphne glanced over to what appeared to be a parlor room and saw a little old man sitting in a wingback chair. He pushed up his thick glasses and set down the newspaper he'd been reading, encouraging a conversation. Daphne went into the room to talk to him further while Mrs. Coleman stood stock still and loudly harrumphed, obviously displeased that he'd spoken up.

Margot stayed by her, watching her body language, and noticed how rigid she was.

"Sorry, you said the police were here earlier?" Daphne asked.

The elderly man continued, excitedly, "Oh, yes, they were here for quite a while, going through that new man's room, 'bout nine this morning."

"Really? Do you know what it was about?" Daphne eagerly pursued.

"Now, now, Mr. Drake, you know it wasn't all that serious." Mrs. Coleman tried to brush off the new line of questioning, but was jittery. "He tends to make things up, exaggerates a little." The girls didn't buy it.

Daphne saw he'd been reading Weathers' article about the man found on the beach and encouraged Mr. Drake to continue. "Did it have to do with this? Do you know?"

"And that's enough." Mrs. Coleman abruptly ended the questioning. "I'm sure it has nothing to do with Miss Fox and therefore nothing to do with you. It's time for you two to go and mind your own business." She began to physically shoo the girls out of the house.

Mr. Drake, happy to have an audience, kept looking in Daphne's direction and carried on. "Oh, I think so. The police took out a couple of boxes of information and talked to all of us here in the house, didn't they Mildred?"

Mildred was flustered. She blurted, "Yes, well we don't need to discuss that with our visitors, do we?" Her remark was pointedly directed at Mr. Drake. He shrank in his chair and retreated back into his newspaper.

Daphne's eyes grew wide. "So you know who the murder victim was!" She kept her eyes on Mildred.

Mrs. Coleman shrugged. "They didn't say that's what it was about and I didn't ask. They just asked me some questions and I let them do what they needed to do." The boarding house owner was adamant. "That's enough. It's time for you to leave."

Daphne was undaunted and tried a different tack. "When was the last time you saw that particular male lodger?"

Mrs. Coleman didn't answer.

Daphne continued. "Did you tell the police about Jeannette being missing?"

"No," Mrs. Coleman sighed.

"Why not?"

"Because it has nothing to do with her. Go back to your store and leave us alone. When Miss Fox returns, which I'm sure she will, I'll let her know her employers were here. Good afternoon, ladies." Mrs. Coleman gave them the bum's rush and slammed the door behind them.

Daphne and Margot rapidly walked down the path out to the sidewalk and burst out laughing for relief. Once they had a sense of composure, Margot remarked, "Well, I don't know what to make of that. Sounds like Mrs. Coleman and her guests may know who that man found shot on the beach was. The police must now know, too."

Daphne thought out the next conclusion before she said it out loud, but she was pretty sure Margot was already thinking it as well. "So, if he was shot in the heart, it sounds like a romance gone wrong, doesn't it?"

Margot nodded. "It does."

"And now we have a young lady from the same residence gone missing."

"Yes."

"So she could have been involved," Daphne surmised.

"Yes."

"And they had a fight."

"A big one," Margot added.

"And so she shot him."

"And ran away," Margot concluded as they reached the Poppy Cove doorstep.

"Well, it's a theory, anyway." Daphne stated.

Margot nodded as they walked through the door. "And maybe we should keep that just to ourselves right now. The police already know about the boarding house and who lives there. I'm sure they have their own ideas."

"Good thinking. Tom hates it when you jump to conclusions."

"Especially when I'm right," she winked.

The girls settled back into the rest of a productive afternoon. Although Jeannette had not turned up, which now they privately didn't know what to make of, work went fairly smoothly. Daphne put the idea of the missing man and Jeannette out of her head, figuring that there was nothing they could do, and that if the police were already on the trail, they would sort it out. Maybe Mrs. Coleman was right. Jeannette's absence was just a co-incidence and had nothing to do with the murder.

Daphne also felt that in her own small way, she had reassured Margot that it would be okay to warm her cold feet to Tom. Now if only she could get Daniel's mind on matrimony, maybe a double wedding could be in the books! She floated off in her dream world, occasionally hearing Margot share her plans about the collection and fashion show, and making appropriate suggestions for the accessories between her thoughts. She had one slight flaw in her plans however. Sophie kept popping up in her mind. Curvy Sophie, with her firm grip and sloe-eyed grin, preening and sidling up to Dan at the Academy. She shook her head, doing her best to clear her mind. She could keep him away from the French tart most evenings, if not all, but during the daytime when they were working was another story. She made a mental note to ask Jane Peacock, the math teacher's wife, if she could keep an eye on things, and just maybe have a reason to 'pop by' and see Sophie when her art classes weren't in session. She nodded and straightened the catalogues on her desk with firm resolve, glad she had another situation under control.

In reality, Daphne didn't notice that all the time she was sorting out her plans, Margot was equally preoccupied, adding appropriate work-related comments while distracted over the decision she needed to make. Truth be known, it wasn't the actual matrimonial yes or no that was a problem to her. It was her history leading up to whether or not Tom's question was still on the table once she told him about why she came to Santa Lucia in the first place. By the end of the day, she knew she had to tell him all, and soon, whether he had an important case or not.

It turned out that it was going to be sooner than that. As the production staff was leaving and the girls were ready to lock up, there was a knock at the shop front door. Tom was accompanied by both Detective Riley and Officer Jenkins. Daphne grinned as she let them in, greeting Tom in particular with an even bigger smile. "Hi guys, any news on the body yet?"

There was a measured silence. Margot was sorting out her handbag on the sales counter. She looked up and instantly knew this was not a social call by the group's demeanor. Daphne's smile deflated rapidly.

Riley took the lead in the conversation. "Miss Huntington-Smythe and Miss Williams, we have a few questions that maybe you can answer for us. We believe you may be able help us." The girls were startled by his formality, thinking that Mrs. Coleman had reported their snooping at the boarding house as a nuisance. Tom was behind him, trying not to meet Margot's eyes, darting his glance awkwardly towards Daphne and the back of his partner's head. Riley nodded towards Jenkins who pulled out a protected image from the file folder he was carrying. By now, the rest of the staff had gathered around, curious to the goings on. Riley continued, "Do either of you know why this would be found on the body?"

He handed the protected evidence over to Daphne who was closest, in a way that blocked her from communicating with Margot. It was a copy of the newspaper photo and article that had run in syndication across the country, featuring Joyce Jones. It also mentioned Poppy Cove in the caption and article, as well as their names and a reference to Joyce's film work and Miss Starfire appearances. It was folded so that Daphne and Joyce were on one side of the crease, with Margot on the other side, by herself. The page was warped and in a fragile state, but the ink and newsprint were still legible. Daphne was puzzled, but couldn't understand why someone would have it. She shook her head. "No, I don't know. It's kind of creepy."

Tom, in the meantime, continued to avoid Margot's gaze, who stood stock-still. Marjorie had come up beside her, curious about what was happening. Margot swallowed hard, waiting her turn, not entirely sure what her friend had. Riley nodded at Jenkins again. "Does this shed any more light on the situation?" Jenkins handed Daphne another protected piece of evidence, this time a small card. It was a Connecticut Driver's Permit, registered to a Nathan Charles Reed in 1955. Again, she shook her head. Riley indicated to Jenkins one more time, who then handed her a photo of the deceased, taken by the police after his body had been found. Daphne paled when she realized what it was and shook her head again. She handed them back to Jenkins.

Riley indicated that it was now Margot's turn. The procedure started the same—she took the article in her hand and said nothing. Her hand started to shake when they gave her the license, then she almost stopped breathing when she saw the photo, saying nothing. She paused a beat, then gave a very clear, concise answer. "That's my husband."

CHAPTER THREE

There was a moment of shocked silence as everyone in the room took in what Margot had said. She blushed furiously as she looked up from the photo in her hand. "Well, my ex-husband, I mean."

She handed the evidence back to Riley, and no one was able to think of what to say. Margot waited, knowing there would be so many questions, not just from the police, but everyone in the room. She didn't know where to look, so she stared off into space, waiting pensively.

The members of the police force quietly conferred with each other on what to do next. Tom would not look at Margot. He inspected his brogues intently and eventually took a step back. Detective Riley and Officer Jenkins took command.

Before they could speak, Daphne blurted out, "What? Ex-husband!?!" She then stepped right in front of her friend, imploring her for a further explanation. Margot focused in on Daphne, yet said nothing.

"Yes, it would be best if you volunteered any information you know about this man," Riley continued. "We could do this here or at the station. It's your choice."

Margot looked around the room. Only Marjorie and Daphne, along with the police were present. She sighed, feeling a sense of relief that she could finally tell her story of how she came to land in Santa Lucia, to the closest people she knew in the world. "Where do you want me to begin?"

Officer Jenkins got his notepad ready. "Wherever you like, whatever you feel is relevant." He poised his pen.

She looked around and motioned to the salon seating area of the store. Ever the hostess, she knew it was best to get everyone comfortable. It was time to tell her tale and it could take a while. She looked at everyone she knew dearly. Tom still stood, hands behind his back, avoiding her gaze, but close by. Riley stood near him, watching both members of the couple, keeping Tom from going too close to Margot. Daphne looked at her with beseeched bewilderment, while Marjorie looked kindly in her eyes, soft and warm, encouraging her to continue. Margot took a deep breath and began her story.

"I've known Nate—Nathan Reed—for my whole life." She paused, catching the surprise in her captive audience's face. "I guess I better explain."

She looked down at her lap, wrung her hands and continued. "I was born on the east coast. My family is actually well known in the fabric industry. My birth name is Margaret Jane Willmington."

Daphne couldn't help herself and blurted out, "As in Willmington Textiles?" They were a well-known firm that for some reason Margot had always hesitated ordering from when textile agent Sam Baker would recommend samples from their product lines.

Margot nodded, wanting to continue now that she'd started. "The same. Anyway, Nate's father worked for my father in the company. He was his right hand man, overseeing all of the day-to-day operations. Nate is, or I guess I should now say *was,* four years older than me. The families had planned all along that when we were of a suitable age, we would marry. So we did."

Jenkins scribbled furiously while Riley paced, waiting for her to continue. The rest of the crowd remained still and silent, reveling in the information their friend was dispensing.

"The idea was that between Nathan and me, we would inherit and carry on the business as our fathers retired," she explained matter-of-factly. "It wasn't much of a love match." She glanced in Tom's direction as she said it, who gave a nervous cough, still not looking towards her.

"When were you married?" Riley asked.

"June 21, 1952."

"Where?"

"In my hometown of Westport, Connecticut. At the Episcopalian Church."

"Do you have a copy of the license?"

"Yes, and the divorce decree as well."

"When was that finalized?"

"July 25, 1955. It was a no fault divorce."

Riley continued with the pointed questions. "Was it truly 'no fault?'"

"No. He had committed adultery many times, but I wanted nothing from him and that's also how my family wanted to treat the situation. It made fewer waves."

"You have the paperwork?"

Margot nodded.

"What about for your name change to Margot Williams?"

"I made it official as soon as I decided to settle in Santa Lucia. I have all of my legal paperwork filed here at the courthouse, and I kept my birth certificate. If you look into it, it's all above board. I just never mentioned I'd done it, I felt it was no one's concern and I wanted to start over. Everything is as it should be, I assure you."

Everyone took a moment to absorb what they were hearing, trying to comprehend in their own way why a person would do such a thing. Margot waited, knowing the police weren't anywhere near finished with their interrogation. Riley conferred with Jenkins, looking over the officer's notes, then the detective continued his line of questioning. "You said your husband committed adultery many times. How do you know?"

She sighed and rolled her eyes. "A wife just knows."

"Meaning?"

"He lied about where he was, came in late, smelling of perfume, and other things." She paused, feeling exposed.

"How long did you know this had been going on?"

"Oh, months. I don't think he was ever faithful."

"Why did you stay?"

"It was expected of me," she stated again. "I finally had enough."

"What do you mean by that?"

"By early 1954, January, I think. One of his women came by the house, telling me she was pregnant with my husband's baby. She demanded that I either give her money or my husband. She had a doctor's note confirming her pregnancy, so I knew she wasn't lying about that. She also stated dates and times she was in the company of Nathan and I could recall that he certainly wasn't with me at those specific times. That was enough for me. And enough for my parents to accept that the marriage was a sham and so was any future business arrangement."

"Do you know her name?"

"That's not something I could forget. Phoebe LaRue. She was a showgirl at a Manhattan nightclub."

"Was that her real or stage name?"

Margot shrugged. "I don't know. That's what she told me, anyway."

"What happened after that?"

"My parents finally encouraged me to divorce him, so I moved back in with them and got started on filing the paperwork."

"And then?"

"I couldn't live with them anymore. They were too controlling and it was stifling, killing me, so I left."

"Where? How?"

"I got into my car and travelled west."

"When?"

"Late April 1954, I think."

"What was your plan?"

"To get away. At first I didn't have one." The information Margot was revealing caused a surprise among her peers. In all the time they'd known her, or thought they'd known Margot or *Margaret*, she'd been very methodical, always with a clear objective or agenda. Impulsiveness seemed out of her character. She took another breath and continued. "I just drove across the country. I wanted to leave them all behind and start over. Eventually, I felt I wanted to settle and work, to do something. I got here to the Pacific and rested. I felt finally at peace and began sketching. I always loved clothes and fabrics, although my mother thought it was unbecoming for a modern girl to have to do such things for herself, when you could have hired help do it for you. I thought I might stay a few days and then head down to Hollywood, maybe get a job as a seamstress in the movies, and just work and hide."

"Why did you stay here?"

"It felt right. I finally felt calm, seeing the Pacific and Santa Lucia seemed so uncomplicated. People were friendly and didn't demand anything of me." She looked at Daphne, who was shocked, but her eyes were still warm, not cold. Margot knew she still had one friend, at least. Marjorie reached for Margot's hand and squeezed it in assurance as she continued.

"When did you first start using *Margot Williams* as your new name?"

"Unofficially, right after I left Westport. I didn't want my family or anyone else to find me. It was easy. No one questioned it along the way. But as I said earlier, I decided to take care of it formally when I decided that I wanted to reside here."

"When were you last in contact with your family?"

"The morning I left Connecticut. They thought I was driving by myself to the mill, but I left a note in my room for them to find later that I was leaving, and asking them not to look for me. They never did, as far as I know."

The fact she was not pursued by her parents gave the impression that they wanted to distance themselves from their daughter's disgrace, as much as Margot wanted to leave them behind.

"And your last contact with Nathan Reed?"

"Personally?"

Riley nodded.

"That January, the day I moved out. We only communicated through lawyers after that."

"You've not seen him since or had any other form of personal correspondence with him?"

"No."

"So you had no idea he was in Santa Lucia?"

"Yes, I mean no." Margot's answer confused the crowd, except for Daphne.

"What's the answer? Yes or no," Riley demanded. Daphne sucked in her breath, waiting to hear what Margot was going to say.

She sighed before continuing, determined to make her answer as clear as possible. "I was not aware that Nathan was in Santa Lucia. I did, however, go to Mrs. Coleman's Boarding House on Bay Street after lunch today because our new cutter, Jeannette Fox, had been residing there and had not shown up for work this morning. Daphne and I went together to check up on her. While we were there, we learned that you—well, the police anyway—had been there earlier and from the sound of it, it was to learn more about the man who'd been shot. You can verify that with Daphne and Mrs. Mildred Coleman, along with one of her guests, a Mr. Drake, I believe. So, now I guess that must have been Nathan, but I didn't know it at the time."

"Are you willing to swear that in a statement?"

"Yes."

"Did you find your employee, Miss..."

"Fox? No, and neither Mrs. Coleman or another resident, Miss Diane Phillips who works over at the

Poppy Lane Tearoom, have seen her since Saturday. You may need to look into her whereabouts, too."

Riley wasn't happy about her remark. "You don't have to tell us our job. We'll handle this our way. Just answer our questions."

"Riley!" Tom spoke up from the back with gritted teeth. "Be respectful, or I'll have your job." Officer Jenkins held Tom back and Riley cleared his throat. He made a couple of notes before speaking again.

"Why do you think he had this on him?" Riley indicated the photo and article evidence.

Margot shook her head and replied, "I guess for some reason he wanted to find me."

"Are you sure you didn't have any contact with him recently?"

"Positive."

Riley continued to interrogate, pushing the conversation in different ways to see if she was concealing any truths. "And what were you doing down on the beach yesterday?"

"Just walking with my friends after the art show. We often walk along the beach."

"Did you lead them there?"

"No."

"Did you know his body was there?"

"No, of course not!" she exclaimed.

"If you didn't know who or exactly what was going on just a few feet away, why did you not continue and also discourage your friends from coming closer? Did you know what you and your friends would find? Seems to me that you've been awfully curious about crime recently," Riley speculated.

"I wasn't involved, nor did I want to be. It was just a pleasant day out and I didn't want anything to spoil it. It was none of our business. Well, not Daphne's, Dan's nor mine, anyway," Margot replied.

Detective Riley continued as if he didn't believe her, goading her for any misstep. "How long had Nathan been in town?"

"I don't know."

"Had he come by your house or the shop?"

"Not that I know of."

"Are you sure?"

"Yes."

"Why wouldn't he contact you directly, if in fact he was here to see you?"

"I don't really know. We didn't leave things well." Margot paused. "I'm sure he'd know I wouldn't want to see him."

Riley let that go for the moment and carried on. "Have you had any strange phone calls, anonymous letters, anything out of the ordinary lately?"

She gave the question some thought and shook her head.

"Were you aware that he had notes in his room, tracking down your movements over the last week or so?" Riley announced smugly.

Margot paled at the information. "No," she replied in a small voice.

"You're sure you weren't aware of this?"

"God, yes. This is news to me. I didn't even know he was the one staying at the boarding house until you arrived just now."

Riley changed his line of questioning. "What about contact from Miss LaRue?"

"No."

He finally turned his attention off of her and directed a question to the rest of the group as he held up the picture of the corpse again. "Now that we have a positive identity of the victim, I'll ask again. Has anyone else seen a man of this description in Poppy Cove or lurking about here, at Ms. Willmington's residence, or anywhere else in town?" Riley was insistent on referring to Margot using her original name and passed the photo around to everyone again. No one recognized him.

When Tom received the picture, he handed the image back to Riley and said, "I can't say that I specifically saw him, but I may have seen something."

Riley turned on his partner. "What do you mean?"

"It was the other night. Friday, I think. We got to Margot's late, around 11 p. m., and I think I saw someone in the bushes."

"Are you sure?"

Tom scratched his head and replied, "No, not really. It was dark and there was only a brief rustle, so I didn't think anything of it at the time. It could have been an animal, even Mr. Cuddles, Margot's cat. Now that we have something to go on, maybe it's related."

Riley turned to Margot. "Did you see or hear anything that night?"

She shook her head. Margot's resolve was beginning to fade. She could only handle the intensity for so long. Riley was almost finished for the night.

"We'll need you to go down to the morgue first thing in the morning to identify the body formally. Bring some proper identification, Ms. Willmington, including your marriage and divorce documentation. And don't leave town."

She nodded. "I don't have to come into the station tonight?"

"No. Not at this point. We'll need to talk to you again." He stared her down silently. Riley faced Tom. "Malone, you're too close to the case. I'll have to mention this to the Chief, and you know you'll be given other assignments and not allowed to be involved in anything pertaining to this one." Although Margot and Riley got along politely, Riley would occasionally become exasperated with her when it came to Tom and her involvement in his work. There seemed to be an underlying tension that caused her to now wonder if he actually didn't like her. *Now he has a reason,* she thought. *Great.*

The police wrapped up their questioning and were leaving, including Tom. Margot looked at him beseechingly, and he responded by coming over to her as she stood up. He put his arm on her shoulder. They embraced in an awkward fashion. "I have to go." His voice was ragged and restrained.

"Tom," Margot ran a hand affectionately through his hair.

He did not reply at first, but set his hat firmly on his head after she removed her hand. "I'll call you when I can. I've got to go." He broke away from her.

"Tom?"

"I don't know," he sighed.

"You said there's nothing I couldn't tell you."

"I know; I mean, I don't know. Look, I've got to go." With that, the police left, leaving Margot alone with Marjorie and Daphne, who had more questions that she had to answer.

CHAPTER FOUR

An awkward silence prevailed as the women were left alone. Margot exhaustedly slumped back down in her chair, wrung out, and sagged her head. Daphne sat still, stunned from what she'd just learned about her friend. "Well." Marjorie slapped her hands on her thighs and stood up. "I'm sure you girls have a lot to talk about and I think it's time for me to call it a night."

Margot looked up at her pleadingly. Marjorie patted her hand as she walked by. "Now, dear, I'm sure there's not much more to say and you'll tell me the rest I need to know in your own sweet time. Don't worry; this too shall pass. You'll see. No one gets through this life without a secret or two."

Margot smiled in gratitude and looked over to her friend and business partner as Marjorie left. Daphne continued to say nothing. Margot waited, eventually having to say something as her friend was still silent. "Daff, it's still me; ask me anything, I'll tell you the truth. Honest."

Daphne glared at her. "I don't even know what to call you."

"What do you mean?"

"Well, who are you? Margaret or Margot?" There was an anger in Daphne's voice that Margot had never heard before.

Margot decided to remain calm. "Margot, please. That's who I am, who I was when we met and who I'll continue to be." Her friend said nothing, so she carried on. "Look, you know I never cared to bring up my past, and, when I was ready, I was going to tell you and, well,

Tom, everything—if either of you are still willing to listen to me."

Daphne sighed and thought for a bit. By now, it was getting dark outside and gloomy in the shop. "What about now? Will you tell me any more?"

Margot nodded, relieved. "What do you want to know?"

"Everything, anything. What didn't you tell the police? Tell me who this 'Margaret' and 'Nathan' were. How exactly did you get here? What else don't I know about you?" Once Daphne got going, she didn't want to stop. She wanted to know all, thirsty for her friend's secret life. "Can you go over everything again, but this time add in the details?"

"Do we still have that bottle of scotch upstairs?" Margot inquired.

"The one left over from the Christmas party?"

"That would be the one."

"It's up in my desk," Daphne brightened with her reply. "I don't think there's much to eat around here, maybe some saltines in the lunchroom. The tearoom's closed by now."

"That's okay; I couldn't eat a bite, but a stiff drink sounds good. Maybe two." Margot responded.

"Or three." With Daphne's comment and following smile, Margot knew she still had some things to confess, but it would be all right—if not now, then not too far off in the future.

The girls made their way upstairs to the stashed scotch in the office. They poured themselves triples and turned on the Los Angeles jazz station on the radio. As Miles Davis' *Straight, No Chaser* played over the airwaves, the girls each took a long swig and Daphne could wait no more. "So you were married?"

Margot nodded. "It wasn't a fairy tale."

"So his name was Nathan…" Daphne prompted her friend to go on.

Margot was willing. "S, yes. I knew him from childhood. He was okay, good looking, but I didn't love him. He was more like a brother to me, but it's what my parents wanted."

"So you're rich?"

Margot blushed. "Well, the mills made money. My family was rich, but I didn't take anything from them when I left, just what the lawyers worked out in my divorce and the savings and investments my parents had set up for me as I grew up. It was enough for me to get here and establish myself. Really, that was it."

"There must be more."

Margot shrugged. "There might be, but I don't want anything to do with it."

"Why?"

Margot looked at her friend as she took another sip and thought about Daphne's life. She was very comfortable in her family. The Huntington-Smythes were a happy lot, with great expectations on Daphne's brother William, the male heir apparent, but little to no demands placed on Daphne or her younger sister, Lizzie, apart from the expectation that they would marry well when the opportunity presented itself. Daphne didn't have the same expectations or obligations that Margot had grown up with. Margot sighed, ready to continue. "My parents had my life all planned out—to their benefit. They knew everything I was going to have, say, do, before I did."

"What about brothers or sisters? Was it the same for them? Couldn't they take on some of the business?"

Margot shook her head. "I'm an only child."

Daphne nodded quietly, allowing her friend to elaborate. She knew of girls who grew up as Margot had. She saw it all the time at the country club, but this was the first time she could understand what that could actually mean when it came from someone so close to her.

"I felt safe when I was a child; I didn't have any worries. I was quite happy, to be honest. I was always drawing and playing, dressing up my dolls in the remnants and samples from the mills, and even created some of my own clothes as I got older. By the way, my sewing and design skills are self-taught, if you are wondering. I might as well come clean that I don't have a diploma or degree in design. That's bound to come out now when they look over my background. It was all fine and good for me to whip up a dress or two in the privacy of my own room, as long as I never wore them to any important social or business function. According to my mother, that would never do."

Daphne waved her hand, dismissing the notion that Margot's skills or formal education were an issue. "That's terrible. Your talents are tremendous. You've created some of the most glamorous garments I've ever seen. Goodness, if they're good enough for Hollywood stars like Joyce Jones, they're good enough for anyone!"

Margot shrugged off the compliment. "My parents would have never let me pursue a career in creative fashion. It was fine that they sold to designers, but that was business and they certainly would not approve of how I am part of such a small shop." Margot phrased it flatly—just another matter of fact. "I was considered to be an asset to the business, first as an assistant to my father, then as my husband Nathan's minion. They meant that for my married life, too. All business, to keep up Willmington Mills. And then, when Nathan was settled in, father and Douglas—that's Nate's father—were to retire, so was I, to make babies and carry on the families."

Daphne's head was reeling. She had a million questions but didn't know whether to interrupt and ask or just let Margot unravel her tale. Sometimes she couldn't help herself and just blurted out. "But that's not you!"

Margot smiled, relieved that Daphne seemed to understand her. Perhaps she was the first person she'd been able to let in who did. "No," Margot agreed. "That's not me." The girls realized they had drained their glasses and poured themselves another. "Now don't get me wrong, I'm not against marriage or children, I just want them to be my choices, when I'm ready and in love."

"You mean Tom?"

"Yes, if he'll still have me."

"Does he know any of this?"

Margot shook her head. "Actually, before all of this happened, I was planning on telling Tom the whole story tonight and then give him a *yes* to his question if he'd still have me after I told him about Nathan."

"And now, he shows up here, dead," Daphne concluded. "Listen, I need to ask you," she added nervously. "Did you know he was here?"

"No, I had no idea."

"What you told the police, was that really the last time you saw him? Back in Connecticut?"

Margot affirmed the question. "I was just as shocked as anyone to find out he was here in Santa Lucia, let alone dead." It was catching up with her again, and she slumped in her desk chair, taking off her high heels. "Wow, what a day."

"I'll say." Daphne quietly sipped, giving her friend a moment. Then she couldn't help herself. "Why do you think he was here?"

"I guess to see me? I mean, he had the newspaper clipping."

"Yes, but why exactly after all this time?"

Margot took a sip and suggested a reason. "I wonder if it's money. I can't imagine he still loved me, or to be honest ever did."

"What was he like?"

"He was a rogue," Margot said slyly. "Always had his hand in the cookie jar, or till, or a girl's dress, for that matter."

"Oh, my!" Daphne exclaimed. "Did you ever love him?"

Margot thought about the question. "No, I don't think I ever did."

"Care to go on?"

Now that Margot was on a roll, she was game to continue and felt safe to tell all. "He was always running around with this girl or another, stealing money from his dad's wallet, running schemes out of his locker at school. He wasn't bootlegging to teens or doing any really nasty stuff, just small things—betting pools, girly magazines, the occasional cheap piece of jewelry, that sort of thing."

"Your parents were okay with that?"

"I don't think they ever knew, or if they did, they never believed it. If he was ever caught by the teachers or the principal, his father would brush it off, saying that's what boys do. Nate was really proud of his exploits."

"He didn't ever hurt you, did he?"

"Physically?"

"Yes."

"No, nothing like that. Emotionally, he could be a real jerk, though. I'd have to say in his defense, however, he actually pretended to behave after we got married."

"What was your wedding like?" Daphne inquired.

"My wedding? It was this big, fussy, finicky event— the so-called perfect June wedding. I had this big, poufy dress that my mother picked out for me. In fact, she took control over every aspect. Between her and Nathan's mother, they picked out everything, registered the gift list and invited three hundred guests including many people I didn't know. They chose the flowers, colors, and attendants—all of it. Any time I gave an opinion or suggestion, it was shot down in a condescending manner.

Eventually, I just gave up and went through it. It's pretty much a blur now. I guess I blocked a lot of it out."

The news of this surprised Daphne. Margot was usually so present in her day, focused and on the ball, not necessarily a controlling person, but very much deliberate in her actions and reactions. She wondered if her past was the reason why she was like that now.

"What about actual married life?"

"Oh, it started out fine. We honeymooned in Europe and were given a brand new house in the 'right' neighborhood—both were gifts from the Reeds. When we got back, I was told I would no longer to be working at the mill and to become the perfect housewife and hostess for my husband. Nate tried to settle down, or at least, made the appearance of being faithful. When I saw how decent he could be, I thought that maybe he was growing up, becoming a real man, so I made an effort to get along as well, to make a real marriage out of it. I thought that was making me mature, too. After all, I was twenty-one at the time. Now that I look back, it seems that he just had his tracks covered and his lies down pat."

"You told the police earlier that you knew that Nate hadn't been faithful and about that showgirl. What happened?"

"Just before Thanksgiving, I got this anonymous call from a girl, who told me that Nathan was hers and I should get out of the picture."

"No!"

"Yes. I thought it was a crank call, even laughed at it. When I got off the phone, I asked him about it, and he just shrugged and brushed it off. I felt a little funny about it, and actually talked to my mother. She shrugged it off too, and told me to focus my skills on making a proper home for an executive and starting a family. There weren't any more calls for a while, so I didn't really think about it. Then he started working later and later at the office and had business meetings in New York, or so he claimed."

"But he wasn't?"

"No, I don't think so now, not at all."

"What happened?"

"Well, it turns out I was right that he never stopped fooling around the whole time we were married."

"The phone call?" Daphne asked.

"It went past that. I got a visit one afternoon at home. From a Miss Phoebe LaRue."

"Really? Did she look like a 'Phoebe LaRue?'" Daphne couldn't help but smirk.

"Very much so." Margot reflected back the same expression. "And if you can believe it, she was a nightclub girl from New York City."

"Seriously?"

"Yes."

"Now do go on!" Daphne could not contain her enthusiasm. For a moment, the girls almost forgot they were talking about Margot's actual life, not some great salacious tale about one of their social set.

"Anyway, she showed up in the middle of a Tuesday afternoon in late January. She said that she had a note from the doctor, claiming she was pregnant, and Nathan was the father."

"No!"

"Yes. At first I didn't believe her. I mean, she was such a cheap floozy, wearing a revealing dress that was far too tight and thin for the weather, with a fox stole draped over her shoulders, fire engine red lipstick, too much powder and perfume, just not a typical Connecticut housewife. She arrived unannounced, in a flap, with a taxi waiting, while she tried to extort me for money!"

Daphne just shook her head.

Margot kept talking. "I told her to get out. She said she wouldn't and stayed seated on my brand new sofa. She took out a black date book, where she'd written in various dates in the fall and even the week before and upcoming, Nate's name and times. I grabbed the book and, believe it or not, his was the only name there. I took a closer look at the book and they were all times when he'd claimed to be working late or out of town."

"What exactly did she want?"

"She said they'd become 'exclusive' and she wanted him or money—one or the other. She said his baby was due in July. He either had to divorce me and make an honest woman of her or give her enough money to raise her child and provide a life like I had for herself."

"And if you didn't?"

"She'd go to the local papers and make a scene. She also knew he was gambling and sometimes in some disreputable places with some questionable people, too. She said it meant nothing in the city, but it could ruin him and the families' business in Westport. She might have been trashy, but she was right. In a community like I lived in, it was like committing career and social suicide."

"Then what did you do?" Daphne was all ears.

"I told her I'd deal with it and sent her away. She left full of threats, and I think she meant them."

"What did Nate say when he got home?"

"I left before he got there. That was it. I knew she was telling the truth and as far as I was concerned, she could have him. I packed in a panic, using just a small case and went back to my parents' house. I told them everything. They were very reluctant to believe me and disappointed that there could be such a scandal. They tried very hard to deny it, but eventually they knew it was true. The next morning, my parents started divorce proceedings on my behalf and it never hit the papers.

"I was at loose ends. My mother kept pestering me, even suggesting that had I been a little more 'accommodating' to my husband's desires, he might not have strayed. Both of my parents started to place some of the blame for Nathan's behavior on me. I was told to stay put, not to go out, not to be seen socially during the waiting period for the divorce. They'd look after it, quash any rumors and after a suitable time, they'd find a better heir and successor for me—and the business—to marry."

"What happened to the Reeds?"

"Well, father 'retired' his business partner—that's Nathan's father—with a severance package, and I had no idea what happened at that point to my ex-husband. He could have married Miss LaRue, for all I know."

"Until yesterday."

"Yes, yesterday. I still don't know what brought him out here."

"Are you creeped out that he's been stalking you, watching your every move for the past week?"

"Yes! I feel like I need a hot bath or shower, like I have to scrub off. It's as if his eyes were on me, and I wonder what in the world he's been doing."

"What about Jeannette? Do you think that she had something to do with it or was involved with him? Or maybe she was stalking him as he stalked you?" Daphne gave a little shiver.

Margot aggressively shook her head, wanting to clear out what she was thinking—real or imagined. She drained her glass for what she thought was the last time that night. "I have to admit, I'm overwhelmed with it all. To find out someone—maybe two people—have been watching me, I can't put it into words. It's weird, but it doesn't seem like something he'd do, which also has me confused. He never stayed fixated on one girl for very long, so why me?"

Daphne shrugged. "What about Jeannette? Did she seem like his type?"

Margot laughed involuntarily. "Any girl in a skirt was his type."

"Do you think she murdered him?" Daphne asked. "I know we didn't know her very well, but she didn't seem like a girl who could get really hung up on a guy."

Margot thought about that. "But, being that she was from New York, arriving at what seems like the same time, it makes me wonder if they were together, or was she trailing him? If you ask me, he wasn't that great of a catch. I traveled across country to get away from him, not to be with him. I mean, he wasn't perfect and I didn't think of him often, but he'd been my husband. I may have been angry, but I never truly wished him dead."

"But someone did."

"They did," Margot agreed.

"And was it Jeannette?"

"Or is she dead or in danger, too?"

Daphne sighed. "I'm stumped on that one. Santa Lucia's finest are going to have to figure that out."

CHAPTER FIVE

The girls sat in silence, while Daphne drained her glass. She turned the conversation back onto Margot's past. "And then you left town?"

Margot stopped, thinking over all that had happened, and how much she wanted to tell her friend. Daphne was so innocent, and Margot was hoping that if she told her every little thing, that Daphne would not think less of her. The last pour turned out to be the second to last, and Daphne held out her glass for a refill as well. Margot knew that she'd done some things she wasn't proud of—either in retaliation or as a gut reaction. Telling the truth was worth the risk, and the scotch was making the telling quite painless at the moment. Why stop now? "Not quite."

"What do you mean?" Daphne couldn't open her eyes any wider. "That would have been enough for me."

"I was placed under curfew and basically house arrest by my parents while they kept a wrap on the social situation. I was going crazy. Mother told me that my life would be how she chose it. I wasn't allowed to talk to any of my friends; I wasn't even permitted to go to a department store. What if I were seen by the neighbors, business associates, or their wives? It was awful.

"Eventually as the divorce got underway and the Reeds were out of the picture, my parents allowed me to go back to work in the office. They realized I had to do something while all that was going on. They still didn't feel it was acceptable for me to rejoin the social scene, but they kept their engagement calendar full as if nothing was happening. They continued to go out to dinner and

parties, leaving me to think about—in their words—
'What I'd done,' as if it wasn't their decisions all down
the line. Most nights I sat in my room, writing in my
journal, thinking, and overthinking.

"My parents started paying less attention to me,
convinced I'd settled down, doing what they said and
that I was quietly waiting for their instructions. Instead, I
started going out when they would leave. I headed to the
city—it wasn't very far by train. I'd go to some of the
jazz clubs and other places in the village, sometimes just
to the Automat, anywhere to be out. No one knew me, so
I could just wander. I'd make it back before they even
knew I was gone.

"I started to understand a bit of the appeal that the
night life had on Nate."

Daphne was shocked. "You mean you gambled?
Illegally?"

Margot laughed. "No, not that, but some of the other."

"The other?"

"Well, the nightlife. One of my favorite haunts during
that weird, yet somehow wonderful time, was the
Vanguard, among other places in the village. The music,
the people. They were all so free and lively. Expressing
themselves through music and poetry. It was so different
from the life my parents deemed proper. It was fun and a
little dangerous, too. I was out on my own with no one
looking out for me, or watching my every move. Except
for the last time. "

"What happened then?" Daphne, by this time was
warmly rapt, a bit from the story, a bit from the liquor,
and was leaning forward with her chin resting in her
hands on her desk, not really caring about her poise or
posture.

"Nate was there at one of the clubs. There was some
barely dressed strumpet on his lap."

"Not Phoebe?"

"Definitely not Phoebe. He practically threw her off his lap when he saw me. I think it was just an immediate reaction, I don't think he still cared for me, or whether I saw him with someone else.

"However, I felt angry. I had wanted to escape from everyone and everything that had a hold on me and there he was. I saw another man making eyes at me from the bar. I'd seen him before, but I didn't think twice about him; he wasn't my type. He was gruff, a bit rough around the edges and seemed to live too hard. Not only had he been keeping an eye on me, but also watching Nate and his lady of the night. Because of that, I decided to join him at the bar.

"Turns out the woman was his girlfriend who was a little too giving with others—Nate in particular that night. He wasn't too happy about it, telling me all about how she liked to make him jealous. Nate was eyeing us too, and when the boyfriend started making advances on me to get a rise out of his girlfriend, I was in just the right mood to play along. I have to admit I had too much to drink that night, and the flirting didn't end on the barstools. I went too far and woke up in a rather rundown apartment and recollected exactly what I'd done. I didn't even know his name. In that one night, I had become *that* sort of girl."

Daphne blushed, and her mouth formed a rounded, soft, "Oh...."

Margot turned the same shade of crimson. "I only behaved that way the one time. I was ashamed and disappointed I'd let my feelings towards Nathan lead me to do something like that. The funny thing is my parents never even realize that I'd been out all night, but that was enough for me.

"The very next day—April 26, 1954—I knew I had to leave. I pretended to be on my way to work and just took off. I did leave a note for my parents telling them I was leaving and asked them not to try to find me, I would be in touch when I was ready. I stopped at the bank, withdrew all the money I could and just drove."

"And you haven't seen them since?"

Margot shook her head. "Maybe I will one day, but not yet." Then she sighed, realizing, "but I may have to now. After all, the police are going to look into Nate's and my past as well."

"So that's when you became 'Margot Williams?'"

"Unofficially, yes. As soon as I had my money from the bank and I crossed the state line, the name popped into my head and I left Margaret Willmington behind and became Margot Williams. It came out so easily, and no one ever bothered to question it, or look at my identification. Even my signature looked similar enough, so I don't think it ever came up in my travels."

Daphne took a moment to contemplate about all she'd learned tonight. She looked at her friend with so many thoughts running through her head. Still, intuitively she trusted Margot, and thought that there was still a person she knew well under all of that. She felt a twinge of worry as she realized, "But you lied to the police!"

"No, I don't think so. When?"

"When you said the last time you saw your husband— well, ex-husband—alive. You saw him at the club, not when you left the house to divorce him."

Margot tensed, realizing that to be true. "Oh, my goodness, you're right. I guess I forgot all about that. I saw Nate, but didn't actually talk to him that night." She shuddered at the thought of having to admit that part, most likely to the police, and possibly publicly while Tom was in the room. "I will have to mention it."

"Riley will have a field day with that," Daphne remarked.

Margot rolled her eyes. "I just hope he doesn't take it out on Tom."

"Are you going to tell Tom *all* of this?"

"Yes," she said with relief. "It's out now, so it's best to really clear the air. He told me he loves me, and there's nothing I could have done that would change his mind. I guess I'll find out."

"Well, if he sticks with you through this, it's definitely love." Daphne concluded.

****

It was nearly midnight by time the ladies had finished talking. Daphne had so many questions for her friend. After the hard discussion was concluded, her natural curiosity lingered. She asked Margot about what she'd done between Westport and Santa Lucia. Margot told her that she basically just drove across the country, taking her time over the course of a few months, connecting up with various highways and byways, taking detours in large cities and small towns. She visited tourist attractions, natural wonders, and art galleries. As she felt her worries and her past melt away, her creativity kicked in. She wrote in journals and picked up a sketch pad, drawing freely anything that caught her eye. The images became shapes, then shapes became flow, flow became structure, structure became garments.

By the time Margot reached San Francisco, she knew she wanted to stay on the west coast. The limitless view and the endless horizon of the Pacific opened up possibilities to her. She didn't want to *stay* in the city by the bay. She loved it, but it didn't fit with her future ideals, not quite. She went south, feeling as wild as the Big Sur waves and groves, getting lost and overwhelmed in their massiveness. Along the way, she'd come up with her destination—Los Angeles—Hollywood to be specific. Her plan was to get a job in the movie industry, as a seamstress or something of the like in a studio wardrobe department. She was sure there would be plenty of work and although she was an amateur, she felt her skills were there. It was mid-July and she had one more stop along the way—Santa Lucia. Margot figured she'd spend one night and then take her chances in the land of glamour.

Then a funny thing happened as she drove into town off the freeway and parked right on Oceanview Drive. She got out of her powder blue Bel-Air convertible sedan and sat on the beach, looking out to the sea. Her whole body relaxed in a way she'd never known. All she could think of was 'home.' She sat on the sand, in the sun, alone, and found a feeling of belonging she couldn't explain, nor ever felt before. She decided to stay another day, which kept becoming just one more day everyday as she explored the town and its surroundings. She liked the town, its setup, the market, fountain, and the pace of life. She stayed in a little hotel just off the beach, gaining a new routine, which involved morning walks along the beach, followed by endless hours sketching ideas in the Poppy Lane Tearoom. Sometimes breakfast turned into lunch while she was creating a portfolio of ideas to take with her to Hollywood, yet she was never quite ready to leave. Occasionally, she would glance at the cute little corner storefront across lane with its 'For Rent' sign. Lana, who ran the tearoom was a great gal, pausing to glance over her shoulder as Margot drew, and complimented her ideas, sometimes sitting down and passing the time of day with her between meal rushes.

In addition, there was a flighty, birdlike woman full of energy always scribbling in a notepad with a young man in tow, carrying a camera and following her bossy directions. She turned out to be Loretta, a reporter with the *Santa Lucia Times* newspaper, who had ambitions to become its Society Editor. She was always pleasant, but always in a hurry, often glancing at Margot's drawings and tossing a 'nice!' or 'I like that' her way as she breezed by.

Another tearoom regular was a girl around her age, with blonde curls and a lively, pleasant disposition. She often came in and picked up take-out orders, but occasionally stayed and passed the time with Lana. She noticed Margot and always smiled her way. After a while, she sat down and introduced herself. Daphne and Margot hit it off immediately. Daphne helped herself to Margot's drawings, genuinely interested in what she saw. Margot opened up and told Daphne of her plans to go south and find work. Daphne's face lit up as she exclaimed, "Say, you know how to make dresses like this?"

Margot nodded and shrugged, saying that she actually thought about constructing them before she even drew them. In her mind, the details always seemed to come first, before the overall look. She couldn't explain it; it's just how she saw things.

Daphne kept pouring over the sketches, marvelling at the ideas, feeling as if she'd struck gold. "Listen, I'm sort of at loose ends myself. I've been toying around with a few ideas for a dress shop, but I was just going to purchase garment lines, accessories and such. Why don't you stay and design your own fashions here?"

Margot wasn't sure, but Daphne was convinced. Her family was very well connected with the right social set for such an establishment and with Margot's talent, they could be very successful. Margot sat quietly and entertained the idea as Daphne enthusiastically prattled on, mentioning that the cute storefront up for rent across the way was actually owned by her father and they could get it at a good price. Plus, it was in a prime location at the intersection of Poppy Lane and Cove Street.

Margot didn't mull it over for long. She did have some money and no real plans for L. A. She had to admit Daphne's idea felt right and so she set about legally leaving Margaret Willmington permanently behind and formally becoming Margot Williams. It would enable her to sign a lease and business agreement legitimately. In September, with minimal hassle and basic business paperwork, Poppy Cove—the girls' shared atelier—took up residence in the vacant building. Although they didn't open for business until the spring of 1955, it was a busy time. Margot started right away on her first collection and helped set up shop, while Daphne ordered accessories and saw to the design of the store. Margot left the hotel and took up residence in the little office upstairs. She didn't have or need much at the time, blissfully content to throw herself into creating her new life of silks and satins.

The girls got on very well, and the new life suited Margot to a T. She still had a need to keep to herself, and found it easy to distance her past with such a bright future. The two were so busy and getting on so well, neither one bothered to bring up the past. Until now.

CHAPTER SIX

Both Daphne and Margot had to admit they were a little worse for wear the next morning. Even though they each had chosen fresh and lively spring dresses (Daphne in a mint green sleeveless shift with a white bolero jacket and a string of pearls, Margot in a powder blue cotton lawn dress with a ballerina neckline, cap sleeves, fitted bodice and wide tea length skirt that had a scalloped white embroidered hem), neither looked their usual top-notch selves. Irene, the sultry store manager who generally worked Tuesday through Saturday, had been unaware of the previous evening's events. She smirked when she saw her two employers' less than sparkling presences that morning. "Looks like some girls got up to something last night," she remarked.

Marjorie gently swatted Irene on the arm. Irene gave a quizzically dirty look at her and the head seamstress shook her head, indicating for her to keep mum and not to bring it up. Margot and Daphne chose to ignore it all, quietly going about their routine.

By the time the store opened at nine, it had already been a long day for Margot. After they'd left the store the previous night, close to one in the morning, she hadn't slept at all from both drumming up her past and also with concern over the whereabouts of Jeannette and what she was up to. Margot had also already been down to the morgue promptly at eight a.m., to identify Nathan Reed's body. It was him without a doubt. Officer Jenkins and Detective Riley were there, watching her every expression and move. They asked Margot about her involvement with the deceased again, which she answered fully, including that she'd remembered seeing Nate for the last time in New York City, specifically naming the date—April 25, 1954—and the place—Moe's in the village—but that she had not actually spoken with him. Riley wrote down the new information and was not impressed.

It was awful. She was unnerved and sad, but numb and felt lost as well after seeing Nate's corpse. Tom was not there. Margot hadn't seen him since the police had left, and he hadn't called or made any contact. She didn't know what to think about that. She knew that he must have been watched by his superiors and warned to stay away from the case and, most likely, Margot personally as well, and she was too worn out to contemplate it.

Margot and Daphne both needed peace, quiet and coffee. They went back up to their private office and pretended to shuffle papers. Their silence was broken when Loretta flew up the stairs and into the room, swinging the closed door wide open. "Loretta's coming upstairs," crackled Irene's voice on the telephone intercom speaker at the same time.

"Margot! What's going on?" Loretta dropped the morning's edition of the *Santa Lucia Times* on her desk as she sat down in the guest chair. "I'm sure you saw this?"

Margot glanced at the headline. BEACH CORPSE IDENTITY KNOWN, screamed the front page with a picture of Nathan on the cover. The article went on to say that the police knew the identity of the corpse and had some leads as to why the stranger was in Santa Lucia. Other than that, the article was short and tight lipped. "Rumor has it that you are in the know on this one, Margot. Is that true?" Loretta sped through her statement and question so fast that Margot had to think of what the reporter actually asked in order to answer.

"Yes, Loretta. I know a lot more about it than I want to," she stated.

"Okay, time to fess up, friend. What's going on?" Loretta was poised and ready to take down any and every word her friend uttered.

"Um, why is the Society Editor on the Crime Beat?" Daphne interrupted.

"Well, I've actually pulled some strings. Jack, the Editor-in-Chief owes me one. His wife got a little too friendly with a waiter or two at one too many social teas and I have the photos to prove it." Loretta grinned. "Weathers was chomping at the bit to get to this story. Who would you rather have? Him or me tell your side of it?" The reporter was barely seated in her chair, twitching like a hummingbird. She undid the button of her fitted grey flannel suit jacket and hiked up her slim pencil skirt, ready for action. Her horn-rimmed glasses perched on her nose seemed to vibrate from her energy. Even her brunette curls bounced.

Margot sighed and rolled her eyes, feeling weary. Last night and the confession had caught up with her. She paused, wondering how much she wanted to say. She trusted her friend, but after all, this was for the *Times*. There was so much at stake—her reputation, Poppy Cove, Tom, and possibly her parents once again. Telling her now closest friends, Daphne and Loretta, was one thing, even talking to the police—she had to tell them everything, even if it did affect her romantic situation with Tom. Honesty was a risk she had to take when upholding the law. But sharing any sordid details with the social set of Santa Lucia and beyond? That was another matter entirely. She perked up when she realized how she could handle it. "On one condition."

"Name it." Loretta stated.

"I get final approval of your article. If I think you've written too many personal things, or it's written in a way that's going to affect my business or personal reputation, you have to change it. Okay?" Margot was firm.

Loretta sighed momentarily. She'd written plenty of salacious tidbits in her former life as a gossip columnist in Hollywood before coming to sleepy Santa Lucia and taking her current position in a rather staid community. "Deal, but only if you tell me everything." Margot was taken aback. "No, no, I don't mean for the paper. For me. I'll be good professionally, but I want to know it all personally. Spill it, sister." She put her pen and paper down. "Talk to Loretta, honey, and we'll work on the story later together." She reached over and touched Margot's hand to reassure her.

So once again, Margot told her whole story to Loretta of how and why she came to stay in Santa Lucia. When she was done, the reporter gave a low wolf whistle. "Well, then, you've had a life! Trust me, you've not been the baddest girl I've known, but you've got some history behind you."

Margot looked a little worried that maybe Loretta was not too pleased with what she'd found out about her friend. Loretta laughed as she looked at her face. "Oh, don't look so fretful! I'm just kidding. Listen, we've all got something we've left behind."

"You too?" Margot asked.

Loretta nodded. "Me too."

"Like what?"

"Oh, no, this isn't my story. We'll get into that another time." Loretta grabbed her pad and pen. "Okay, let's see what I'll say about you and your relationship to the deceased, Mr. Nathan Reed."

Margot fiddled at her paperwork while Loretta scrawled manically and flipped the pages of her spiral notebook, pausing every now and then to think, her green eyes scrunching up and flashing, shifting her position every now and then in her chair. In about fifteen minutes—which seemed like an eternity—the reporter asked, "How's this so far?"

She handed her notebook over to Margot. "Sorry it's a bit messy; I tend to scrawl when I write in a hurry."

There was silence as Margot read over what Loretta had produced to that point. It was good; tasteful, but accurate and informative. Loretta had reported the truth of the murder victim's identity and that Margot had been his former wife, citing her birth name and place. She stuck to the most basic of facts, but not revealing the reasons for divorce or why Margot came out west, and she did state that the two had not been in contact since Margot had left Connecticut in 1954. In the article, Loretta stated who Margot is now, her place of business and position in society, and also confirmed that Margot had no idea that Nathan was in Santa Lucia, until after the police had informed her that he was the deceased corpse washed up on the shore. She also wrote that Margot had no idea why he was in Santa Lucia.

Margot nodded her approval, then Loretta started up on a new tack. "Great. Let's look at what's happening now. There's the buzz about both Jeannette Fox and Nathan staying at Mrs. Coleman's Boarding House. Do you think they were in cahoots? She just came out from New York too, didn't she? Do you think Jeannette's part of it, or in danger?"

Margot related the recent developments regarding Nathan's recent actions in Santa Lucia and what she knew of Jeannette's appearance and disappearance in town to the reporter. Loretta scribbled furiously, while Daphne added her two cents in, feeling glad to be part of the story.

"Oh, that Mrs. Coleman! I'll say she runs a tidy ship, but, wow, don't mess with her rules." Loretta laughed.

Daphne asked, "Do you know her?"

"Yes. I boarded there when I first came to town from Hollywood. I lasted less than a week!"

Daphne's eyes went wide. "What did you do?"

"She didn't like how I tromped down the stairs and I left my papers everywhere. She also said I was too nosy for my own good."

"You? Never!" Daphne commented.

Margot asked, "When did you get here, Loretta?"

She thought for a moment, recalling the years. "I can't quite believe it, but I've been here since 1952."

"Why did you leave Hollywood?" Daphne wondered.

Loretta blushed and commented abruptly, "Oh, I don't have time to go into that now. Give me a tick and I'll just finish this up." She put her head down and wrote faster than ever. In a few minutes, she remarked in triumph, "Done!"

Margot was surprised. "Already?"

"Yep," Loretta confirmed. "And it's good. You'll be pleased; trust me."

Loretta sat anxiously while she waited for Margot to finish reading the article. "As I said, Jack still owes me one, so I'll guarantee that he won't change the story once I put it to bed, but he's going to want to run a picture, probably of both of you. He may even see if he can pull a picture from one of the locals back east of the two of you together. Are you ready for that?"

Margot breathed heavily, but relented. "I guess. Let's just get it over with. If I don't agree, it'll show up sometime anyway." She paused, then touched Loretta's arm. "Thanks. I guess if this had to be done, I'm glad it was you handling it."

Loretta gently swatted her friend's arm, giving a laugh. "Ah, don't worry about it. There'll be a bit of a flap and it'll blow over. Who knows? It might even be good for business. And hey, now the Nancy Lewises and all the other moneyed ones know that you're one of them, not just some clever girl with a needle and thread. Might actually get you more business."

"You think so?"

Loretta was emphatic. "Absolutely. Once they get past the rumor and idea of scandal, they'll know that you're one of those *Willmingtons* and also that you know how to keep a secret. You've known how to be discreet about naughty bits. You've done it for years."

Margot wasn't sure, but at that point, she was too tired for it to matter. Loretta started gathering up her things. "Well, I've got to fly. This is front page news and I need to file this now." She took another look at her friend. "Mar, it'll be okay. By the way, how's Tom handling it?"

She gave her head a slow shake. "He hasn't spoken to me since he heard me talking about it all while he was on official duty."

"No!" Loretta sat down again. "Nothing? He hasn't called, dropped by?"

"Nothing," Margot said. "I'm not sure how he's taking it."

"Oh, pish-tosh! He's a big boy, a man of the world." Loretta tried to pass it off as nothing. "Listen, like I've said, I've heard worse stories by some of the most upstanding and square clean-cut people you could imagine. And I'm no saint either. Look, Tom's probably just busy. It's a big case, even if they do have a lead."

"He's been taken off the case. Um, I don't think I told you, but he'd asked me to marry him."

"Oh, wow, that's fabulous!" Loretta exclaimed. "When's the big day?"

"That's the thing. He asked me before all this came out. I was actually going to give him an answer last night, just before all this happened. I was going to tell him everything, privately, but then it turned out that Nate was the corpse on the beach." She gave an ironic, self-defeated chuckle. "I think it might all be over now. I don't think he thinks that highly of me anymore, and he certainly won't want to marry me, even if I was coming around to the idea."

Loretta was finally at a loss for words, a rarity for her. Daphne, who'd been in the room the whole time, quietly listening and absorbing the conversation, finally chimed in. "Well, gee, I'm feeling a little left out," she genuinely pouted.

Loretta looked at her. "What do you mean?"

Daphne had a funny look on her face. "I don't think I've lived. Not yet, anyway. I don't have any secrets. I've not really done anything wrong, really. And my parents have been good to me. They've never made me feel guilty, or told me what to do. They talk about the new teens rebelling, but I certainly never felt the need to do that."

"Well, that's great, Daphne. That's good. I wish that had been how I grew up. I wouldn't have gotten myself into this mess if I hadn't felt forced to run away," Margot encouraged.

Loretta agreed. "I never would have left Vermont if I hadn't had such strict parents."

"Yes, but it gave you a reason for an adventure. Loretta, you moved out to Hollywood and made an exciting life for yourself. I've always been in Santa Lucia."

"That's right," Loretta said. "And some of those activities made me have to run away and come here."

Daphne and Margot shot Loretta inquisitive glances, which she defiantly dismissed. Eventually, Margot turned the focus back to Daphne. "Well, you've been to Europe," Margot encouraged.

"Yes," Daphne confirmed. "A two month fully chaperoned tour, with my former nanny in complete control of my activities and never out of her sight. Next thing you'll say Loretta, is that you have a husband— alive or dead in your past!"

Loretta laughed. "No, that I can say hasn't happened. I have had a couple of serious affairs, though." She paused, drifting off in thought. "One in particular... No, now is not the time." She gave a wave of her hand. "You've had your share of romance, though, Daphne. You've always had a man on your arm, ever since I've known you. Heck, even before that."

"Yes, but nothing serious."

"What about Daniel?" Margot questioned.

"Oh, well, Dan. Yeah, I love him, but well, you know, he's safe. Such a gentleman. Don't get me wrong. I would even marry him, if he asks. But he's the first really serious one. None of my flirtations were ever even close to compromising my virtue. I certainly don't have a past, or have done anything worth keeping secret."

Loretta snorted in a very unladylike manner. "Those bruises from 'Peter' have certainly faded from your memory as well as your arms." Loretta was referring to one of Daphne's dates who was decidedly questionable from last year.

"Oh, that. Well, yes, 'Peter.' That was something, alright," she acquiesced. "But there was nothing I had to hide, or did anything that could be considered an indiscretion. I've always been the good girl. I still am!"

As far as her friends were concerned, that was okay with them. Margot and Loretta started fussing and making tutting references, trying to make Daphne feel at ease. However, Daphne wasn't really listening to them and absentmindedly started rummaging through her handbag. She pulled out a business card. "Here it is."

"What?" Margot asked.

"That artist's business card."

"What artist?"

"Adonis."

"Who?"

"The man at the art show. You know, the one who wanted to give me the painting. He told me to come by his studio. He also said I had a classic shape and wanted me to model for him."

Loretta raised an eyebrow. "Model for him? He used that line?"

Daphne's eyes were clear and wide. She was happy to be considering a new adventure. "Yes, and I think I will. I'd love to be an artist's muse."

Loretta wrinkled her forehead in concern. "You know what that means, don't you?"

"What do you mean?"

Loretta cleared her throat. "You know what artists and their muses get up to, don't you?"

Margot couldn't help but smirk, while Daphne looked at Loretta innocently, then formed her mouth into an 'O.' "Oh, I'm sure he didn't mean *that*."

"You don't think that's what he intended?"

"Oh, no." Daphne shook her head. "This is Santa Lucia, not Paris!" Her friends looked skeptically at her, both Margot and Loretta knowing full well what Adonis was most likely after, inviting Daphne up to his private studio. Daphne registered the looks on their faces and became indignant. "Well, so what? Maybe it's time I did something I'd regret!"

"Do you know what you're saying!?!" Margot asked incredulously.

"Yes!" Daphne affirmed.

"Well, what about Daniel?"

"What about Daniel? That Sophie made it sound like all the men at the school, including him, were wrapped around her finger."

"Well, that's beside the point. You don't know that; she might just be putting on a show. Do you really think he'd like you to go to Adonis' studio, let alone 'pose,' for lack of a better word?"

Daphne tossed her curls dismissively. "He doesn't need to know. Maybe I need my own secret, a slight indiscretion."

"Are you sure? You might be sorry," Margot cautioned.

"Good, then I'll have a history too."

Loretta broke in, "Well, girls, this has been fun. Enlightening too, but I've got a deadline to meet. Margot, don't worry. This will all blow over as soon as Nancy Lewis does something stupid again. And you, Daphne, don't you be the one to do anything to top the headline. I mean it. Think twice before you get in over your head. We don't know this artist fellow. There's having an adventure, then there's just plain old trouble." The reporter left in a flurry, leaving an uncomfortable void in the room.

Daphne sat, flipping the artist's card in her fingers, contemplating if she would or wouldn't. Margot drummed her fingers on her desk, staring out of the office's arched window onto the fountain in Avila Square. Finally, she spoke and the declaration was a Pandora's Box. "None of this changes the fact that Nathan Reed shows up here and is murdered. I've got a missing employee who may be in danger or after me and, for God's sake, I don't know why. What does this have to do with me?"

For the first time since it had all come out, she put her head down on her desk and cried.

CHAPTER SEVEN

Daphne slipped quietly down the stairs, leaving Margot to herself. She had sat with her for a while, letting her friend let it all out until Margot felt she couldn't cry anymore. There was nothing Daphne could do to make it better, and Margot thanked her, sending her down to deal with any Poppy Cove business that had cropped up.

They'd been upstairs for hours. Irene gave Daphne a sideways curious glance, wanting to know what was going on. Customers had come and gone, with rumors and innuendo buzzing in the air. She'd heard Margot's name crop up, as well as the name *Margaret* and references to the dead man on the beach, but whenever she came near the speakers, they clammed up and asked questions about the clothes or just bought items to appease Irene. With Daphne now on the sales floor, Irene felt she was entitled to some answers, which she demanded none too politely of her employer. "Look, there's obviously something going on and if it affects business, I have a right to know." Irene was a sleek, steely-eyed beauty, with dark hair and a curvy, formidable figure that commanded attention.

Although Daphne was not pleased with her tone or demanding attitude, she was not in the mood to fight or reprimand her. She chose to ignore Irene and pretended to fuss with the appointment book on the sales counter, then remembering another direction she could take. "Has Jeannette shown up today?"

"No, and when I mentioned it to Marjorie, she said nothing about it."

Silence ensued and after a while when Daphne did not respond to her, Irene took a closer look at her boss. When she noticed that Daphne's hand was shaking as she turned the pages and she appeared near tears, Irene mellowed her tone. She looked around the shop and seeing that there weren't any customers in at the moment, whispered to Daphne, "What's going on? I've heard rumors that Margot's somehow involved in the murder of that guy on the beach, and now the new girl's missing, too."

Daphne double checked that no one else was around before replying, "We have no idea what's going on with Jeannette, but I can say that Margot's not exactly involved in the murder, but she knew the victim on the beach."

Irene sucked in her breath. "How well?"

Daphne momentarily paused, then replied, "Very well. As in ex-husband."

"Wow! Really? Who knew?"

"Well, pretty much no one from here."

"Not even you?"

"Not even me."

"How about lover boy?"

"Nope, Tom didn't, either."

"Huh, that must have come as a shock to our 'Eliot Ness,'" Irene remarked. "Well, well, well. So I'm not the only one who's come here to start fresh."

"Oh, God, you too? Everyone seems to have led a much more colorful life than I have."

"Well, that's true. Most of us have. Come to think of it, most nuns have, Daphne." Irene couldn't resist making such a comment. She got along well enough with her employers, but she did view Daphne as sheltered and privileged—more so than Margot. She always wondered what Margot had up her sleeve. Irene had been moved to Santa Lucia from Los Angeles by her parents to live with her grandmother after she ran into some trouble in the city. She didn't talk about it, but she did have a taste for the wild life and was able to find it even in Santa Lucia. Her dates were often small time hoods who sometimes ran not-so-fine illegal establishments, gambling halls and other unsavoury activities.

Irene, however, had a good head for business and filled out the shop's fashions perfectly. She shared the right gossip with the right clients, and flattered the customers just enough so that they believed her praise that boosted their egos and they rewarded her with plenty of shop purchases. Today was no exception. Mrs. Morgan had been in, looking for a new blouse and matching slacks. Not only had Irene outfitted her with a new sleeveless lilac midi-blouse that tied at the waist and lime green Capri slacks, but also had her add a full-circle skirt in a lilac gingham check and a white twin set that paired with both the slacks and skirt, all the while promising the client Mrs. Morgan that as soon as she knew what was going on with the dead man on the beach and Margot, that she—Mrs. Morgan—would be the first to know. Of course, Irene had no intention of breaking any truths or confidences about her boss, but it was enough to keep Mrs. Morgan shopping, as she talked, willing to add more to her purchase. By the time she left, she had added another set of pearls, cotton gloves and a new handbag as well.

The day progressed. Margot had pulled herself together and had come back downstairs after reapplying her makeup thoughtfully and carefully. By mid-afternoon, she was able to carry herself with enough composure that the staff no longer had the need to pussyfoot around her or try to protect her from customers. The general impression was that whatever was being said out in town could not possibly be true; no one could behave in such a manner and have anything to do with such a situation, especially as the gossip was coming out that Margot was actually one of their kind, not just a dressmaker from out of town, but of their same social level—a society peer.

Some customers came in to reassure Margot that it would all be okay, other ladies came by, some who were infrequent shoppers or who had never set foot in the store to just get a glimpse of her. Very few of them actually said anything to Margot, just took a quick glance and then left when they saw her. In spite of all this, she was glad that in tomorrow's paper, Loretta would have it all out in the open, honestly telling her facts and her history in the role of Nathan's life. Margot was actually beginning to feel that it might blow over once it could be figured out what exactly happened to Nathan, and now that was the most important thing. Above all, he was murdered. That was far worse than her running away and changing her name. His killer, whether it was Jeannette or not, would have to be caught and justice served. For all that had happened, as far as she was concerned, he did not deserve to die.

Mind you, no one knew what he'd really been up to during their marriage and afterwards. It didn't make sense that he had just shown up in Santa Lucia. He wasn't that attached to her and he must have known she couldn't have been able to help him financially if it was indeed money he wanted. He couldn't have involved her in any schemes since she'd left that would have put her in personal danger, so that didn't worry her. They weren't that close. It may have been just one of those weird things that out of all the places he ended up in Santa Lucia. Every moment that she felt she might relax, her mind would run over it all again. How long had he been around? Is it possible she'd seen him at a distance and it didn't register with her who he was? There were so many questions and he wasn't alive to answer them.

It was closing time and Tom still hadn't telephoned or come around. Margot didn't dare call. On top of everything, she didn't think her heart could break any further. She'd realized just before the discovery of Nate's identity, how much Tom meant to her, and that she was willing to tell him all. At that time, she thought he might be a little surprised by her past history, but not enough to distrust her. But now, her ex was dead and her private life was exposed to Tom's suspicious colleagues, with questions surrounding the murder. Being that he was a cop, she had no idea what Tom thought of her.

There was a rap on the closed shop door and Riley and Jenkins appeared, without Tom. Irene let them in without a comment, which was unusual for her. She gestured in the direction of Margot, as if she clearly knew why they were there. Officer Jenkins appeared awkward and uncomfortable while Detective Riley looked straight in her face. "Ms. Willmington." He still refused to use her now legal name.

"Y-yes," Margot stuttered and gulped.

"Do you own a Smith & Wesson .38 revolver?" Detective Riley inquired.

"Yes."

"Our records indicate you purchased it in New York City at Bob's Hardware and Sporting Goods on Monday, April 26, 1954. Is that true?"

"Yes."

"And what was your purpose for purchasing such an item?"

Margot paused, thinking carefully how to answer him. She had a sinking feeling she knew where this was going. "I got it for protection."

Riley sniggered. "Protection?"

"Yes. I was leaving on my own and I felt I needed to have some form of self-defense. It seemed like a good idea at the time."

"How often have you used it?"

"Never," Margot replied clearly.

The detective sneered, making a note. "Never?"

She shrugged. "Thank God I never had to. I was never in any real danger as I travelled."

Riley stared her down, but she did not flinch. "Do you have the gun in your possession?"

"Not on me, no. It's at home, tucked away in my lingerie drawer." Margot licked her lips, beginning to feel nervous. She had a sinking feeling she knew where this conversation was going and she didn't like it.

Riley muttered to Jenkins, who made a note regarding the search of Margot or *Margaret's* residence.

"Excuse me, Detective Riley?" Daphne walked up to him and tugged on his suit sleeve.

He glared at her before responding. "Yes?"

She couldn't help herself; she was feeling bewildered and couldn't believe what was happening. "What's going on here? Can you explain why you're asking my friend these questions?"

Riley turned and faced her with a self-confident swagger in his motion. "Well, Miss Huntington-Smythe, your *friend* has a gun registered in her original name that is the same make and calibre as the one used to shoot and kill her ex-husband."

The room stopped. The only people left in the store at the time were the police, the owners, and Irene and Marjorie. Margot stopped breathing. She thought she was going to pass out. Marjorie saw her sway and caught her from behind, just before she fully swooned. She gently but firmly patted Margot's cheek. "Stay with us, dear. Take a deep breath, that's it." As Margot regained her air, Marjorie righted her.

"Margaret Jane Willmington, also known as Margaret Jane Reed and Margot Williams, you are under suspicion for the murder of Nathan James Reed, on Saturday, April 19, 1958, by a single gunshot wound from a Smith & Wesson .38 at close range, through the heart. Come with us." Riley ignored the outburst of the women in the room as he handcuffed her and the two officers escorted Margot out of the store.

"Sorry, Margot." Jenkins felt bad and apologized under his breath while he did what he had to do.

"Officer Jenkins!" Riley barked. "Just do your job. I want you to stay here and supervise the rest of the uniforms when they get here to search the store. Also, I want you to ask everyone what they know about the disappearance of Jeannette Fox—when they last saw her, the usual. I want a thorough search, do you hear me? That means workroom, shop, office, everywhere on the premises. I want this place gone over with a fine-tooth comb. The same goes for her residence. There's a team going back to Mrs. Coleman's as well. Got that?"

"Where's Tom?" Margot blurted out.

"Funny you should ask that. Chief's got a lot of questions for him, too." Riley replied.

"What do you mean?"

"A .38 is one of his guns, as well. He's got his own set of questions to answer regarding his involvement in the murder."

"That's ridiculous. He knew nothing of Nathan, or my past for that matter. Tom should be helping solve the case, not be part of it."

Riley turned his focus back to Margot. "He's the one that may need help now, if you had him take part in it. Tom's on an ordered absence. Not only that, but his background and premises are being searched, too. He's under surveillance and under no circumstance is he to contact you," the detective stated coldly. "I suggest you listen to us and get yourself a good lawyer. You'll need one."

Margot was being railroaded out the door at breakneck speed. There was a female officer waiting outside, someone she'd never seen before. She continued as part of the escort to the Santa Lucia Police Department, saying nothing, just doing her job.

CHAPTER EIGHT

The rest of the Poppy Cove women were left momentarily silent. They couldn't believe what had just happened. Marjorie started talking first. "Well, it's no good if we just stand here. Let's just, well, something…" She started fussing with the appointment book, finally finding something productive to do. "Tomorrow I can take the appointments, and we've got the garments under control." She stopped. "What about her cat? Mr. Cuddles, isn't it?"

"I'll take him," Irene spoke up.

Both Marjorie and Daphne were startled. Irene was never one to step in and offer to help. "You?" Daphne asked.

"Yes, I've looked after a cat before." She softened. "I have to do something. Last year when I was messed up with Eddie and the cops went and bothered my grandmother and her home, Margot was good to me. I owe her—I owe both of you. I don't say it often enough, but thanks for giving me a chance here."

"Okay. Well, I'll get one of father's lawyer friends to step in. I doubt Margot knows who to go to here in town," Daphne remarked. She went to the sales desk and found Henry Worth's home phone number. After a brief call, she was relieved to report that he was heading down to the police station right away.

There was not much more they could do before three more uniformed police officers came in and began searching Poppy Cove under Jenkins' lead. He personally asked all the staff regarding the whereabouts and last sighting of Jeannette, but came up with nothing.

No one had seen or heard from her since her last shift on Friday, nor could they give any idea of her weekend habits or activities. She had not been there long enough to really connect or socialize with anyone yet.

Irene left to get Margot's cat. Presuming she'd run into more officers there, searching the house, she said she'd stay and keep a close eye on them. Daphne offered to stay downstairs and watch the proceedings while Marjorie accompanied a young man who looked like a rookie upstairs as he searched the office.

Irene ran into Michael Weathers as she was leaving. "What are you doing here?"

"It's a big story, baby. I've got to blow the doors off this one." He was in full press mode, with his card in his hatband, striding in and watching every move of the police, flashing pictures as he went.

"Creep," Irene exclaimed as she left. Weathers smirked at her comment.

"Just a minute. I don't want you here," Daphne said when she saw him. "Loretta's covered the story already. The Editor-in-Chief gave her the go ahead. Hasn't it already gone to press?"

"Oh, that? They've bumped that to the Society Page. They've now stopped the presses for this. It's bigger news and I don't care what Loretta's got on Jack. No society dame's gonna get the front page on a story like this!"

Every ounce of adrenaline kicked in to help Daphne defend her business and friend. "Get out!" she roared in a tone and volume she'd never heard from herself. She never knew she had it in her, but she did.

The sound stopped everyone in the room. All the police looked at her. Jenkins, in particular, gave a wide-eyed blink, then had them resume their search. Weathers, however, was still cornered by Daphne. In her rage, she had backed him into the window display, wedged between two female mannequins in sporty, flirty playsuits. He didn't know exactly where to put his hands to balance himself, falling against the plate glass window.

"Daphne?"

She turned her head, saw Daniel walk in and immediately smiled. "Oh, hi!"

"Hello. What's going on here?" Dan was a little perplexed. As he was walking up to the store, he'd heard a rather loud woman, which he now realized was his easy going, darling Daphne.

"Well, I don't know where to start, but I do know that our friend Michael was just leaving. Good night, Mr. Weathers." She grabbed him by his checked sports coat collar, pulling him out of the display.

He straightened himself up and, under the eyes of Daniel and the police, he left. "I'll be back. I'll get the whole story, mark my words. You can either work with me, or I'll work against you. It's up to you how you want it all to look. I don't care; it'll be a good one. You may want to think how you want to come out of this one."

Michael brushed past Daniel, who moved out of his way, giving him a wide berth. "So what's going on?" Dan asked.

"Oh, what isn't?" Daphne exclaimed and collapsed in his embrace.

She took him by the hand and led him to the seating lounge, hoping they were out of the range of police ears. She discreetly gave him a brief rundown about what had happened in the last two days since she saw him on Sunday evening. She included the problem of the missing employee and most of all, the revelation of Margot's history. He sat in silence when she was done, trying to take it all in. "Hmm. How are you?" He stroked her hair gently. His first concern was her welfare, and she could not believe how good that made her feel.

"I don't know. I mean I'm fine; it has nothing to do with me really, but well, she is my best friend and business partner and I've just found out about this whole new person. She's still the Margot I know, even if I'm learning more about her. It's just confusing and so much to take in. You know what I mean?"

He nodded, letting her continue, which she did. "And the gun. I didn't know about the gun. I still don't believe she did it, or that Tom had anything to do with the murder either. Do *you* think either of them could do something like that? I mean, she never spoke about an ex-husband, or her past for that matter. If she was that upset about it, don't you think something, somehow, sometime would have come up? I know she was gun-shy about marriage—oh pardon the pun—but she was coming around to it, even ready to talk to Tom about it right when it all happened." She started to shake and ramble. "I can't believe she had a gun!" she repeated as she put her hands in her face to cry.

Daniel sat quietly with her, stroking her head and back, letting her sob. In the meantime, Marjorie had come back downstairs and had a brief word with the officers, who were leaving with a file box of miscellaneous things. She brought Daphne a cup of tea and spoke with Dan, announcing her departure and letting him know that if there was anything he or Daphne needed before tomorrow morning to call her at home. She gave Daphne a quick squeeze on the shoulder and left them alone.

Eventually, Daphne did calm down. She faced her boyfriend head on. "Do you think she did it?"

"Do you?"

She shook her head. "No, I can't believe she would. Not Margot, not the Margot I know." She paused. "You know, she never mentioned him."

"She didn't?"

"Not once in all the time I've known her. But then again, she never said anything about her past at all. I never thought to ask her, either. It never occurred to me that she had much of one."

"Why not?" Dan asked.

"I don't know. I guess I don't, and we don't seem that different from each other."

He brushed a curl off her forehead and gave a gentle chuckle. "Of course you are."

Daphne paused, considering his demeanor when he said his comments. "But is that good?"

Dan studied her face, unsure of how to proceed. Although he'd done his share of mingling and dating, he was not a lothario. He knew enough that he was now in the middle of a romantic minefield. One false step either way that would make her feel more naïve or suggest her friend's past was bolder than hers could offend Daphne, and that was the last thing he wanted to do. "It's very good." *Simple was best,* he thought, proud of his thinking.

"How?" she pressed.

"Well." Dan paused scratching his head. "You've never had to be pressured into a marriage you didn't want or told you couldn't have a career. You've been allowed to make your own decisions from the comfort of your family home. You weren't threatened to be disowned if you didn't marry someone to keep the family industry afloat, or have to hide a bad relationship."

"Bad relationship? If you recall, Peter wasn't exactly good for me," she remarked, bringing up a rather sordid fellow in her dating history Daniel knew only too well.

Daniel nodded, but carefully continued. "Yes, but that was two dates and *you* chose him. He didn't come along with a matching china pattern from your parents."

There was a frosty silence while she thought about what he'd said and what it must have meant for Margot to feel she had no say in her future while remaining with her family. Daphne sighed and leaned into his shoulder. "Okay, fine. I understand what you mean. I saw a lot of the girls I grew up with go straight from their parents' homes to a husband's. Some of them seem happy, but I see some of them now, and they're pretty tight-lipped and don't have many good things to say about married life."

"But you, my darling, have this wonderful career and a friend who needs your support." Dan hugged her close.

"And such a handsome man in the bargain, too!" She smiled and leaned in closer. "Who is all my choice."

"And you're mine, too." He smiled and they had quiet peace for the moment.

Daphne sat up straighter and turned to face him. "You never answered my question."

"What question?"

She repeated the inquiry that got the whole conversation started. "Do you think she did it?"

Daniel opened his mouth, paused and closed it again. "No," he eventually replied.

Daphne looked at him critically, reading his face for a lie. "Hmm, it took you a while to give your answer."

He shrugged and rubbed his neck. "I wanted to think about it. I don't believe she could kill anyone, but I do understand why she left her husband and everyone else behind."

"Really?"

"Yes, yes, I do." Dan read the perplexed look on her face and elaborated. "I didn't have the same pressures as Margot did, but I had to leave my family, in a way."

Daphne blinked and shook her head. "But you're still close to your parents."

Dan nodded slowly. "Yes, but I still had to leave home and start out on my own. I didn't want to be part of their ranch and just do as they did. I had to make my own way, without their connections or money, and they were sore about that for a while." The Henshaws ran a successful horse breeding ranch in Ojai with plans to leave it to Daniel and his brother, Victor. Victor was keen to take it on, but Daniel wasn't. "You're just getting to know my parents now, after they've gotten used to my departure." Daniel had settled in at Stearns Academy and was very happy and successful in his post, which his family was now recognizing was an ideal decision for him.

Daphne sat quietly for a moment, thinking about what he and others had recently said to her. She did have a relatively carefree and easy life, save for a few recent adventures. But maybe her problem-free life *was* a problem, to her. They were right about her. She never had to worry about money, always had the love of her family who never pushed her in any direction, fairly well behaved boyfriends, except for one or two, and work she enjoyed. Topping that off with a lovely personality and figure to match, well, she realized that maybe that wasn't enough. Everyone else had something—a past, a secret, some sort of hardship that, as was said, 'built character.' "I need a past," she murmured, more to herself than to Dan.

He screwed up his face in a puzzled manner. "What do you mean?"

"I could become a woman of mystery. Travel somewhere new, where they speak a different language and don't know me." She paused. "Like Sophie."

"Who?"

Daphne rolled her eyes. "Are you kidding? You know, Sophie, the French tart art teacher who was crawling all over you at the art show."

"Oh, her? She doesn't count; she crawls all over everyone," Daniel replied.

"What happens up at that school when I'm not around?"

"Nothing," he said flatly, honestly.

When he didn't comment further, she brightened up with a new idea. "I know what I need to do. I have to have an adventure!"

"Daphne, you are an adventure," he chuckled.

She gave him a playful slap on the arm. "No, I mean I have to *do something*, be a bit wild, have a regret, a secret."

Dan shook his head. "What!?! No, Daff, wait. You don't understand. People go their whole lives wishing they've had it as comfortable as you. You don't plan hardships, errors. They just happen."

"Not to me, they don't." Daphne crossed her arms stubbornly.

Dan looked at her quietly, stroked her hair, which was starting to look frizzed under the stress of the day. "Maybe your time just hasn't come. Look, don't wish these things on yourself, and don't do something foolish or dangerous. Trust me, your adventures, as you call them, will come."

She sighed, resting back into his body. "I suppose you're right. I sure wouldn't want to be in Margot's shoes tonight." She got up and started pacing, suddenly feeling agitated. "I don't know how to help."

"You know, that's probably it, darling." Dan got up to stop and hold her. "Margot could use your support, more than anything. We believe she's innocent, but it's hard to say how Santa Lucia will react to the news. She's going to need her friends."

"Yes," she resolved firmly. "That I can do. I'm sure she's innocent. I can look after Poppy Cove until this blows over and stand by my friend, no matter what the Nancy Lewises and the like will say."

"That's it. Now why don't we put this out of our heads for the evening and have a nice dinner. It may be the last moment's peace we have for some time."

Daphne smiled at Daniel, knowing he was right. Somehow, he always knew how to make her feel better. She checked all the doors and lights as they left, ready to spend the time focusing on her date. She just wouldn't mention that nagging unrestful feeling to him, and sort it out for herself. He didn't need to know everything about her, did he? The corners of her smile went a little higher as she planned to keep the back of her mind busy on, well, something…

CHAPTER NINE

"Let's go over this one more time, Ms. Willmington," Detective Riley droned on. "Tell me again about your relationship with the deceased."

Margot sighed wearily and looked over to her lawyer. Daphne had generously arranged for his attendance at the police station for her. Henry Worth got there shortly after she was taken in, and she told him everything, not leaving a word out. She had nothing to hide now. He took it all in, without passing outward judgement on her, letting her talk without interrupting with very few questions when she'd finished. The first of which was a request for her to level with him if she was in fact guilty of murdering Nathan Reed, followed by what exactly she'd done while on the road, and not to leave out anything small, even an outstanding parking or speeding ticket. When he was satisfied she'd been honest, he continued a polite but straightforward line of questioning, which included various ways in which she could have hidden or forgotten any small detail that might incriminate her. Then he told her to get ready—the police wouldn't be so easy to convince. She gulped audibly.

The lawyer looked as rumpled around the eyes as she felt. They'd been in a gray, airless interrogation room all night. "Look," he replied for his client, "She hadn't seen him since she left the east coast and she had no idea he was here. She moved on with her life, with no malice towards him anymore. Other than superficial evidence, you have no reason to keep Ms. Williams, as you well know is her legal name, detained any longer." Margot glanced at the wall directly in front of her while her representative spoke, looking past Riley and the female officer's shoulders to the clock, which showed 5:30, which she guessed was a. m. Frankly, she was so tired and wrung out, it could have been the next evening, for all she knew.

"Hmm, let's see." Riley looked at his notes. With his rolled up shirtsleeves and a skewed tie, he was in no better shape or humor. "I think we have enough to keep us all talking, don't you? Reed doesn't have any other apparent ties to the community, only a picture of you in his jacket, and you *are* here under a false name and identity. He comes to town, gets killed, with a gun that's the same make and model as the one that's registered to you. Care to tell us why we didn't find the gun where you said it would be?"

Margot was shocked. She couldn't remember the last time she'd seen it, but did remember she'd stored it where she'd told them—in the back of her lingerie drawer. "Then it's missing!"

"Why didn't you file a report?" Riley asked.

"I didn't know it wasn't there!" Margot turned to Henry. "I thought it was behind my papers, wrapped up in an old slip."

Henry made a few notes, then asked Riley, "Are you sure you looked where my client specified?"

"Of course, we did! I know what lingerie looks like. We found the papers and most likely the slip, but no gun." He directed the following question to Margot. "Where's the gun?"

Henry eyed his client who gave a bewildered shrug. "Well, then, we need to file a missing weapons report."

Worth then looked Riley in the eye until the policeman gave a slight flinch. "That make and model of pistol is very common. The majority of local police departments have that exact same weapon including yourself, I might add. Are so sure the bullet came from her gun?"

"We're working on that," he flatly stated.

"And again, what's the delay in your proof?" Henry sat back and folded his arms. He knew he had him.

"We're still searching and testing for the exact murder weapon," Riley muttered.

Henry nodded. "That's right; you don't have the right gun yet. You've torn my client's workplace, car and home upside down and have no trace of it, so you can't say that it was Margot's, let alone that she's the one who used it. Especially now that it appears to have been stolen." He paused for effect. "Riley, let her go or I'll pursue unlawful detainment, even harassment on your badge number."

Riley tried the 'stare down' treatment on the older and wiser lawyer, but to no avail. He was stalling for time, hoping that either the search would come up with the literally smoking gun or that he could get 'Margot' to crack and tell him what he wanted to hear. "There's also a concern regarding her identity. Although the records show her name was officially changed in 1954 upon arriving in Santa Lucia, there's still some question as to her behavior prior to the name change, while she was interstate traveling. What had Ms. Willmington been up to that we don't know about?"

The lawyer gave a dismissive wave with his hand. "You know that's neither here nor there. It has nothing to do with the case. Check my client's background all you want on your own time, but stick to the charges, Riley. Either charge her with murder or let her go."

But Riley was nowhere near finished with his questioning. He reviewed his notes again, then started with, "So, you were at Mrs. Coleman's Boarding House."

"Yes, I was."

"Miss Fox is your employee?"

"Yes, a cutter."

"From New York?"

"Yes."

"Did you know her previously?"

"No."

"Are you sure?"

"Yes. Positive." Margot was direct. They'd gone through all this earlier that night, and her responses had been the same. They couldn't have been anything else. She knew what was coming next. Why didn't she report Ms. Fox's absence? Did she think that Jeannette and Nathan were in a relationship? Was jealousy or obsession a motive? Did she know about where Jeannette was now? Did Margot do anything to hurt her or was she aware if Jeannette was after her as well? It all lead back to the same thing. She knew nothing, because that was the truth.

Once Riley had gone through his routine again, Margot sat nervous and tense, not sure what would happen next. Riley was quiet, shuffling his notes. He left the room and closed the door behind him. Margot looked at Henry, who patted her hand. The female officer, Rose Marie Hartley by name, didn't know where to look or what to do, either. Margot guessed she was young, a rookie really. In an odd way, Margot felt sorry for the girl. Officer Hartley didn't look like she wanted to be there anymore than Margot did. Riley came back in shortly and did not sit down.

"Ms. Willmington, you are allowed to leave. You are still the main suspect under suspicion but at this point not formally charged. Pending further evidence that may change. You are not to leave Santa Lucia County limits and you may be called in for further questioning at any time," Riley stated flatly, then turned to face the attorney. "You must file a report regarding your client's missing handgun today. Does that satisfy you?"

Henry gave a curt nod with his head and zipped up his attaché case. He motioned for Margot to stand and gently moved the chair out for her. "You make sure if you have any formal questions, you contact my office directly, not my client. Is that understood? No underhanded behavior because you know Margot through Tom. I mean it."

Riley tightened his jaw but relented and got out of Margot and Henry's way. Henry took Margot's arm and escorted her through the station. He stopped at the reception counter to reclaim her purse and gloves, which had been taken from her when she was placed into the restrictive interrogation room. As he did so, Margo noticed that Bruce Jenkins was sitting at his desk. Margot broke away from her lawyer to speak with the officer. "Bruce, have you seen Tom? Has he been around?"

Officer Jenkins looked around the station bullpen to see if anyone was paying attention, and spoke quietly to her. "I don't think I'm supposed to say anything."

Margot knew that Tom had been told to keep his distance, and as much as she didn't like it, she could understand why. Now she had a sick feeling like something was really wrong, for him as well. Even if she didn't want to, she had to know. "Why? Jenkins, what's going on?"

He furtively looked around again and replied quietly, "He's being questioned. About the murder."

"What?" Margot blurted. "Why? He's got nothing to do with it. He never knew about Nate, or anything. For goodness sake, he was there when the body was discovered."

Jenkins shrugged. "Chief still has called him in on it. He's pulled him off the case and all others, for the time being. They're interrogating him, too."

"Here?"

"Yep." Jenkins nodded. He saw the look on her face. "Hey, Margot, it's a weird situation, but it'll get cleared up." He gave her a smile.

"Thanks, Bruce. I take it you believe me. You know I'm innocent."

"Jenkins! What are you doing?" Riley barked from the doorway.

Jenkins blushed. "Sorry, can't talk about it. Orders."

Margot nodded and moved to join Henry who was waiting to take her home. As he glanced out the main doors, he said: "I should warn you, it looks like the press is outside. They can be nasty."

She couldn't believe what she saw. When she thought about the press, she figured that would be, say two or three men—Weathers, from the *Santa Lucia Times*, a reporter or two from both the local radio and television stations, but that would be it. To her surprise, in the early morning light, there was a crowd of thirty to forty people—men and women with notepads and cameras, jostling and clamoring at the door, jumping forward as soon as they got a glimpse of her. "My goodness! Henry, why so many people?"

He looked calmly at them and then back at her. "Well, it's big news. A stranger gets murdered across the country from his home, and you're the only one who knew him locally, as far as we know. You're a policeman's girlfriend, and he's suspected as well. You've been living under an alias for many years and now it turns out you're an eastern business heiress who ran away to start a new and secret life. The fact that we're just miles from Hollywood and its various and sundry reporters just adds fuel to the fire." Henry's eyes softened when he realized he was frightening her. "Now, dear, I don't mean to sound cold or alarming, but you're today's news. It'll be a while before some other scandal bigger and more sordid makes this story a fish wrapper."

Margot was flabbergasted. "But how did this get out so fast?"

Henry puffed his cheeks and exhaled forcefully. "Probably through the news wire service. It goes fast and

doesn't stop until they have their headlines." He looked
her in the face and gently asked, "Now do you want to go
through it here, or for me to find a back exit and bring
the car around? I'll warn you though, if you don't meet
the press now, they'll follow you till you do."

"Might as well face the music here. I'll never be ready
for this," Margot sighed.

Henry smoothed down his hair and gave a tug at his
suit jacket and gave his client the once over. He guided
her over to the restrooms. "You may want to freshen up a
bit before we go out."

Margot nodded, realizing that with all that had been
happening, she hadn't given much thought to her
appearance. Bad form for a person in the beauty business
as she was, regardless of the situation. The washroom
was as she expected—serviceable, reasonably clean, but
not a country club powder room by any means. The
mirrors over the sink were dingy and scruffy, but even in
the shoddy reflection, she could see she was a little worse
for wear. Her auburn pageboy had no bounce and the top
laid flat against her scalp. She'd never seen such dark
circles under her eyes in her life. Her lips were pale and
chapped, and she guessed she'd chewed on them
unconsciously throughout the questioning. Then she
looked down at her dress. The beautiful powder blue
cotton lawn had lost its crispness and volume. It hung
like a wrung out limp rag, creased around the waist and
through the skirt where she'd been forced to sit on the
hard chairs. Her stockings were twisted with a run on her
thigh from when the female officer had given her a pat
down looking for hidden weapons. *Really!* she thought. *I
can't believe they could think that of me.* She shook her
head, saying to herself, *It doesn't matter; I'll just have to
get through it.*

The taps ran only cold water. Margot gave her dress a
light spritz, thinking if she could blow the hot air from
the automatic hand dryer, it would perhaps steam some

of the wrinkles out. The dryer would not co-operate. There was virtually no air flow, although the motor sounded like it might take off from the wall. Whatever air there was, could not be directed from the small vent; it was stuck and ineffectual. *Oh, well,* Margot sighed. *It'll look a bit better from the front, anyhow.*

Then she began on her face. It was a major reconstruction. She piled on the powder so thick it was as if she'd disappeared. She drew a thick line of kohl on the top of her lids to detract from the underside and with a re-sculpture of blush and two coats of lipstick, she felt that at least she could show her face to the crowd.

Her hair—well—there was only so much a girl could do without Mr. Anthony, the beautician extraordinaire, or at least a can of hair spray. All she had was a comb, so she lightly teased her roots, gave the ends a quick, damp finger curl and deemed herself as physically presentable as she could be.

Mentally, she was nowhere near ready. She could not believe what was happening. Nathan was apparently in town, now he was dead, shot in such a way that seemed so emotional and final. Tom had been dragged into this, before she'd had a chance to tell him all about everything, just before she was going to tell him. And to be accused of something so awful that she could never even think of doing. She certainly knew Tom didn't have anything to do with it. He knew nothing. Not usually one to entertain what people thought of her, she couldn't help but feel sick over what others were believing of her now. What would that mean to her personally? To Poppy Cove? To Daphne? The thoughts and conclusions reeled in her aching and throbbing tired head. She gave herself one last glance before subjecting herself to the judgement of others. As she did, a few new thoughts came to her. *If they didn't find the gun, where was it? And who has it? And what about Jeannette?* The situation was getting worse rather than better.

Going through the press gang was blurry. Henry had advised her before they went out the door to not say anything, to not look up or directly at anyone. As they moved through, there were so many faces she didn't recognize, save for Weathers, of course, and a couple of media locals. The rest must have been out-of-towners. Margot had noticed, by that. People were calling out her names—both Margot and Margaret—trying to get her attention, but she did as her lawyer said. He issued a statement that his client had not been formally charged with anything and had no comment at this time. If there was any official news, he'd be the one to notify them and for the press to respect Margot and leave her alone. He swiftly delivered her to his car, a substantial and imposing brand new, black and chrome Cadillac Eldorado, which was parked out front, and he whisked her away.

As they were driving, Margot noticed Henry had a satisfied grin on his face. He seemed to be enjoying himself! "Are you finding my situation amusing?" Margot asked, incensed. She wasn't generally short or punchy, but she was failing to see the humor in the current events, given how she'd spent the last few days.

Henry looked over at her and dimmed his smile. "Oh no, don't take it the wrong way, dear. It's just been a while since I've had any cases such as this. My original background was in civil law, then I dabbled for a few years in criminal in my early thirties, but when we started a family, Clara suggested that I look at something that was a little safer, generally with regular hours, so I changed my focus to business law. Most of my cases in the last twenty years have been all mergers, acquisitions, and the like. They haven't fired my blood up like this one has." He smiled broader again. "I apologize, but I'm very glad Daphne called me."

Henry Worth had been a great friend of Gerald Huntington-Smythe's since boyhood and now represented him in all his legal business matters. He was the first person Daphne had thought of that she could trust with her friend's future.

"I don't think I've had the chance to thank you for coming so quickly and staying by my side. I have no idea what your rates are, or how you'll charge me, but I can assure you I can pay. Would you be willing to continue representing me? I mean, I know it's no longer your specialty, but..." Margot looked at her hands that had been wringing unconsciously in her lap.

He reached over and patted her shoulder. "Don't think twice about it. I'll clear my books and see you through. We'll work out the financial details in the end, but don't worry, I'll be fair. The opportunity to handle such a case has made me love my work again."

They drove on silently for the rest of the trip home until they parked in front of Margot's bungalow on Beacon Street. He turned to her before they got out of the car. "Margot," he said firmly. "I need you to be completely honest with me. I know you said you haven't seen Nathan Reed since you left him years ago back east, but is that the truth? Is there anything you are hiding? About yourself or Tom? In order for me to represent you, I need to know everything, even if it's small. Or big." He paused. "Did you see him here in Santa Lucia?"

She knew he wasn't joking, being harsh or pulling punches. She answered sincerely, "No, I did not."

"And you swear, to God and all else, you did not kill him or have anything to do with his demise?"

"No. Nothing." Margot had told him everything, including about her indelicate indiscretion and purchasing the gun.

"And Jeannette?"

Margot shook her head. "I wish I did. I think I have a few questions for her now myself."

"And the gun? You're not hiding it? It's truly missing?"

She nodded.

Henry took a deep breath and exhaled. "Good. That's the last time I'll ask you. I'm glad to get that out of the way." He took the car key out of the ignition and put it in his jacket pocket. "Let's get you home."

Fortunately, either the press had a good enough story or good enough taste to not follow her home. The street was in an early morning mood—quiet, except for Margot's nosy neighbor, Mrs. Sharon O'Leary, walking her precious little white terrier, Sparky. For the life of her, Margot swore that woman and her dog were always out whenever she came home late, or early for that matter. And she was always raising an eyebrow at Margot's activities. Mrs. O'Leary stopped Sparky to give Henry Worth a visual going over. "Good morning, Margot. Are you just getting in? I saw such comings and goings from your house last night, I had half a mind to call the police, but then I realized that they were the ones there. Anything wrong, dear?"

Margot stopped and looked at the middle-aged woman in her house dress and curlers with a smarmy grin on her lip-sticked face. She knew that Sharon kept up with the local gossip and read the papers, so she must have some idea of what was happening. Margot's eyes squinted as she put a brave grimace on her face. "Oh, just helping the police with a case."

Henry removed his hat and scratched his scalp, waiting for the 'friendly' interrogation to be over. Sparky was whining and pulling at his leash wanting to continue on his way. Sharon wanted to stay put. "I see. The police were here for a long time. They took out quite a few boxes, too. I can't imagine what they were doing, can you?"

Margot was in no temper for such cattiness, but carried on as lightly as she could. "They were just looking for some things they might need. Now if you don't mind, Mrs. O'Leary, it's been a very long night and I'd like to go home."

"Humph, well by all means. I wouldn't want to keep you." She made a grand gesture to move out of Margot's way. She shouted loudly just as Margot and Henry were about to enter the front door. "By the way, I didn't see your Tom among them. Isn't that funny? Him being so high in the police force and all."

Margot stopped, shoulders high, but she didn't turn around as she put her key in the lock. Deciding that she really didn't owe Mrs. O'Leary any fodder for her gossip, she let herself into her home with Henry following her.

She sighed when she saw the state of her usually tidy bungalow. There were drawers open, doilies and ornaments askew. Papers and sofa cushions were haphazardly discarded in a careless array, without any thought to the sanctity of her home. Henry started tidying, while Margot put her hand on his arm and shook her head in a gentle no.

She went through to the kitchen and saw it was in no better shape. On the Formica and chrome kitchen table was an official carbon copy list of everything the police had removed from her place. Her tired eyes were blurry and she stared blankly at it without comprehending the words. She set it back down and noticed another note on the table. It was from Irene, stating that she'd taken Mr. Cuddles to her grandmother's and he was fine to stay until Margot was ready to pick him up. In her emotional and exhausted state, she was so touched by Irene's uncharacteristic thoughtfulness that it brought a tear to her eye. As much as she would have appreciated his loud purring and nuzzling, she was so relieved he hadn't been around when all the strangers were routing through her things. He was a skittish and shy cat; who knows what he would have made of it? He probably would have hidden and been scared out of his wits. She shook it off and began unconsciously to clear and tidy the room.

"Now there's plenty of time for that," Henry softly spoke as he put his hands on Margot's shoulders. "You need to rest. Why don't you lie down for a while? You haven't slept all night."

Margot opened her mouth to protest, which turned into a quivering yawn.

"All of this can wait." Henry took charge of the situation. "There's nothing you can do right now about the accusations; we've gone over everything more than once. I'll drop by Poppy Cove and inform Daphne of what she needs to know and nothing more. I'll tell her you'll be in when you're ready. And not a moment earlier, hear me?" He looked at her kindly but firmly. "I've got things I can follow up on myself, so I'll be in touch either later today or tomorrow. For now, there's nothing you can do. Take your telephone off the hook, have a hot shower and get into bed."

She nodded, knowing he was right. Henry popped his hat back on his head and let himself out. Margot went to her bedroom, which was in the same state as the other rooms in the house. Her eyes narrowed onto her dresser, noticing that the top drawer had been removed and was leaning against the side of the cabinet, empty. Her silky unmentionables were scattered on the floor around it, and none of the important papers—her legal name change, gun license, birth and marriage certificates, and divorce decree were there. She imagined they were mentioned on the removal list. Noticeably missing was also her pistol. She knew that wasn't on their list and the police didn't have it in their possession. For the life of her, she couldn't remember the last time she'd seen it. The entire time she'd had it, she'd never used it, or frankly felt the need for it, and had almost forgotten she had it. When she'd moved into her own home, around three years ago, she'd wrapped it in an old full slip and tucked it away in the back of the drawer. Occasionally, she would catch a glimpse of it when she would take things in and out, but could not recollect when the most recent time was that she'd actually noticed it. Feeling defeated, she took a deep breath and walked over to her bed. Margot didn't even feel like taking a shower. She cleared a spot on the cluttered mattress, kicked off her pumps and crawled into bed, in her wilted dress, stockings and all. Sleep overtook her even before she'd covered herself with the sheets.

CHAPTER TEN

Daphne arrived first to work, long before nine. The morning copy of the *Santa Lucia Times* had been folded up on the doorstep. She picked it up, tucked it under her arm, not interested in reading the headline news. She knew what it was, having glanced at it in the family breakfast room earlier. The Editor had kept Loretta's tasteful interview and story on the front page as promised, which must have irked Weathers to no end. There was, however, a side bar from him, added at the last minute, stating that Ms. Williams appeared to be the main party under suspicion by the authorities in the murder of Nathan Reed, along with a hint of the possible involvement of a high-ranking police detective, whom he did not name, but he made it very clear to those in the know who it was, with details to follow. Filling out the rest of the page was a wedding photo of Margot (*Margaret* at that time) standing beside her husband, Nathan. Neither were smiling, but standing close to each other, looking at the camera.

For all the troubles in their little world, Daphne knew the Poppy Cove show must go on. At her own sense of loose ends, she felt the best thing for herself to do would be to go in and face what the day would bring. Her evening with Dan had gone fine; he'd done his best to romantically hold her interest. They'd gone for a nice dinner at Antonio's where she'd picked at her veal *piccata*, then for a moonlight walk on the beach, which should have been perfect, but she'd kept thinking about Margot's (*Margaret's*, no, Margot's—she'd always known her as Margot, and that was her legal name now) deceased ex-husband washed up on the beach after being shot through the heart. She knew that Daniel had meant well, even took her in the opposite direction and out of sight of the events, but still…

Her man knew her well enough to patiently and quietly let her sit there in the restaurant and stew. No matter how hard he could have tried, she would have remained in her own thoughts anyway. Daphne knew she was being self-absorbed, but couldn't help herself. The events were happening to Margot, not her, but they were affecting every one of them.

Now this morning, and—all in all—the shop front was fairly tidy from last night's police raid, for lack of a better term. There was an itemized list of what the police had removed to consider as evidence in the murder and Daphne looked it over. It seemed that most of the items taken were paperwork and such, mainly from the upstairs private office. The clothes had been left unharmed, and the sales desk—although rifled through—had not taken her long to straighten out. She'd leave Marjorie to the lunch and back workrooms, she reasoned, not wanting to get in the way of the head seamstress' method and sense of order. She didn't want to face the upstairs private office or Margot's desk until she had to. She'd wait until either Irene or Marjorie came in, leaving someone else to take care of the shop, while she tackled what she assumed would be the worst of the disorder.

Daphne wandered about the sales floor, straightening a rack, playing with a button or hem here and there. She absentmindedly traded a pink patent purse for a white one in the front window, all the while milling over everything that had been brought to light. Even her father had all kinds of questions for her to answer about her business partner. When she got home after midnight last night, Gerald Huntington-Smythe had made her go through her business papers regarding Margot's legal legitimacy, at the suggestion of Henry Worth. Gerald had always liked Margot and had never had a problem with his daughter's involvement with her—both as a friend and a business partner, but Daphne couldn't help but notice a slight reserve and hesitation in his demeanor regarding the recent events and the knowledge of Margot's past and present predicament.

At breakfast, Henry had dropped by the Huntington-Smythe residence after leaving Margot, letting them know of the state of the situation and that all the papers regarding Margot's identity and business dealings under her current name appeared to be legal and above board. Henry felt they shouldn't concern themselves regarding any false claims or illegitimate representation about Margot Williams' identity. He also vouched for her character, and informed his long term friend and community peer that he truly believed she was innocent, although he was concerned over the matter of the missing gun and why Nathan had shown up in Santa Lucia. He'd let them know if he came across anything to the contrary, but he did not believe he would, so they should rest assured in their association with Margot.

Henry had also informed Daphne that her business partner needed the day off and not to expect too much from her over the next few days, as they needed to get to the bottom of the case. Daphne understood, knowing there was a long road ahead of them. She was grateful for the capable staff Poppy Cove had. Irene, Marjorie and the sewing room crew showed up just before opening, except for their newest employee—Jeannette Fox—whom they still had heard neither hide nor hair from, but at least it was out of their hands, and in the police's now. The staff greeted each other quietly, and then got to work, unsure of what the day would bring. They all wondered how the public would react to the news. Would they stay away in droves? Would the social set avoid the store as if it carried the plague? Irene had already begun tactfully canceling custom appointments while Marjorie had ordered that production be stopped temporarily to tidy up what the police had disorganized and taken apart. Marjorie then informed Daphne that other than what they currently had in production would be completed, but they would not start any new garments until further notice. Daphne agreed and there was no uproar or protestation from the team, just a quiet acceptance of that's what was to be. The team did not even appear to want to gossip, which was shocking in itself.

With things in capable hands, Daphne went up to the private office. She shut the door behind her, ready to roll up her sleeves. She knew it was going to be hectic having to wear many hats, covering for both herself and Margot. To get through her day, she'd chosen to wear something cheery, but not showy. She was in a new pale yellow small checked cotton dress, with a small white daisy print scattered all over. It had a white pointed collar and buttoned at the neck, right down the front. The sleeves finished at just below the elbow with matching white wingback cuffs. The bodice was fitted, yet demure with a full, sweeping skirt. It was bright and fresh, without being garish, and comfortable enough for Daphne to handle whatever came her way in a pretty and flattering manner.

Her desk was relatively unruffled with its usual assortment of piles. As accessories buyer, Daphne had many catalogues and brochures scattered all over. It wasn't a rat's nest, but she had her own way of organizing, and appreciated being surrounded by the materials she needed available at a quick glance.

Margot's workspace, on the other hand, was usually neat and orderly—everything in its place and a place for everything. Today, however, it was not the case. Daphne figured Margot would have had a fit if she'd seen it. She always knew Margot was reserved and secretive; now she understood why. She could not fully imagine how exposed and raw her friend must be feeling. She wondered what her home looked like, if this was what they did to her desk.

Systematically, Daphne went through the steps of reorganizing how she thought her partner would want her desk and filing cabinet. Being that all her past and secrets were now out, it probably wouldn't make any difference to Margot if she went through all her drawers now. She re-pinned her fabric swatches on her bulletin board as they should have been, with current spring/summer fabrics being used on the left side, and ones on the right for the upcoming fall/holiday orders. She placed swatches for custom orders in the middle, along with Margot's current sketches in their appropriate regions. The actual papers and materials themselves were in fine condition, not ripped, torn or dirty, just out of order.

As Daphne continued her work, she was relieved to notice that there was only one surprise waiting for her regarding her friend. Way in the back of the left hand bottom drawer was an old photo which seemed to be of a younger Margot, standing between what looked like an older version of her, which Daphne guessed to be Mrs. Willmington. On Margot's other side was a tall, handsome older man, who surely was her father. It was an outdoor shot, set in a well-manicured back yard garden. The family was formally dressed, and they all looked very attractive, but stiff—not very comfortable with each other. No one was smiling and they were all standing close to each other, but not touching. The picture told Daphne a lot. The subjects looked like each other, but did not appear friendly to one another. She wondered what that must have felt like and understood a little better about why Margot had wanted to leave. Daphne could never recall a family snapshot, or posed photograph for that matter, that the subjects from her family were not smiling, or at least relaxed and happy to be in each other's company. She put it away and finished up her task.

In a short while, she was satisfied with her efforts and thought that Margot would be pleased, or at least able to find what she wanted when she got back to work. Daphne wondered when that would be. Henry couldn't give her any indication. He mentioned that Margot would need her rest today to be certain, but after that, what would happen? With the room tidy, Daphne felt at loose ends. She didn't know what was happening downstairs and honestly didn't feel up to facing what she thought would be an empty store, with employees wanting answers that she didn't have. She sat at her desk, drumming her fingers on top. She picked up the phone receiver, an automatic reaction when she had questions and Margot wasn't at her desk. Normally, she'd just call down to her on the telephone intercom, then realized she couldn't do that. How could she forget? She sighed, flipped through a magazine, just to pass the time, while her mind continued to race.

She pawed through the piles on her own desk, but nothing was leaping out and taking her attention. Then she came across a colorful business card. It had an abstract splash of glossy, bright, contrasting paints on the front and simple, bold, black lettering on the back. "Adonis—Artiste" and a local phone number. It was for an area in the foothills. She turned the card over and over in her hand, recalling his invitation. *Wonder what he meant by 'posing' for him?* She mulled over his words in her mind. *He seemed like a free spirit, a bohemian, a beat, even. Would he have meant 'nude?'* Was Loretta right? She grinned secretively, blushing at the thought even though she was all alone. *Wouldn't that be such a daring adventure? No one would expect that of me!* She picked up the phone and dialed the number before she could change her mind.

Daphne practically skipped down the stairs after confirming a four o'clock appointment at Adonis' private studio for Friday afternoon. *I'm telling no one,* she decided. Irene caught the look on her face and gave a quizzical glance, but then motioned towards what was happening on the sales floor. Daphne was shocked and stood dead in her tracks when she saw how busy the store was. It appeared that anyone and everyone who'd ever heard of Poppy Cove was crowding the shop floor. Betty Young, their shop assistant had come in for her shift, and was moving through the patrons, nearly flying back and forth, to and from the dressing rooms. There was buzzing and clattering from the hoard, as they absentmindedly flipped through the racks, not really looking at the garments, but talking all about Margot, the murder, and the man. One particular conversation caught Daphne's attention specifically.

"I've heard she's been plotting this for years!" Mrs. Morgan hissed.

"Well, they say that the gun's missing. They've combed the beach and had divers searching off the wharf and came up with nothing." Mrs. Marshall added.

"It's probably washed out with the tide," A woman Daphne didn't recognize concluded, then added, "I've also heard that Detective Malone was in on it, too."

"No!" Mrs. Marshall exclaimed.

"Yes," the third woman confirmed. "He's been pulled off all cases and told not to contact Margot, or whoever she is. He's not in custody, but he's not allowed to talk to her or see her, either."

Daphne was surprised to hear this turn of events, especially from a stranger and decided to step in. She tapped the woman on the shoulder. "Excuse me, but where did you hear that from?"

Mrs. Morgan and Mrs. Marshall stepped back, red-faced. The other woman shrugged and replied, "Why, from Nancy Lewis, at the bank. She was talking for all the world to hear. She said that she knew all along that 'Margot' was probably up to no good. Too mysterious and, after all, she's not from here, either," she sniffed.

Daphne considered her comment. "And you are?" she asked the stranger.

The woman sized up her shoulders and gave herself an important stance. "Mrs. Lucille Givens. How do you do?" She held out her hand. "And you are?"

She took Lucille's hand and looked her dead in the eye. "Daphne Huntington-Smythe. Co-owner of Poppy Cove, along with my dear friend, Margot Williams, of whom you are speaking."

"Oh, well," Lucille stammered.

Daphne paused a little to let her squirm. "I don't believe I've seen you here before."

"I, er, well, I don't think I've been in before."

"And what brings you in today? A new dress perhaps? A playsuit for summer? What would you like to try on?" Daphne persisted.

"Um, well, I just came in to…" Lucille was having great difficulty keeping up her end of the conversation.

"To snoop? To spread ugly rumors? Or, would you like one of our shop assistants to help you pick out a flattering garment or two, maybe a matching hat and necklace? That way, you can tell all your friends what a good Poppy Cove patron you are." Daphne had never felt so bold. And it felt good.

Lucille looked around and saw that not only her group had come to a standstill, but also everyone else in the shop had stopped to listen in. It appeared that the majority of women were regular customers, therefore entitled to put in a word or two, but virtual strangers adding their own opinions in was not acceptable. Out of the corner of Daphne's eye, she noticed another figure she didn't recognize scurry out the door before being visited. Daphne then ran her hands through the hangers and picked up a couple of dresses and playsuits she thought would show Poppy Cove in its best light on the woman and waited for Lucille to answer.

Lucille looked at the garments Daphne had handed to her. She tilted her blonde wavy hair to one side and gave the items a good look. She had to admit, she liked them. She fingered the dresses and took the hangers. "Yes. I'll try them on." She gave a surrendering grin. They do look nice." Betty led the new customer to a dressing room.

The room was still quiet and Daphne took the opportunity to make an announcement. "Ladies, I'm aware that there are many stories flying around right now about our good friend, Margot Williams. And yes, that is her name. She's had it legally changed and we have all known her as that. She has proven to be a valued and loyal member of our community and Santa Lucia society. She's opened up publicly about her past, and we should respect her for that. As for the murder of Nathan Reed, she's said she had no idea he'd come to our town and therefore had nothing to do with his demise. I'd appreciate that if you are all spreading the news around town that you share that with your grapevines."

Daphne walked over to Irene at the sales desk and the conversations continued, at a quieter tone. "Yeah, that'll help," Irene commented out of the side of her mouth.

Daphne shook her head. "I had to say something."

"Look, people are going to talk, and they're going to say exactly what they want to say—truth or not, whether you like it or not," Irene stated. "It's big, but it'll blow over. Believe me."

"Yes, but what will it do to the business?" Daphne wondered out loud.

Irene laughed. "Look around you. Things like this bring people in."

Lucille brought a turquoise halter style playsuit with a matching overskirt and a popover shirtdress in a lavender windowpane check to the sales desk. "I'll take these." She fingered a necklace and earrings with cut glass flowers in the same lavender hue. "And these. And that." She picked up a paisley print scarf to go with the playsuit. Irene grinned as she wrote up the purchase and completed the sale. Daphne quietly—albeit somewhat smugly—wrapped up the items in tissue and sealed the paper bag with a signature Poppy Cove sticker. The new customer faced Daphne. "You do have some lovely things here. I'll be back. I'll bring my friends, too. You know, they may become collector items if your friend isn't as innocent as she claims." She briskly made her way out the door before Daphne could think of a response.

"What did I tell you?" Irene drawled.

Daphne's forehead developed worry wrinkles. She grabbed Irene by the arm and quietly asked, "You do believe she's innocent, don't you?"

"Of course," Irene answered without hesitation. "You don't?"

"No, no, of course," said Daphne. "I know with all my heart that she didn't have anything to do with the murder. Remember, I was there when we came across the body. She was as surprised as the rest of us. Even more so when she realized who it was. There's no way she was pretending. No way." She crossed her arms firmly.

"Well, then, you have no need to suspect her. Stand behind your friend. She's gonna need it. There's going to be more like your new best customer 'Lucille' before it's over." Irene grabbed the newspaper that was sitting on a shelf under the front counter and had a long look at the front page photo. "You know, I think I saw him."

The remark sparked Daphne. "Where? When?"

Irene paused, thinking carefully. "Saturday night, in the back room at Bud's." Bud's was a local dive bar with an illegal gambling den in the back. Everyone knew about it, including the police. It was usually pretty quiet without harming or involving the general Santa Lucia public, so it was left to itself.

"Eddie's not still in town, is he?"

"No, I haven't seen him since the fall." Eddie and his family had been involved in other nefarious duties that either had them behind bars or hiding out of town. "The back pretty much runs itself. There's a couple of muscle men who think they own it. They just basically keep it in order, tossing out the real riff raff."

Daphne knew the kinds of people that Irene enjoyed being in the company of and wondered what exactly that group would consider as 'real' riff raff. "So you think you saw Nathan?"

Irene nodded. "I was already in the back, just watching a couple of games and he came in. With Teresa Abbott."

"The police chief's daughter?" Daphne was shocked to hear that Christopher Abbott's daughter would frequent such a place. She knew the girl had been drifting since finishing high school two years ago without college plans, but really…

"Yep," Irene confirmed. "I see her around a lot these days. Fun gal."

"So she was on the arm of Margot's ex-husband?"

Irene shrugged. "I guess so. Strange bedfellows, huh?"

Daphne cringed at the term. "Tell me everything. What were they doing?"

"Well, he was playing cards, Black Jack, I think, and she was just hanging on his arm, sipping her drink and watching." She glanced at the picture again. "He was a looker."

"Did you talk to him or hear anything he said?"

"Nope. I was at another table. I just remember thinking he was new and attractive, wondering how hard Teresa had her hooks in."

"Had you seen him before?"

Irene shook her head. "Or since."

"What exactly happened that night with him?"

Irene understood the importance now of what seemed so small and insignificant that night, so she took her time recalling everything. "Let's see. I was there, just having a drink and watching the tables. It was a lively night, almost a full house. There's usually about five tables going, cards, roulette wheel, and sometimes a combo playing in the corner for tips, a private bar at the back wall. It's pretty smoky and kind of dark, but happening, you know?"

Daphne imagined. She'd never been in a place like that, but she'd seen her share of gangster movies. She motioned for Irene to continue, which she did, quietly. They were still at the sales desk, so she put the paper away and continued talking while pretending to look at the appointment book, which prompted Daphne to feign equal interest as they talked. Betty brought up a customer to the desk and wondered what they were talking about while she took care of the sale on her own.

"I'd been there since about nine-thirty, and they came in a little later, say ten o'clock," Irene recollected. "He sat down at a table right away while Teresa got a couple of drinks at the bar. He did not have a lucky streak."

"He was losing?"

"I'll say. He put down some big bets and none of them paid off. He had Teresa dip into her purse once or twice. He didn't say much from the beginning, but got even more moody and sullen."

Daphne was fascinated. "Then what happened?"

"It seemed like Teresa got tired of backing a loser and took off, probably around eleven. She left with some local guy. I know who he is by sight, but I couldn't name him. A regular. I think I went out with him once, but I'm not sure."

Daphne motioned for her to keep going.

"He wasn't the only one who was on the loser train that night. There was this really old beatnik guy at the table I was watching. He was wearing loose trousers, a rumpled and untucked shirt, and sandals. He also had a ponytail, of all things. He was going on about 'truth is beauty, beauty is truth,' while telling me he wanted to sculpt my form. I hightailed it away from him."

Oh my, that wouldn't be Adonis, would it? Daphne thought. She blushed but said nothing, waiting for Irene to turn her focus back to Nathan.

"Anyway, I went over to see what was happening at his table and I wasn't the only one. The big guns came over when they noticed he was all out of cash."

The store was busy, but Irene kept Daphne in rapt attention. Betty, on the other hand, was run off her feet, giving them as dirty a look as the perky blonde could do. They didn't notice her. They had their own priority matter.

"Nathan looked at the thugs. He asked them if they could spot him for a few bids, he'd give them back the loan from his winnings, with 'fair' interest. He said that his luck would turn around any second. They just stood there, not budging. Then he told them that he had money, but just not on him and if he lost, he could return it to them tomorrow night. So they footed the bill for a few more rounds. Inevitably, he lost and they escorted him out the door. That was the last I saw of him."

"You really should tell someone about this."

Irene nodded knowingly, but sneered. "Right, who? The police? I don't think Chief Abbott wants to know about his precious Teresa being there, let alone hanging around with a dead guy probably just before he was bumped off."

"You could tell Henry!"

"Who?"

"Henry Worth. Our family's lawyer, well, Margot's now, too. He's representing her and will defend her in court if it comes to that as well. He'll know what to do about the information. He'll go to a higher authority, if he has to."

Irene sighed. "Yeah, give me his number. I'll call and tell him. I owe that much to Margot, especially if it helps set her free."

Daphne eagerly got out the phone book while Irene picked up the receiver. Daphne put her hand out to pause her for a moment. "By the way," she asked, "any sign of Jeannette? Was she there, too?"

Irene shook her head. "The last I saw of her was when she left work on Friday." She became more alert as she remembered something new. "I did, however, catch her snooping last week, though."

"Really? What do you mean?"

"I came out from the changing rooms, Tuesday or Wednesday—I'm not sure which day exactly—but she was routing through the sales desk drawers and madly through the appointment book, tearing the place upside down."

The production staff rarely came to the front of the store during business hours, except to bring out new garments or to walk through while on their break times. "Did she say what she was looking for?"

"She said she was missing her favorite marking chalk, but I didn't buy it. I mean, what would it be doing up here?"

Daphne tried to recall if she'd seen her up in the front herself, but wasn't sure. "Did you see her do that more than once?" Irene shook her head.

"If you don't think she was telling the truth, what do you think she was doing?"

"I haven't a clue, but it did strike me as odd. I told her that if she needed anything, she should check with Marjorie and stay in the workroom. Those girls track all kinds of lint and thread all over the place. I'm forever cleaning up after them when they're out here."

Daphne smirked. Irene was always impeccable about her personal grooming, but couldn't remember when she would   actually   be   concerned   with   the   store housekeeping. She would rather delegate the task to Betty or Abigail, the weekend help, if she could. Daphne repeated her inquiry. "So you didn't happen to see Jeannette anywhere on your weekend?"

"Nope. We don't know her that well, but do you really think she'd be the type to be at a place like Bud's? That's about as likely as seeing you or Betty there!"

Daphne ignored the slight in turn for all of the useful information Irene had shared. She found Henry Worth's office number in the telephone directory which Irene then dialed.

The day progressed in much the same fashion. Both legitimate customers and curiosity seekers continued to keep the shop lively. Sales were good, which created both a blessing and a curse. Having the cash drawer full was swell for the business, but without Margot available to make decisions on the new stock and replenishing sold out garments, it could leave them bare. At this stage, they had no idea how long she'd be away. Daphne was lost in thought, wondering how to handle it all. She was comfortable with her share of the work—ordering the accessories, costume jewellery and the new swimwear. She could rely on Irene to manage the day to day running of the shop, and Marjorie was very capable to keep the stock flowing with everything already planned and most likely could make up more garments from patterns of items that had sold well in extra fabrics they had. Marjorie could also take up some of the custom appointments, if necessary. And then the May fashion show was coming up. A day or two delay on everything could be okay, but what if… *What if Margot's not up to working? What if she can't come up with designs? What if the public really does turn on her? What if she's caught up in a court case? And what if, God forbid, she can't prove she's innocent?* Daphne couldn't believe she was thinking that way. This was the first time she had so much sole responsibility for anything, and usually she wasn't prone to worry, but she felt so much responsibility on her to make this right—for the shop, the town and especially for Margot, who had enough to deal with.

"Excuse me," a young girl—who looked vaguely familiar—came up to Daphne, breaking her out of her reverie. "I wonder if you could help me."

Daphne blinked, realizing that Diane Phillips, the new waitress from the tearoom was standing in front of her. "Oh, right! Do you have any news about Jeannette?"

Diane's face registered disappointment and her perfectly poised shoulders sagged. "No, I was hoping you might."

"Sorry, no. So you don't know anything either? How worrying. Have you talked to the police?"

Diane nodded. "They came back to the boarding house last night and I told them the same thing I told you at the tearoom."

"Did they take much, find out anything new?"

"No, I don't think so." Diane awkwardly stood there for a moment. She looked at her hands, waiting politely for Daphne to either continue or let her go.

"Well, if you find out anything more about Jeannette, can you drop by and let us know?" Daphne asked.

Diane asked her to do the same and left.

Five o'clock came before the Poppy Cove crew knew it. The work room was packed up for the night and Daphne was straightening the last of the garments. She was the last employee about to leave when she heard the bell over the front door jingle. Looking a tad weary, Margot had arrived.

CHAPTER ELEVEN

"What are you doing here?" Daphne was surprised to see her. "I thought you were resting."

"I did," Margot said calmly. "I'm fine now. I can't just sit around at home."

"No, of course not," she agreed. "But are you okay to be here?"

"Yes. Where else would I be?"

Daphne didn't know what to make of Margot's behavior. She was used to seeing her cool and collected, but she didn't expect to see her at the store so soon. "I mean, it's yours, you're welcome to be here, of course, but..." Daphne also realized that like it or not, now that she knew more about her friend, her past and troubling present, she felt awkward. Immediately after Margot had told Daphne about her flight from Connecticut, she could come to terms easily with what her friend had done. However, the new facts that her friend had a gun and the police were treating Margot as the main suspect troubled her. She'd spent the whole day defending the character of her best friend and truly believed her, but now, being alone in the same room, knowing what she knew and it was just them, it felt raw.

Margot sat down in one of the lounge chairs and motioned for Daphne to join her, which she did. "Look," Margot sighed, defeated. "I'm still the same person you knew and went into business with. I never lied to you about anything in my past; I just never told you everything. There's nothing left for me to tell; you know it all and I'm glad. It's okay if you need time to absorb it; I do understand. But if you don't think you can do that, let me know and I'll move on once the situation with Nathan is behind me." She paused, waiting for Daphne to answer. When she didn't, Margot continued. "I'm going upstairs. I've got some things to sort out, and we've got so much to do. If you don't feel it's good for business to have me around, just say so and I'll make myself scarce. I'll need to leave some directions for Marjorie, however. I don't know what's going to happen and I want to make sure things are looked after."

Daphne started to cry and embraced her friend, who became weepy as well. After a few moments, she said, "Margot, I know you're innocent. You never outright lied or did anything to me or the store that I would even consider to be untrustworthy. Now that I know more about you, I just have to get used to it. I mean, I look at you now and think back to things you've said or haven't said, and the inklings were there all along. The way you didn't want to talk about getting married, your family, even your ease with being around Tom. I don't know if you realize it, but sometimes you acted like a married woman around him."

At that, Margot had to laugh.

"No, it's true." Daphne laughed as well. "The way you'd fix his coffee, straightened his tie, physically be near him, just a certain knowing and ease of being around a male, if that makes sense." She blushed when she realized what she was intimating. "Anyway, when I think back, we all just assumed things about you and your past, which in all fairness, you never claimed or denied. You never said you'd never been married, or came from money, or what you did in your past. I think we all just filled in the blanks in our own heads, and I'm probably the guiltiest of that."

Daphne continued. "I guess what I'm trying to say is that I don't know what's going to come, what will happen next and I hope for the best. And also, that you're not alone. We'll face this all here together and there's no need for you to hide your past from me or keep any more secrets. I don't believe you've done or could do anything so bad that it couldn't be overlooked or forgiven. I know you're not a murderer, but a victim in this as well, and I'll do my best to help you get to the bottom of it—and keep Poppy Cove running smoothly for the both of us."

Margot was crying in earnest, in a mix of relief, sorrow and fear. They sat silently for a moment in the dark lounge while she pulled herself together. When she could, she replied, "To be honest, even though it had to come about because of such a terrible thing, I'm glad to have told my story. I'm not sorry that I did what I did— well, maybe a couple of indiscretions I would change if I could—but I'm relieved in a strange way to have spoken it all out loud. You've been a true friend, letting me be, sending Henry and not judging me. I know you don't fully understand what my life was like, yet you accept me. Thank you." She looked around, feeling lost, then brightened. "If you're not in a hurry, do you want to catch me up on the day? What's the latest news? Oh wait, spare me the details if I was the subject. Did Nancy do anything embarrassing?" She smiled.

Daphne grinned back. "Now that you mention her, she did say something out of turn about you in public that brought a customer in who ended up buying a few things." With that, Daphne recollected to her friend the day's events, both monumental and trivial, and by the end of their good talk, it almost felt as if there was nothing wrong in their own little world and that was good.

****

Margot's Thursday morning started out calmly. Even though the case was far from solved, she'd had a full night's sleep. She picked out one of her favorite new dresses, a white cotton lawn with a bold red rose print, nipped in at the waist, with short capped sleeves and a flaring skirt. She thought about dressing more demurely, but it wouldn't matter what she wore, people were going to talk, so she might as well put her best foot forward, choosing matching patent red leather pumps. Feeling good about herself gave her a fragile sense of hope, just keeping her worries and fears tucked under her carefully made up surface.

She knew she was still under suspicion and also wondered what the heck had happened to Jeannette. Should she be worried for *or* about her? She'd conferred with Henry, who said everything was under control, with nothing new to report, other than that Irene had spoken with him and he in turn had spoken with Mayor Stinson who was having the proper authorities look into Teresa's whereabouts and connections in a hush-hush manner. She also wondered how cozy the girl had been with Nathan. Enough to have a jealous or angry streak? Would she have access to a .38 and the inclination to use it? Most of the media had temporarily gone away as there was no new news, save for Weathers who kept popping up around corners, asking questions and getting nowhere. Given the circumstances, it was all quite normal.

She was, however, aware that all throughout her day there was a somewhat discreet police presence. A cop car was down the block from her house, which did not escape the eyes of Mrs. O'Leary, who added her own thoughts on the subject. Also a patrol vehicle circled by Poppy Cove on a regular basis, with officers lunching at the tearoom, watching the shop windows. She imagined that Mrs. Coleman's was probably under surveillance as well, which would irritate the woman to no end. She could imagine Mr. Drake rubbing his hands in glee and watching them through the lace parlor curtains.

Margot was surprised she could concentrate on work, and was so relieved that she had that solace to dwell in. Her staff gave her a respectable berth after letting her know they were there for her, all within an air of believing her innocence. Not a word was spoken or implied that she would be found otherwise. Marjorie patted her on the arm, told her that her door was always open to her and then moved on. She watched her employer, giving her just enough to handle, without overwhelming her, deciding what could wait for another day and what would feed her mind and heart, such as the focus on the garments for the next fashion show, and suggesting which custom appointments to reschedule.

Irene looked at Margot with a new level of respect, which Margot noticed and was grateful for. She also asked Irene to keep Mr. Cuddles for a few more days. As much as Margot would love to have his purring fuzzy little body to comfort her, with all the turmoil still surrounding the situation, including the police watching her yard, she felt it was best not to have him underfoot. Irene felt proud, knowing that Margot personally trusted her. In turn, Irene was now understanding how Margot had been in many ways not that different from her. She wasn't pure and lily white without facing some of life's seedier choices. Not that she believed Margot was a killer, but a strong woman who lived up to making a future by now living up to her past. It was something that Irene would have to do, but not yet, and Margot could teach her a thing or two on how that was done.

Betty's heart was open to her employer as well, even though her upbringing and past was nothing at all similar to Margot's. Betty Young was pretty, perky and a happy three-year newlywed, always making it home every night to have dinner on the table for her Dwight, a star salesman at Smart's Oldsmobile. What she did know was how to stand by a friend whom she believed in when they were falsely accused of murder, no matter how dark or damning it seemed for them.

Margot retreated up to the office to see if she could get her mind on new design ideas. Although they had a handle on the current 'Making Waves' summer line, in their production schedule, fall was looming. With all that had been going on, she'd forgotten that a new catalog of fabric swatches had arrived, featuring some exquisite lightweight woolens in warm earthy browns and greens which were a change from the uniform grey flannel that had been so popular over the past few years. She flipped through the colors without focusing, as she was not able to find a cohesive thread of ideas. She moved through the various European fashion magazines, looking to see if anything there would inspire her. As she was left alone with her quiet mind, restlessness welled up and productive thought went out the window.

Margot picked up the Poppy Cove design book where she had sketches, swatches and written details of every design they'd ever made for the shop floor. There was information about what pattern they used for each garment, how much fabric, a button sample, tricky problems and also how well something sold, such as the navy shift in the first year that did not even hit the floor before selling out, to the raincoats that didn't move until the next season due to a dry spell. She still felt restless.

She grabbed her sketchpad and sat down in the easy chair by the big arched window that looked out onto Avila Square. Still nothing was coming, so she turned on the radio, and just began to mindlessly draw, not clothes, but just free form to clear her thoughts. Johnny Mathis' *Chances Are* came on and she realized what she was actually drawing. That song was the last one she and Tom had been dancing to just last week. As she looked closer at what she thought was a nothing sketch, she realized she was drawing his face. She threw the pad down and ran out the door, not hearing Daphne's "Where are you going?" far behind her.

Margot was about half a block away from Poppy Cove, headed in the direction of Tom's apartment, when she slowed down, realizing her rash decision. Both she and Tom were under strict orders not to have contact with each other. She looked around, and, of course, down the block was a patrol car. Fortunately it was unoccupied, and there was no sign of any officer or detective around. She took the risk and briskly walked by. Tom's place wasn't too far away, about another three blocks, but she had to go by the courthouse, police station and civic buildings to do so.

Due to taking detours so as not to be seen, it took her twice as long as usual to walk to Tom's. The sky was cerulean blue, with no sea breeze making it quite hot off the pavement. In her impetuousness, Margot had left without a hat or sunglasses and she kept pausing to shade her eyes and look over her shoulder, hiding in various spots—doorframes, behind a barber's pole, a mailbox, and even sneaking down a back alley. She was pretty sure she hadn't been seen. At least, no one stopped her.

Her feet and ankles were killing her from her beautiful but pinching red shoes and her heart was beating a mile a minute when she reached his apartment building. It was a well-kept three-story walk-up, in white stucco, with the classic Spanish flare shared in most of the Santa Lucia architecture, finished with a terra cotta roof and black wrought iron balconies and trim. Jacaranda trees were in full bloom in front as well as red geraniums and white impatiens framing the entrance. It was sweet smelling and bucolic on a beautiful spring day, giving the illusion that nothing could be wrong. Margot wondered if her decision had been rash. Would he even want to see her? Was he mad? Not only had she been hiding her past from him, avoiding his marriage proposal, but also now putting his career in jeopardy. She reached into her patent leather handbag to find her key for his place, but thought better of it. She may be presuming her welcome too much. She looked around once more to make sure she wasn't followed and pressed the intercom button for his apartment.

Tom did not hesitate to let her in, even though he was surprised to find her showing up at his home. He opened up his door cautiously, looking around as she came in and gently whispered, "You shouldn't be here." He did, however, let her in.

As soon as the door shut, he took her in his arms for a full embrace. He trembled, while she began to melt and cry in relief. "I had to see you. I know I may get you into more trouble for doing this, but I just couldn't stop myself."

He smoothed her hair, holding her and saying nothing for a moment, sensing her anxiety but unconsciously caught up in her beauty. Finally, she asked, "Have I completely destroyed our relationship?"

Tom was gobsmacked and gave a nervous chuckle when he could. Nothing could be further from his mind. "I thought you'd be the one mad at me."

"Why on earth would I be mad at *you*?"

"I feel like I let you down, deserted you. But honestly Mar, I didn't have much of a choice. When they figured out who the victim was, they locked me away for questioning."

"Oh, Tom, I feel so bad."

He shrugged it off. "They were just doing their job. They didn't do anything I wouldn't have done. It was odd being on the other side of the table, that's all."

"What happened?"

He hesitated. "I'm not to say."

"And I'm not supposed to be here."

"No, you're not. Well," he grinned while he led her by the hand to the sofa, gave her a peck on the lips and they sat down very closely together and began to elaborate. "They went through my desk at the station, took away all of my guns and my badge. They also went over this place, too." He motioned around his apartment. "They asked me questions over and over again, even brought in someone from the state level to make sure that it was all officially done."

She took off her pumps, curled up her legs, and nestled in his arms. "That must have been terrible for you."

"It was tiring, but nobody got rough or out of hand. They just kept repeating the same questions over and over again. 'Did I know or know of Nathan Reed? Had I come into contact with him? What did I know about you and your past? Where is your gun? Had I fired my .38 recently? What exactly did I hear or see that night outside your place?' Pretty much everything you would expect, no surprises." He pause looking at her. "How were things for you? Are you okay?"

She nodded. "It was all right. Daphne called Henry Worth to come defend me."

"Worth? I thought his practice was business law."

"Turns out he has criminal law in his background and he's very comfortable with defending me. I almost think he's getting a kick out of it."

Tom laughed. "They told me they let you go home yesterday."

She nodded. "When did you get home?"

"Late last night. I just finished getting things in order around here."

For the first time since arriving, Margot had a look at her surroundings. Tom looked all right, but his green eyes were flat and weary. His short, dark hair was tidy, but not Bryl-creemed, as if he'd just towel dried it out of the shower. He was in a navy polo shirt and tan chinos, barefoot, which was a touch out of the ordinary for him. The place was tidy, as he usually kept it, but there were a few things slightly askew that his housekeeper would catch that Tom didn't, such as a dead fig leaf here, an old newspaper there.

They sat quietly for a moment, relieved to be alone together. A bubble of anxiety started to well up in

Margot's chest. "Tom," she started, "You know I had nothing to do with Nathan's murder. You do believe me when I say I had no idea he was here, don't you?"

He nodded emphatically. "Margot, of course, I believe you. You may have told me things I didn't know about you, but I know you didn't do this. I've seen a lot of things that have happened in this world, and many unsuspecting people do some pretty awful things, but I saw your reactions and I'd have to say I'm a good judge of character. I believe you when you say you hadn't seen him recently. Your word is good enough for me."

Margot couldn't believe her luck to be so trusted, especially from someone whom she'd deceived about some very important and personal things in her life.

"I do have a question for you, too." Tom said.

"I'm sure you have a few," Margot replied slyly, prepared to come clean. "Ask away."

"You know I didn't have anything to do with it either, don't you?"

She sat back and blinked. "Honestly, Tom, it never even crossed my mind. Of course not! How could you? You knew nothing of him!"

"Just asking. Margot, if we're going to be on the level with each other, then I need to know you trust me, too."

She immediately replied. "I don't think I had any doubt, ever."

"Well, I'm not perfect. I know I get obsessed with work. I forget that other people need attention too, not just the criminals." He looked into her eyes and caressed her arm. "I don't think I ever told you I had been engaged once."

It did come as news to her, but not a complete surprise. After all, he was an attractive man in his thirties, coming to Santa Lucia a few years before she had. "What happened?"

"Emily was a daughter from an old society family. They weren't pleased with her seeing a copper," he answered lightly. Tom had told Margot that he came from a couple of generations of police officers and still had an uncle in the force back in the bay area. "They forced her to break off our relationship when they found out I was determined to stay in law enforcement."

"So that's the reason you came here?"

"Yes and no. Margot, I saw some pretty wild things in San Francisco, far worse than you've ever done. I was sick of it and being a beat cop, always having to prove my worth because I came from a line of Malones. There was an offer here for junior detectives, so I answered the call and worked my way up on my own merit." Which Tom certainly had. His position was as Lead Detective of the Santa Lucia Police Department, even if he was removed from duty at the moment.

"And now by knowing me, you're involved in all this. I'm so sorry." Tom did not reply, so Margot continued. "You must not think that highly of me anymore now that you know all about me and I don't blame you."

"Listen, every good cop gets in hot water at least once in his career and it all gets worked out. Just by our association, we get to know some pretty shady characters." Tom realized what he said made her blush. "Not meaning that I think that of you. But, do I know *all* about you now?" Tom asked gently, but wryly.

"Yes, yes, I think so. I don't think there's anything left to tell." She slumped. She sat up and pleaded, "Tom, that's not how I wanted to tell you about me, about my past."

"And did you want to actually finally share that with me?"

Margot nodded. "I was actually going to tell you that night, before all of this happened and you were called away. I wanted let you know all about who I am, where I came from, and how I got here. And, to answer your question..."

Just as Margot was about to give Tom the reply to his life changing proposition, there was a buzz from the lobby intercom, followed by a male voice. "Malone? You'd better let me up if you're in there. I need to talk to you."

CHAPTER TWELVE

Tom told Margot to hide in his bedroom while he waited for his guest to arrive. She stood behind the partially closed bedroom door and scanned the room. It wasn't as orderly as the rest of the place. She saw his damp bath towel thrown on the bed and resisted the urge to pick it up and put it where it belonged. She made a mental note that if he was indeed going to accept her reply, there were a few habits he'd have to change.

Hearing the knock on the door brought her back to the current situation. "Hey, Tom." She recognized that it was Officer Jenkins.

"Bruce, what brings you by? Any news?"

"Yeah. Listen, I shouldn't be here, but I wanted you to know. The results came back from your gun. It's clean. It's locked up at the station till they say you can come back."

Tom eyed the bedroom door and saw it move slightly. "What about Margot's? Have they found it? Run any ballistics reports on it yet?"

Jenkins removed his cap and shook his head. "Nope. They haven't found it." He hemmed and hawed around before he spoke again. "Margot, come out. I know you're here."

She debated on whether or not to walk out, but didn't want to get Tom in worse trouble. Margot decided it was best if she did and greeted Officer Jenkins, who was in uniform. "Hi."

"You know you're not supposed to be here, but I'm not surprised," he said firmly. "Don't worry. I won't say anything. I'll help you get out, too. If anyone sees you, I'll say it was official business."

"Did I hear you say that my gun is still missing?" She sat down and the men followed suit.

Jenkins nodded. "And you have no idea where it's gone?"

"No. I've been trying so hard to remember when I last saw it. I have no idea. I've never used it. Once I moved in, I put it in the back of my drawer and just left it there." Even though she was concerned about the gun being at large, Margot was at ease to read into his comment that it sounded as if Jenkins truly believed she was not the murderess. "What about Jeannette? Has she shown up or has anyone reported seeing her?"

"Nothing on her, nobody turning up in any hospitals that fit her description either. She is definitely being considered as both a missing person and a person of interest."

"It's unnerving, to say the least. I don't know her well, but last night Daphne informed me that our manager caught her routing through papers and such that had nothing to do with her at Poppy Cove. I think Daphne had her call my lawyer to tell him."

"Tom, you'll be glad you aren't around," added Jenkins. "Not only did Henry Worth call and mention that, but he also said that Teresa Abbott had been one of the last people to be seen in public that night with Reed, and left him in rather a hurry. She evidently wasn't happy with his behavior and made it public."

"Irene never mentioned seeing them row," Margot added.

"No, they didn't fight," Bruce agreed. "But she did leave with another man, and made a point of it. Teresa also has access to a gun of that description, if she so desired." Although there were only the three of them there in the privacy of Tom's home, Jenkins looked around before quietly continuing. "It's really hit the fan down there. Chief's ticked off with his daughter and he's being questioned about her involvement and how secure the station is. Riley's walking around with the Commissioner and Mayor like he's the one in charge. I'd be happy to be on leave, let me tell you!"

Jenkins stood up out of his chair. "I better go before they start asking where I am. Margot, it's probably best if I escort you back. Home or Poppy Cove?" He extended his arm to her in a jovial manner.

Tom looked at her and as much as he didn't want her to leave, he knew it was best if she did. "Bruce is right. Don't worry. We'll get to the bottom of this." He looked her straight in the eyes. "Trust me."

Margot melted. It was too much.

Tom looked over her shoulder at Jenkins. "Give us a moment? Can you just wait out in the hall while I say goodbye to my girl?"

Jenkins did what was asked of him while Tom did his best to assure Margot that one day not far in the future all would be well. "Have faith, darling." Tom kissed her as if the world was standing still, because for that moment, it was.

Bruce escorted Margot back to Poppy Cove. It was fairly steady in the store, but she greeted her customers and staff with a brief nod and ran upstairs. Irene returned a perplexed look, but stayed with her customer at hand. In Margot's trip to Tom's, she'd left without letting anyone know where she was going. She checked her lipstick in her compact mirror. "I'm such a mess!" She reapplied her face powder and gave her hair a bounce as well.

Daphne had been sitting upstairs in the office, looking at Julia McKay sample purses. "I figured that's where you went after I saw your sketchpad. Nice likeness," she remarked. "How'd it go?"

"Good. He believes me," Margot replied with pleasure.

"Oh, as if there was any doubt. What else did you find out?"

"That he leaves wet towels on the bed."

"Well, well, well. Care to tell how you know that?"

Margot gave a bigger laugh than she had in days. "It wasn't because of *that* reason. Jenkins showed up to give him some news."

"Do tell about that!"

Margot filled her partner in.

"Well, I'm glad to hear you're not the only suspect." Daphne held up a new tortoise shell Lucite purse Margot's way. "What do you think of this?" The purse was of medium size, rectangular-shaped, tapering to the top with same handles and brass hardware closure.

Margot looked at the handbag Daphne was holding. "Nice. I like the mother of pearl one, too."

Daphne picked up the one on her desk that Margot was referring to. It was small and square, not much bigger than a wallet, with tiled, pale iridescent hard sides and a brass clasp as well. It would be delightful for evening, where it would gently reflect candle and mood lighting, giving a light glow on the arm of the woman carrying it.

Margot felt invigorated after seeing Tom and knowing that he still loved her. All was not right in the world quite yet, but it gave her hope. She got a new sense of inspiration seeing Daphne playing with the accessories. She started thinking about the swatches she'd seen earlier and walked them over to Daphne's desk. The wool crepe browns and mosses were perfect with the tortoiseshell and gave direction for the new fall daywear line. Margot picked up the small iridescent one, thinking about the upcoming Miss Santa Lucia pageant in May. The regular summery items that the contestants would be wearing in the show were well underway, and they'd have to schedule fittings soon, but Margot was still deciding what fabric they would use for the queen and her two princesses.

When the new court was announced at the pageant that the fashion show was part of, Poppy Cove would create the first set of formal gowns immediately, for the winners to wear in their public appearances. She found her samples of dreamy, opalized taffetas that would make beautiful and shimmery evening wear. The more she thought about it, the more she started to see the new version of the Miss Santa Lucia dress they made every year. It should be a complete departure from the previous dresses that they'd created for the pageant functions. Poor Miss Santa Lucia, Nora Burbank, had met a tragic end and Caroline Parker had had to carry out the reign. Given what had gone on, it would be best to create something in a different color altogether. The creamy, muted white that picked up pastel hues would be very different from the fiery red of the last Poppy Cove queen's gown and would lend itself to so many other complementary tones for the princesses, who always had a slightly less dramatic version of the queen's dress. The contest wasn't judged until that night and therefore the winner declared then. Margot had to act fast with her team to get the dresses done before their first elected public appearance, where they were expected to be in their court attire, so her ideas needed to be ready to be made as soon as she had the measurements of the new royalty. As hectic as it was, it was a challenge that she enjoyed, especially at that moment.

"Mar?" Daphne broke into her friend's design reverie.

"Hmm?"

"Are you okay if I leave early tomorrow afternoon?"

Margot didn't look up. She was pairing lilac, mint, and pale tangerine swatches to the choice she'd for the queen's dress. "Sure, fine. Can't see why not."

"Good, thanks." Daphne circled Adonis' name on his card with her finger. Margot was so lost in thought she didn't ask her friend anything about where she was going, or what she would be doing. Daphne sat quietly wondering, *So what does one wear to pose nude?* She laughed out loud, realizing that it didn't matter.

Margot looked up. "Did you say something?"

"No, no, just thinking out loud. Nothing." Daphne opened up her mouth again, thinking she could say something, anything to plant some bait, to lead her friend in the direction of questions, but then thought against it. For the time being, Margot was happy and at peace, not curious. Daphne sat there with a grin on her face, but felt deflated. She guessed she had a lot to learn about how to lead an intriguing life.

The rest of the day went fairly smoothly. Margot even felt comfortable enough to see customers on the shop floor. She was aware, however, as she circulated the sales room, that certain pockets of customers stopped talking as she went by. Sometimes they would pick up a light conversation with her, or just nod and resume talking after she passed. Of course, there was always one outspoken member of society who had to put her two cents in, and Margot was not surprised when she did, coming from the casual day dresses section.

"Well, of course, I'll still come in, but I don't think I'll be letting my Barbara come here alone. I'm just grateful that Betsy and Anita are still away at boarding school—Lords—to be exact and not here in town at that Stearns Academy. There are certain influences that young girls should not be exposed to," Nancy Lewis sniffed.

Mrs. Lamb, a wife of one of the bank's employees and a sometime Poppy Cove customer, nodded her head in answer to her shopping partner, mindlessly agreeing with Nancy.

Nancy continued to prattle on to her captive audience. "Of course, it's much easier to live the whole starving artist routine when you have the money to draw upon. I mean, I understand where a creative person needs a colorful past, even a little danger to make art. I completely empathize with that, being a prolific contributor to the art community myself, but my daughters—Barbara in particular—being at that crucial marrying age, still need my guidance. Regardless of what the final outcome of the case is, my sources say that what Margot did, including involving her policeman boyfriend, is just one of those wrong things."

Margot rolled her eyes. *Prolific artist? Oh, please, that bunch of misshapen clumps of clay in the park that she put together in a couple of afternoons,* she thought. *And Babs and her sisters need better influences than their mother.* As for the rest of Nancy's comments, Margot had had enough and couldn't keep her response in her head any longer. "Mrs. Lewis, how wonderful that we have you to be judge, jury and justice all wrapped up into one person. Why, it's so great that we have someone like you able to spread conclusions so rapidly and correctly to anyone within earshot." She turned to Mrs. Lamb and smiled sweetly. "Thank you for coming in. If there's anything we can help you with—say a new spring dress, or a lovely swimsuit—do let my staff know."

Nancy blustered, realizing that perhaps she'd gone a titch too far. She pinched her small face into a tortured smile, trying to appease Margot. "Oh, come on, we're all friends here. I'm only repeating what I've heard. I can't help it if people are talking about you." She picked up a blue and white striped seersucker dress and held it up to herself, as if nothing she'd said was remotely hurtful.

"Nancy, it wasn't that long ago that I stood up for you, believing when you said you were innocent," Margot said softly, then continued louder, "Mrs. Lewis, I do appreciate your patronage in my store, but I demand that you show me the same respect and courtesy that I extended to you when you needed it."

The room fell silent and watched the showdown with baited breath. Margot met the redhead's blue eyes, head on and not flinching. "I, er, well. I'll just take this," referring to the dress in her hand. She scurried away to the sales counter where Irene looked at the tag, slowly walked back to the rack, exchanging it for one in Nancy's size and leisurely completed the purchase while all the customers were entertained.

Mrs. Lamb followed Nancy Lewis quietly out the door. Over by the formal dresses, the buzz of conversation started again from a couple of newcomers. Mrs. Morgan and Mrs. Marshall, pawing over the chiffon cover-ups, tittered nervously, but resumed their talk.

Margot looked around, feeling surrounded by vultures. Daphne had come down from the office during the floor show and was about to approach Margot, when another lady beat her to it. "Don't let them get to you, Margot."

Margot turned around to see Betty's friend, Rebecca Goldberg, touching her elbow. "I think I know a little about how you feel. It doesn't seem like it, but believe me, it'll pass and people will gossip about something new and leave you alone."

Margot looked at the woman and smiled. Mrs. Goldberg certainly had had her share of attention last year. "How are you? Is Efrem well?"

The diminutive dark-haired girl smiled shyly. "We're doing fine, coping along. The jewellery store is steady, people are liking Efrem's ideas and we may actually see a profit soon." Goldberg's Jewelers was just down the street and the two businesses helped to support each other. Rebecca's husband Efrem had recently taken over the business from her father Isaac, who'd been involved in his own scandal last year.

Margot didn't know if she should inquire about the old man, when Rebecca volunteered, "We see Isaac every few weeks. It's hard, but he is family. People may not understand, but I have to stand by him." Rebecca looked down at her feet, self-consciously.

Margot felt a twinge of loss when she thought of her own family. She hadn't seen her parents in years and they obviously weren't interested in her well-being. As far as she knew, they'd never tried to follow or contact her when she left, and she didn't want to admit it made her sad. She could feel her throat well up, but replied, "Good for you; you should. He needs to know you care."

Rebecca nodded and left to say hello to Betty. Margot sighed, her façade completely fading. Closing time wasn't too far off and she decided to leave the rest of the business day to the others and just go home.

Unfortunately, when she got there, all that was in her refrigerator was a bottle of milk that had gone bad and a loaf in the breadbox that was growing a lovely blue fuzz. Margot groaned as she looked in her cupboard and saw it was practically empty. Not in the mood for dining out but still hungry, she changed into a pair of navy capris, a sleeveless floral blouse and matching navy flats and headed to Montgomery's Fine Foods to pick up a few things.

If she thought the scrutiny and judgement was bad at Poppy Cove, she was nowhere near prepared for what she was in for at the large supermarket. Right at the entrance was a stack of the *Santa Lucia Times*, with, of course, Nathan's murder still the cover story, with references to her past life and current place in Santa Lucia society. Women pushing carts down the aisles would either stop dead in front of her or avoid her. If they had children with them, they did one of two things: either blatantly pointed her out as a bad example or shield their children from her.

Margot tried to go about her business as if nothing was going on, but then she looked at the end of an aisle and saw a uniformed officer giving a tip of his hat to acknowledge her, both letting her know they were observing her every move and watching to see if Jeannette was after her. She didn't realize what it was doing to her until she went to grab a jar of pickles and her hand shook so badly that she dropped it and it shattered all over the slippery waxed linoleum floor.

"Now don't you worry about that, Miss Williams. I'll get it looked after. You didn't cut yourself, did you?" Before Margot had time to react, Reginald Montgomery had appeared at her side, taking her hands in his and checking them over. "Why don't you come along with me?" He signaled for a stock boy to clean up the mess and a grocery clerk to take her basket while the store owner took her by the arm and escorted her to his office.

He gestured for her to sit down and pulled a bottle of brandy out of his desk drawer, pouring a nip for both of them without asking and placed a glass in front of her. The kind, mature gentleman sat behind his desk opposite her, raised his glass in the air, invited her to toast in greeting, which she did and both took a sip before talking. "Margot, how are you doing?"

She looked at Reginald and saw he meant what he was asking in genuine care and concern. She sighed, emotions ebbing again. "Oh, Reginald, just awful if you want the truth."

"You know, I've been in your shoes. Why don't you tell me all about it?" He put his wing tips up on his desk, lit a cigar and waited for her to continue.

She knew that Reginald would know exactly what she was going through and opened up, telling him everything, including the fresh emotional ups and downs of the day, from knowing Tom still cared and believed in her, the unsure worry and fear about Jeannette, and her own thoughts of grief/non grief of dealing with the death of her ex-husband. And how everyone had an opinion about her personal life.

Reginald sat quietly, letting her get it all out. "People are funny, Margot. What it'll boil down to is that you'll find out who your real friends are. And I'll bet you'll be surprised how many you've made right here in Santa Lucia. And the rest? Well, leave them to their own messes."

She looked at him, so grateful for his kindness, knowing that he was showing her he was one of the true ones. He was soft and a little round, with life experience showing on his features. Just last year he'd his own tragedy, complete with its own rumor mill and accusations that haunted him. And here he was, surviving and living on the other side. "You'll see," he said.

Margot smiled and the two finished their drinks amiably. They talked about how well business was going for both of their ventures, dwelling on what was right and good for a short while. Reginald walked her out of the office and left her at the customer service desk to pick up her basket. She thanked him, feeling much better once again. He continued on to deal with his own shop matters.

"Margot? Is that you?"

She was pleased to see Marjorie, picking up some groceries right after work. "Do you have dinner plans?"

Margot smiled and shook her head.

"Then why don't you join me? I'll whip up something and we can sit and talk," her head seamstress suggested.

Margot agreed and the two ladies continued picking up what they needed, including a nice bottle of red wine. When they got to the till, the clerk put his hand up and declared with a sense of pride, "Ladies, your purchases are free of charge, as per the orders of the owner of Montgomery's Fine Foods."

Margot and Marjorie began to protest and when the clerk was insistent, laughed and thanked him. They looked around for Reginald who was nowhere to be seen, then made sure that the clerk would let the owner know of their gratitude.

CHAPTER THIRTEEN

Both of the women had driven to the store, so Margot made a quick trip home to put away her purchases before going to Marjorie's. In all of the time the ladies had worked together, Margot had never been to her home. She only knew the basics about her trusted right hand— that she was a widow and an accomplished sewer.

It was still light out, with a lovely fresh scent coming up from the ocean as Margot pulled up to Marjorie's Spanish-style bungalow, a block away from the shore at Water Street and Lotus Avenue, which was moments away from the main thoroughfare of Cove Street. Margot took a deep breath as she got out of her powder blue Bel Air and forced herself to relax. She noticed Marjorie's house. It was modest, as so many in the neighborhood were, nondescript but tidily kept with azaleas and rhododendrons blooming wildly in bright orange, pink and yellow tones. The front of the house had a small rounded porch, containing an oversized wicker chair, facing the street. Margot smiled as she realized that Marjorie had it positioned at just the right angle so that she could see the ocean between the houses across the street. The scene made her feel comfortable. She knew she'd done the right thing by coming to spend the evening with Marjorie, who she fondly regarded as a perfect mothering figure.

"Come in!" Marjorie exclaimed as Margot knocked on the front door. She was immediately welcomed with the aromas of roasting meat and garlic, of herbs and savories. Perry Como was crooning on the stereo, asking his listeners to *Dream Along...* with him. A fuzzy old cat wrapped itself around Margot's feet as she stood, taking in the tidy little living room. All the passageways had curved walls and a smooth stucco finish, and hardwood floors polished to a shine with well-worn rugs lovingly maintained. In the corner was an easy chair with a lamp and a magazine stand, chock full of the latest issues of *Life, Look* and *Ladies' Home Journal* and a copy of Mary Stewart's *Madam, Will You Talk?* on top of the pile. In the opposite corner from the chair was Marjorie's Admiral television. It was a scene that provided such warmth that Margot was almost in tears.

"Right through here to the back, dear! I've got the potatoes on to boil and I don't want them going over," Marjorie shouted from the kitchen. "Wine's poured, come join me!"

Margot happily did. She realized she was so hungry and couldn't remember the last time she'd eaten a good meal. Marjorie fussed and fretted around the kitchen, which was just as homey as the front of the house, decorated in cheery white and yellow, with red accents here and there for color. She wouldn't let Margot lift a finger, even after her numerous offers to help. She insisted Margot stay seated at the kitchen table and saw that her wine glass was never empty.

In a very short while, dinner was served. Meatloaf, mashed potatoes, peas, and corn, all smothered in a mushroom gravy. There was an apple crisp sitting on the counter waiting for dessert. Throughout the meal, they made light conversation about nothing—the weather, flowers, music, favorite television shows, just things they liked.

At the end of the meal, Margot sighed contentedly. Marjorie smiled. She allowed Margot to help wash up the dishes. As they cleared up, Margot commented, "Thank you so much. This is exactly what I needed."

"Well, it's really nothing. I figured you could use a little looking after, someone to take you under their wing, what with your mother so far away."

It was a direct, fishing comment. Being that it came from Marjorie, Margot felt comfortable to say more. She tried to respond lightly, but there was an emotional pull in her voice. "My mother is not the nurturing kind."

"No?" Marjorie made work with her hands in the sink to keep Margot talking. It was working.

"No, she never cooked or did any domestic tasks. We had a housekeeper and a nanny to look after everything."

"What did your mother do?"

Margot paused while drying a plate and thought. "Come to think of it, not much. I remember her being busy with beauty parlor appointments, committees and bridge club."

"Well, surely she must have seen to you and your needs."

Margot shook her head. "No, I had a nanny when I was little and once I was in school, she sent me outside or up to my room to figure out my own things." At the time, it seemed perfectly normal—if not a little lonely—to Margot, but now as she was seeing more and more of how others lived, she realized that they'd had very different experiences of home life. "Don't get me wrong, my parents never hurt me, and I had every and any little thing I ever wanted."

"She just wasn't there for you like a mother should be," Marjorie concluded.

"I guess," Margot replied.

"Oh, dear! Well, I'm not perfect, but I did my best with my own."

The ladies finished with the dishes and the wine. They moved to brandy in the living room. Margot continued the conversation. "You have a son, don't you?"

Marjorie nodded. "He's a grown man now. Patrick lives in Chicago with his wife Laura. They've given me a lovely grandson, Richard. He's seven now and named after his grandfather. Bright as a button, that one! They send me pictures often, but I do wish they were closer." She gestured to a table along the wall that was covered with photographs.

"You must have had a lovely marriage," Margot said.

The comment surprised Marjorie a little. The whole time she'd known Margot, the girl had always avoided the subject. She was pleased that Margot was showing her vulnerability and proceeded carefully not to push her too hard. "Yes, we did, but it was over too soon."

"Your husband was in the army, wasn't he?" Margot saw the photograph of a handsome man in uniform, smiling proudly.

"Yes. He was killed in '43 in the Solomon Islands."

Margot had known Marjorie was a war widow, but didn't know any more than that. "I'm sorry; that must have been tough on you and Patrick."

Marjorie agreed. "Richard had been away for most of the war, but it still wasn't easy. I missed him terribly. I was so relieved that my son was never called up. He got a letter to report to basic training just weeks before the whole thing ended."

"Is that when you took the job at Martin's?"

"No, I started there long before that when Patrick entered school. Richard didn't mind. I ran out of things to sew around the house," she laughed.

Margot kept pouring over the family photos while sipping brandy, and Marjorie let her, interjecting with comments or descriptions of people, places or events. When Margot had gone through them all, she sat back down. "I know it was terrible for you to lose your husband at such a young age, but I envy you. You have such wonderful memories."

Marjorie sipped quietly at her drink before replying. "It hasn't all been a bed of roses."

"Oh, no," Margot was quick to answer. I didn't mean it was all easy, just well, nice."

"It wasn't all that, either."

Margot said nothing in response and Marjorie continued. "I know what you're going through."

"I'm sure you do in a way, but I wasn't in love with Nathan when he died. Not like how you felt about your husband."

"Margot, don't be offended by me asking this, but you didn't shoot him, did you?"

She took the question in the respectful spirit Marjorie had asked and answered, "No, I did not. I truly didn't know he was here."

"Right, I thought not. Well, I did such a thing. I shot a man and killed him."

"What!?!" Margot's eyes widened and she wasn't sure she'd heard correctly. "What did you just say?"

"I shot and killed a man," Marjorie quietly and calmly repeated. "It was in self-defense, but I did it all the same." She sipped her drink and continued. "I was on my own. It was in 1932. Richard was away, at some base for a training and maneuvers course, and Patrick was just a young boy at the time. I heard some noise down in the kitchen. Richard had left me a pistol in his bedside table and taught me how to use it properly. Santa Lucia was always a pretty affluent town, but even then we had some effects from the depression, and there were strangers drifting up and down the coast, looking for work. Some of them were honest, but some were looking to loot and steal. It was unfortunate but true, and Richard didn't want to leave me unprotected." She took another gulp and carried on. "Anyway, I checked Patrick's room; he was sound asleep, so I knew it wasn't him. I went back to my bedroom and grabbed the gun. I saw in the dark a man rooting through the kitchen drawers and cupboards. He was grabbing food and the coin tin I had tucked away behind the flour canister. I asked him to stop, then yelled at him to leave, but he wouldn't. The next thing I knew, he dropped what he had in his hands and grabbed the butcher knife. He reached out and tore my nightgown with his other hand. I screamed again, but he wouldn't stop, so I fired. And I shot him. Right in that very room." She pointed to the kitchen.

Margot took a deep sigh, realizing she hadn't breathed through the whole story. "What happened after that?"

"Well, Patrick woke up crying from all the noise. I could tell that the man was obviously dead, it was awful." She sighed, looking out the picture window at the long sunset before continuing. "I was shaking, but I knew enough to set the gun down and run up to comfort my boy and keep him from coming downstairs. I told him it was just a bad dream and once I settled him back to sleep, I called one of my husband's friends, someone you don't know—he's older and long since gone. Anyway, he took care of it all. He called the police for me and kept it out of the papers."

Margot was amazed at what she was hearing. "What did the police do? Did you get charged?"

Marjorie shook her head. "There had been a series of break-ins, mischief, and some other rather nasty things in the area. The police were actually aware of this fellow and had pegged him for many of the crimes, but couldn't catch him. He wasn't from around here and all he did was terrorize and cause trouble for the community. Eventually, they agreed that what I did was in self-defense and not much more was spoken about it."

"Not even in the papers? The Weathers of that time didn't come after you?"

"They didn't know, or Richard's friend persuaded them to be quiet about it."

"What about the neighbors? No one heard the noise?"

"They did," Marjorie nodded. "And saw the police and the coroner. Richard's pal called a neighborhood meeting and when he told them the whole story, they were relieved it had never happened in their homes and that the drifter had been stopped in his tracks. Together, they concocted a story if any outsider asked, that it was the boiler blowing a gasket. That was what made the bang and the damage needed investigating. It gave a reason for me to call Richard's friend in the middle of the night and such goings on, and either other people believed it or chose to believe it. Back then, folks were so busy looking after their own and keeping their heads above water that they kept to themselves. It was explained all neat and tidy for them, and that made them happy. The less they had to worry about others, the more they could concern themselves with their own needs. Our closest friends felt it protected the neighborhood as well as Patrick and me. No one ever mentioned it again. It was a different time."

"Did Patrick ever figure it out? Did you tell Richard?"

"Patrick overheard the story about the boiler blowing at the age of eight, and he easily accepted it. I did tell Richard everything when he came back a few weeks later. It was too important to let it pass and he was my husband. I didn't keep things like that from him. He was grateful that his friend had come to help and nothing worse had happened."

"At least you weren't publicly exposed. People didn't point fingers at you, shielding their children from you, or have Nancy tell strangers about you," Margot said.

"No, but I did get grilled by the police force at first, and, let me tell you, the officer in charge at the time made me feel more like a criminal than the one I shot. They completely disregarded my fear for my own safety and Patrick's. Once I broke down in tears, they relented and believed my story. It was a short time, but I remember it well. I'll never forget it.

"I also have to live with what I've done. I took a life. Even though he came at me and meant me harm, he was still one of God's creatures, and it seemed to be a desperate one at that. There's not a day that goes by that I don't relive at least one moment of it—the glint in his eye, the knife in his hand, the bang of the gun." She gave an involuntary shiver.

"Now, Margot, I'm not telling you this because I think you killed Nathan, not at all. I know you're innocent in this, but what I'm saying to you is that all things shall pass. Things happen by choice or randomly, in a long spiral or a quick burst, but it's how you pick yourself up and carry on that lasts."

Marjorie walked over to her and rubbed her back. "It's going to be all right and you're not alone in having secrets. Give it time and your life will all fall back into place." She placed her hand under Margot's chin and gently tipped her face up to look straight into her eyes. "Trust me, I'm living proof." Marjorie's smile couldn't help but reassure Margot.

The sun had finished its day, leaving behind a glorious and radiant display. "It was certainly an awful thing that happened to you, Marjorie. I understand you had to do what you had to do. I don't think you honestly had any choice. At least you know what happened and why, even if you're the one who did it. I'm still wondering why Nathan was murdered."

Marjorie asked, "Could he have wanted money?"

"That's a distinct possibility; he could have thought I had a lot of it—which I don't, by the way. I used what I had setting up my home and Poppy Cove. Business is great, but I'm definitely of the working class, now." She smiled.

Marjorie reaffixed the bun at the back of her head and moved through ideas. "Irene saw him leaving Bud's back room with a couple of thugs. Could it be them?"

"It could be. He was roughed up before he was shot."

"But through the heart? According to everything I've read, those type of goons tend to aim for the head." Marjorie spoke authoritatively.

"Teresa? How attached was she to Nathan? Could she have been mad or jealous?"

"Sounds like Teresa's not that attached to anything or anyone for that long," Margot commented.

"True. No sign of Jeannette, though."

"No."

"Do we know if they knew each other?" More and more, it seemed to come back to the missing girl.

"No clue. Did you know that Irene found her rummaging through the front desk?"

"Hmm." Marjorie recalled something. "You know, last week, she started asking all kinds of questions about you."

Margot felt a chill. "Such as?"

"All sorts of things, including things I couldn't answer at the time. She asked about your designs, and where did you get your ideas, that sort of thing. Then she started asking about where you were from, how long you'd been in Santa Lucia, where did you go to school, even about your relationship with Tom. Eventually, I told her to pay more attention to her work and that what she was asking was none of her business. She never questioned me anymore after that."

"Okay, so if she wasn't involved with Nathan in some way, why would she ask such things?"

Marjorie shrugged. "It certainly seemed more than just making conversation. She didn't ask the same about Daphne, just of you. My guess? I think she was involved with Nathan, either for a while or just since they met at Mrs. Coleman's."

Margot felt even less at ease about Jeannette the more they talked. "She was from New York, wasn't she?"

Marjorie nodded. "Her references checked out when I telephoned her former employers and her skills are definitely there."

"Do you remember how long she said she'd been here in town?"

Marjorie squinted her eyes, thinking. "Not long, a few weeks. She left her last job just over a month ago."

"And Nathan hadn't been here that long," Margot stated. "Could he have been following her?"

"And did he drag the mob to both of them?"

"And she's hurt or lying dead somewhere?"

"Or does she have your gun and is just waiting for an opportunity to come after you?" Marjorie warned.

Margot shuddered. "Well, that's one thing about being watched by the police. After all, they are on the lookout for her and if she came near me, I'd hope they'd be able to step in in time."

"So is there anyone else who'd want him dead or may have had a grudge against him?"

Margot gave a cynical laugh. "Almost anyone he tried to seduce or swindle." It was apparent they had more questions than answers. Overcome with the day's events, Margot yawned and decided to go home, with no more of a solution, but far more understanding of herself and her friends in Santa Lucia than when the day had begun.

CHAPTER FOURTEEN

Friday morning came and Daphne had nervous expectations for her afternoon appointment with Adonis. She'd decided if he suggested it, she would definitely pose nude. *After all*, she reasoned, *he's an artiste—an appreciator of the human form and without a doubt would be professional about it, and do it in a tasteful manner.* She would not expect anything less. However, she was not going to tell anyone, no way. She didn't want to be talked out of it. It was daring and bold, and so unexpected from her. They'd all know when they saw the final work. She planned on purchasing the commission when it was done and give it to Daniel as a gift, and she'd do it in front of all their friends and family, maybe at his next birthday party or something. She'd think of the occasion later. Wouldn't they all be surprised?

She took extra care getting ready that morning, making sure her body was properly groomed and was happy to see she still had kept her trim, slight athletic form. She was also pleased that she didn't have any mysterious bruises or blemishes, so often caused by furniture and other objects leaping unexpectedly in her path. She wasn't exactly a klutz, but could have her less than ladylike moments.

Lizzie, her seventeen-year-old sister came bounding into her bedroom without knocking as usual. Daphne was able to wrap her pale yellow silk dressing gown around herself in just enough time. "What are you doing?" Lizzie asked with a note of disapproval, flopping on Daphne's bed.

"How many times have I asked you to knock?"

"I dunno." Lizzie wiped her nose, tilted her head and looked at her sister sideways. "What *were* you doing?"

"Nothing, just getting ready for work." Daphne made sure her robe was cinched shut. She wasn't sure what to wear for, well, disrobing later. If she wore something with quite a few buttons or fasteners, it would take her a while to get it off, which may annoy the artist. If she wore something with lots of seams, they may mark her flesh as would a girdle and most of her foundation garments. But if she didn't wear a girdle, then she would look sloppy. What was she to do?

"Taking you a long time to figure out what you're going to wear today," Lizzie observed. "Got something important happening?"

"No, nothing much," Daphne replied lightly. She could not imagine what her younger sister would make of what she was going to do. Or who she would tell. The last people she wanted to know about it were her parents, and that's exactly who Lizzie would blab to first. She'd jump at the chance.

"So," her sister lolled on her bed and slyly drawled out her word, then finished her sentence, matter of factly, "Your friend Margot's a murderer."

Daphne whipped around and faced her sister. "That's not true! Who told you that?"

"No one, but I keep up on things. I read the story in the paper and I keep my ear to the ground, you know?" Lizzie snapped her gum, doing her best to act wise. "She's like those dames in *Prime Crime Magazine*. They've got a past and will do anything to keep it quiet, you know the type." Lizzie was constantly reading dime store detective novels and salacious 'true crime' rags. Their mother always had a fit when she came across them, but Lizzie's fascination was not deterred.

"No, I don't and neither do you. Not that it's your business, but Margot is innocent of it all. If you don't believe me, ask James. His father's helping her in the case." James Worth, a long-time friend of Lizzie's, possibly boyfriend (who could tell with her these days—punching him in the arm one day, making cow eyes the next, all the while wearing lipstick) was Henry's youngest son.

Lizzie was skeptical, rolling her eyes, then brightening up with a new theory. "Policeman Tom did it! Oh, a crime of passion!"

"Lizzie, stop it. You know that's not true and I'd appreciate it if you'd keep your overactive imagination to yourself." Daphne looked at her bedside clock and was grateful it was 8:15. It gave her an excuse to rush her sister out the door. "Better hurry up. If you're late for school again, they're going to put it on your permanent record."

"Aw, really? I'm in my senior year. I'm already accepted into college; what are they going to do to me?"

Daphne glared at the girl in response.

Lizzie got off the bed. "Okay, okay, I get it." She looked at her sister, then herself in the dressing table mirror. She re-tucked the end of her blouse back into the waist of her circle skirt and tugged at her ponytail, which was straggling out of its elastic. She calmed down while she fixed her hair and continued talking in a more pleasant manner to her sister. "But what are you doing today?"

"Going to work, why do you ask?"

Lizzie shrugged. "You seemed kinda funny when I came in."

"I did?"

"Yep."

"No," Daphne demurred. "I just can't figure out what I want to wear, that's all."

Lizzie had finished with her hair and stood up. "Nah, I don't buy that." She gave a flip with her hand. "Later, gator. I gotta fly." Lizzie was gone with as much care and concern as she'd come in with.

In the end, Daphne figured wearing the proper foundation garments was far more important than Adonis seeing the seam impressions on her body. He could always not paint them, couldn't he? He was an artist, he was bound to be looking for overall form rather than anything else. She did, however, choose a wraparound dress in pale turquoise that had a sweeping circle skirt that would be easy to remove by untying the one big sash bow on the side. It had an overall print of abstract florals that she thought he'd find creatively interesting. Wouldn't he?

Daphne skipped out the door with just a quick good bye to Eleanor, the family maid, and her parents, rather than sitting down to breakfast or coffee with them. She didn't want to be put in a position where she might have to say more than she wanted to about her plans. She didn't think her mother would approve and, although she was a grown woman, Daphne was concerned that her father would put a stop to her decision. No, it was her choice and hers alone. It was time she did something risky, or at least risqué. She smiled at her own thoughts.

She got into her red Thunderbird convertible and immediately put down the top. It was another glorious day with the fog bank a ways off, past the Channel Islands. Their family home was a large estate and it was a pleasant drive down to the town center. As she cruised down Oceanview Drive, she tapped along with the new hit song by the Champs—*Tequila*—on KESL, the popular local radio station. The lively tune kept her spirits going. As she hummed along, it crossed her mind about how she could bring up the subject of both Adonis and Nathan being at Bud's Saturday night to Adonis. She thought casually about ways she could do it. She could hint that she sometimes went there herself, but Adonis would probably catch her in that one, or she could ask him if he knew of any good places to play cards, but that didn't seem natural to her either. Maybe she could just ask him what he liked to do on the weekends. *Yes,* she smiled to herself, *that would be casual, friendly, open, not specific. I could do that.*

Daphne greeted her coworkers and found out there were no new revelations in the case, giving an illusion of normalcy. Customers came and went, and the more they carried on with business as usual, the more it confirmed Margot's innocence. Hopefully, their patrons would agree.

Neither Margot nor Marjorie mentioned their conversation from the previous night. Margot was honored that Marjorie had taken her into her confidence and she wouldn't do anything to jeopardize that. She had a twinge of guilt keeping it from Daphne, especially after all she had told her and not wanting to keep secrets, but Marjorie's tale wasn't Margot's story to tell, and if Marjorie wanted Daphne to know, she could tell her herself. Besides, although Daphne was in a fine, if not giddy mood, she seemed to be somewhere else. She hadn't mentioned Daniel much in the past few days and Margot chalked it up to everything being in such turmoil. Maybe Daphne's appointment was a secret rendezvous with Daniel. *Well, good for them,* Margot thought.

Margot shared her plans with Marjorie for the Miss Santa Lucia court dresses, as she trusted her input. The experienced seamstress made some new suggestions that helped refine the ideas further. She would work out an estimate of how many yards they'd need by the beginning of next week. They also realized they were well on track with the inventory for the 'Making Waves' collection.

Excitement ensued when a new shipment of Swan Dive swimsuits, which had been Daphne's task to order, arrived and were equally as impressive as the first batch. The company was new to them, but the girls were impressed with their use of fabrics, that included cotton or nylon blended with Lastex that gave plenty of sturdiness and stretch and always snapped back into shape. There were some lovely, daring two piece numbers in white with an overall tropical print, and others with big, bold red or blue polka dots. Halter neck straps, with buttons for easy removal on the inside of the bust line for the elimination of tan lines gave flirty versatility as well. The roucheing on the sweetheart neckline style was darling, and the bottoms covered the most ample of backsides modestly. Some of the one-pieces had a flouncy peplum, while others a sporty boy short length. The colors were bold—tangerine, lime, scarlet, cerulean—and would certainly make a splash poolside or impress any boss when an executive brought his wife to a company summer barbeque.

Daphne tried on a new arrival—a one-piece with a halter neck, gathered sweetheart bust, low in the back with the modest straight cut boy short hem, in a pink grapefruit hue. It looked delightful. "Well, I'm good for a day at the beach now!" she laughed. "Say, this suit fits really well. I could hang ten in this." She crouched down and was pleased to feel that it didn't ride up or expose too much as she moved her arms.

Margot took a chiffon wrap skirt in a floral pattern that picked up the color and tied it around her friend's hips. "And you're good for cocktails now!"

She grabbed a suit herself to try—a strapless one-piece, with full roucheing along the sides, and a neat little fold along the top, in a royal blue with white piping along the top and a straight modesty skirt hem. It looked equally as fetching and she hoped that once everything was settled, she'd be able to feel comfortable going out in it anywhere and doing anything, once the gossipy snipes had moved on.

Business went briskly with the day so sunny and warm, and outside news at bay. The swimsuits and caps sold well, as well as the playsuits and newly-created sundresses. Daphne could hardly believe it was 3:45—

time for her private adventure to begin. She went upstairs, gave herself a quick modesty check and was pleased she was still as fresh as a daisy. She hurriedly flew down the stairs in such an excited manner that she almost forgot to say goodbye.

"Now that's got to be one hot date," Irene remarked.

"I think you might be right," Margot agreed.

Adonis' studio was up in the hills on the opposite side of town. The landscape was wild, dry and scrubby, not like the well-manicured and watered lusher side of town. Daphne followed the directions he'd given her on the telephone, looking for the hand hewn markers along the dirt road. After a few dusty turns, she came upon his place. It had a sign that was a chunk of driftwood with the familiar, "Adonis—Artiste" carved out and painted in white letters. There were a couple of cars parked on a flat area. One was a rather derelict Packard, at least fifteen years old. The other was a newer model, a nifty little two-seater that Daphne didn't recognize. She removed her sunglasses and looked further around at the property which had a few different buildings. One of them appeared to be a vacant horse stable and there was what looked like an old prospector's shack with a rather sorry porch, surrounded by sage and scrub brush. The third building looked like a small shed, but it had a paned window with homey printed curtains drawn back and an open door. Beside it was another handmade sign— "Studio."

Well, I'm in the right place, she thought to herself. *Daphne, it's now or never.* She got out of her car. She boldly walked to the door and heard some kind of squawky, avant-garde jazz she didn't recognize. It was way out and a little disturbing. She also smelt a kind of funny sweet smoke, which had an almost skunky scent to it. She could hear the trill of a female laugh come from the studio. She was a little surprised and disappointed that someone else was there.

She nervously knocked on the open door, which was followed by louder male laughter. Daphne walked through the doorframe. "Hello?" she timidly asked.

Adonis turned around and greeted her with a big smile. "Daphne, you're here. Welcome, welcome! Can I get you a drink, or something…" He pinched his thumb and forefinger together and brought it to his lips with a wink.

She was shocked when she realized what that smell was and what he was implicating. "No, it's fine. Just water, thanks." Her heart was beating loudly in her chest and her mouth felt sticky and dry.

"Ooh, let 'er be! Do not tease zee girl, Donny. You know she would not do zat," the laughing woman spoke.

Daphne looked behind the artist's shoulder and saw who was speaking. Sophie, the art teacher and flirt who had clamped onto Daniel at the art show. *Hmmh,* she thought before replying. As Adonis moved over to fill her request, she had a better look at Sophie. She was reclining on a chaise lounge that was draped with a variety of colorful cloths. The young woman lay there calmly, without a stitch of clothing on, as naked as the day she was born. Daphne couldn't help but notice how voluptuous the woman was. Daphne's face turned red, but she did not want either Adonis or Sophie to know she was embarrassed. *Play it cool, Daphne.* She didn't know where to look, but thankfully Adonis reappeared at her side with a tall, cool glass of water. She took a sip and it gave her a chance to compose herself.

"Um, sorry if I've interrupted your, uh, date, but I thought we had an appointment," she managed to say to Adonis, keeping her eyes on him.

"Oh, it is just me, I just came by to see mon ami! I am so sorry if I am in zee way." Sophie laughed again, draping one of the shawls around her body, almost covering some of herself. "I will go." She got off the lounge and walked over to an end table where she had draped her clothes. She unceremoniously dropped the shawl and began to dress. "Do not worry, Daphne. You are in good 'ands." She laughed again.

Daphne sat and glanced around the small room while she waited. It was basically a one-room wooden shack, with non-insulated siding weathered to the point that the wood was a silvery brown, with a couple of paned windows. There was a small kitchenette. It was more of a wet bar with a counter, a bank of cupboards and a sink, but no appliances to speak of. There was a bare light bulb in the ceiling, and the chaise lounge, of course, and a couple of tables at either end. In one corner was an old dressing screen, with more of the shawls or cloths draped over the top. In another corner by the sink was a taller table, about waist height with a chiseled piece of stone, in a rather nondescript state, making it rather hard to tell what it might actually turn out to be. All along the walls against the floor, were paintings, mainly abstracts but some of people, in various stages of completion—some finished and some still in rough sketch form. In the center of the room was Adonis' easel, directly in front of the chaise. On it was a stretched canvas and a penciled in female form that Daphne imagined was the glorious Sophie.

Adonis caught her staring at the canvas and removed it, stacking it on the floor behind other works. He took Daphne by the hand and sat her down on the lounge. "Now sit, relax. I will see Miss Sophie to her car. I'll be right back and we'll get started." He patted her knees and stared into her eyes. "You're a vision, darling. It will be my pleasure to capture you!"

Sophie finished primping her hair and applying a new coat of lipstick. "I really must come see your leetle shop. People say it is charmant, no? I will come to your Poppy Cove." She swayed and trilled out the door, dressed now in a simple cotton lawn popover dress that she was able to make look sophisticated and alluring. She was still barefoot, with her sandals slung over her shoulder, holding onto their straps by just a finger. Adonis trailed behind, carrying her purse.

Daphne was relieved when she heard Sophie's car squeal and peal out of the yard. *Leetle shop, charmant, ugh. If I didn't know better, I'd say she's a big fake from Pittsburgh, or somewhere like that.* Adonis came back in shortly, shutting the door behind him, then facing her and rubbing his hands together. "Let's get started." He took a close, critical look at her, then stepped back, turning his head to one side, then the other, squinting and winking, critically giving her the artistic once over. He motioned with his hands to have her stand up, which she did. He walked closer to her then reached out to feel her body. She jumped back, to which he soothed, "Purely for artistic reasons, do not be alarmed, Daphne." All the while, he had been making *hmms* and *aahs*, to which she was gradually getting accustomed.

The record reached the end and out of the corner of her eye, she caught the movement of the playing arm lifting up, sliding back and setting down again, replaying the odd tunes. "Okay," he finally said. "Now you do understand that when I asked you to pose for me, it would be *au naturale*, right?" He lit another skinny, smelly cigarette, offering a puff to her, which she refused and he shrugged off while he waited for her answer.

"Y-yes, and I'm ready!" she blurted out quickly before she could change her mind.

Adonis smiled. "Yes, I believe you are." He ran his hand over his balding pate and redid his straggly pony tail at the back of his head. With a jerk of his shoulder, he indicated the screen. "You can take off your clothes over there. There should be a robe or something you can use if you wish."

She nodded silently and went behind the screen. She carefully removed and draped her dress, full slip, brassiere, girdle and garter, and stockings. She noticed that her skin did not seem too lined or marked, so that was good. There were a couple of robes stacked in a pile and she chose to put on one that appeared to her to be clean and fresh. It was a red chinois kimono which she draped around herself, holding it tightly closed.

Adonis' eyebrows went up in approval when he saw her. "Yes, you are magnificent!" he exclaimed.

"Where do you want me?" Daphne asked.

The man paused for a moment then shook his head and came closer. He took her by the shoulders and gently sat her back down on the lounge. "Now then, just lie back and make yourself comfortable, as if you were just relaxing at home, as if there is no one seeing you."

The room was stuffy with the door closed, but at least it was warm. She thought about what he said as she tried to loosen up, but she couldn't remember if she ever had reclined naked, even in the privacy of in her own home. Then she imagined Lizzie walking in on her and subconsciously pulled her robe even tighter.

Adonis sighed. "Are you sure you want to do this? We don't have to."

Daphne firmly shook her head and loosened her grip on the robe.

"Why don't we do this?" Adonis walked over, gently pulling the kimono off her shoulders, settling her down in a more reclined pose, while guiding her to cross her legs. He loosened her robe so that the fall showed her top thigh exposed but all her private regions were covered. "This, I think would be enough for you," he said kindly.

Although she was relieved at his suggestion of modesty, she decided that wasn't daring enough for the new, bold, and adventurous Daphne. She untied the sash, pulled her top shoulder out of the sleeve and let the robe fall as it may.

Adonis glared at her for a moment more, made a few suggestions on how she should lie, physically moved her arms and legs to get them just so. He stepped back with one last satisfied nod. "Yes, that is it. Hold that pose."

She held her head at the tilt he'd placed it in, but glanced down at her body. *Well, that's not too bad,* she realized. *Some might say even tasteful. Except for maybe my parents. But I'll bet Dan will love it, at least I hope so.* One of her arms was draped across the majority of her breasts, while her legs were crossed, covering everything she wouldn't want anyone else to see. Her rump was a little more prominent than she desired, and hoped he wouldn't paint her to look too bottom heavy, but there at least there was nothing rude showing.

He got to work, drawing her outline, quickly with his pencil. He was working quietly, concentrating. He would stop, scrutinize her, then focus back to the canvas and draw some more.

Daphne started to drift off into nothingness, thinking that it wasn't too bad, although it didn't take long for her to feel stiff and shaky from staying in one position for too long. Just as she thought she was going to lose her pose and fall asleep, there was a brisk knock at the door.

"Adonis, we know you're in there. Open up." The gruff male voice startled Daphne. She jumped, immediately, grabbed the kimono and tied it tightly around her while she sat straight up. She could see through the gauzy floral curtain on the door window that there were two rather large men in hats standing outside.

Adonis exhaled, slumped his shoulders and set down his charcoal pencil. He did, however, appear to take the intrusion in his stride. "Please excuse me; I'll be right back." He got up and went outside, shutting the door and leading the men away from the shack.

She frowned as she listened, then her face brightened. In all the excitement regarding the pose, she'd forgotten to ask Adonis about Bud's back room! She wondered if that's what the two men were there for. Irene had said something about a couple of mob heavies talking to

Nathan that night. From the lounge, she could hear that they were talking, but couldn't make anything out. She got up and crouched under the window frame of the door, where she could hear better what they were saying.

"Look, I know, but I'll have the money for you by Saturday, no later," Adonis desperately pleaded.

"Huh, you said that last Saturday. Now you owe us double," grunted one of the strangers.

"I know, I know. Look, I've been working. I've got another show on the weekend. I'll have it for you by Sunday; all right?"

"Sunday? You just said Saturday," growled the other thug. "Which is it?"

"Sunday, definitely then. I'll sell a couple of paintings and get cash. I've got a show down in Malibu. They always buy my stuff there," Adonis replied.

Daphne tried to see through the slim crack but saw nothing. She pressed her ear firmer to the opening. "You'd better have it and don't even thinking about asking us for any more. You're cut off until you've paid up with interest, got it?"

There was silence, and Daphne imagined that Adonis must have nodded. "Good. If you don't, just remember what happened to your friend from Bud's. We don't want to have to do that to you, do we?" Daphne couldn't tell which thug that was, but it didn't matter; they were both bad news. In her mind, she was putting the pieces together, thinking they must have been talking about Nathan. Were they the ones who killed him?

Daphne's foot cramped while she was crouched down, making her lose her balance. She toppled, knocking over the easel.

"What was that?" said a thug.

"Er nothing, I have a cat. It crawls around the studio and knocks things over. It's a nuisance, but..." Adonis covered quickly. Daphne sat still, flat on her butt.

"Yeah? Well, don't let kitty keep you from getting your work done. Sunday, or we'll do more than this."

Daphne heard a sick thud and an "ugh" from Adonis. Then the sound of heavy doors slamming, an engine revving and the car driving away. Adonis came back in, holding his eye. She rushed over to him. "Let me have a look at that."

He moved his hand away. It was swelling, but not looking too bad. She found a clean towel by the sink, rinsed it with cold water and patted around his eye. After it was clear the punch wasn't too serious, she flat out asked him, "Adonis, were you in the back of Bud's, gambling on Saturday night?"

He nodded.

"And did you see a man named Nathan there?"

Adonis shrugged. "There was this new guy, just came into town. Maybe."

Daphne described him and what Irene had said.

"Yes, I think so. They left with him."

"They did more than that, I think," Daphne remarked. "Don't you know he ended up dead that night?"

Adonis was genuinely shocked. "What?"

"Don't you read the papers?"

"No, they're too depressing. I'm too busy for all that news."

Daphne filled him in on what they knew about Nathan being murdered, including the information that he was with the police chief's daughter, but leaving out Margot's past and present involvement. She didn't think he needed to know that, especially if it was a mob hit.

He gave a low whistle. "Man, they are serious."

Daphne agreed. "You have to tell someone that you were there and what you know about those guys. They may be Nathan's killers."

"Oh, no, I can't do that. They'll come after me," Adonis cowered.

Daphne gave an exasperated sigh. "Yes, you have to. If you don't, I will. Look, if you don't want to call the police, call this man." She found a scrap of paper and took a charcoal pencil that was lying on the floor. She wrote down Henry's name. "He's a lawyer involved with Nathan's murder. Someone needs to know about this. His office number's in the telephone directory."

Adonis looked at the paper. "All right, for you, I will. But you have to promise me something."

"What's that?"

"That you'll come back so I can finish my masterpiece of you!" He grinned.

She crinkled up her nose, thought about it, then replied, "Okay, but next time could you play more pleasant music and not smoke those funny cigarettes?"

He laughed. "It's a deal! See you next week same time, same place, Daphne." He took her hand and kissed it. She was only slightly repelled, as she realized that by coming to his place, she'd found out a key to solving the murder and proving Margot's innocence.

CHAPTER FIFTEEN

Poppy Cove had quieted down after Daphne had left, and Margot felt the back room was well prepared for the next work week. Stock production was in operation Monday through Friday, as were the custom appointments—unless a patron had a special request. Margot briefly discussed with Marjorie about the second cutter position and they decided that they'd give the situation until over the weekend to see if there was any news about or from Jeannette and consider advertising it as a vacant position next week, if necessary.

Margot stayed a bit longer at the store, just tidying up and putzing around after hours. She felt at home in the shop. Touching the fabrics, feeling the textures and seeing the colors often made her feel at ease. The shop front door handle rattled and Margot looked at it automatically, ready to mouth, "We're closed," but she couldn't believe who she saw. Standing on the other side of the glass were two faces she hadn't seen in years, but would recognize anywhere. Dorothy and George Willmington had come to see their daughter Margaret.

Margot panicked. She froze, unsure of what to do. They'd seen her, so she couldn't hide. She also hadn't changed that much, and from her mother's expression— one of familiarity, but not of overwhelming warmth—she knew that she'd recognized her. Margot decided it was best to face the music.

Her mother had her hand firmly on the door knob, still rattling and trying to turn it. Margot's hand trembled as she unlocked the deadbolt and let them in. The three of them stood in silence, no one knowing what to say to each other.

"Margaret," her father George stated, jaw tight. He took off his Homberg and held it in his hands, unsure of what to do.

"Actually, it's Margot now, Margot Williams," she said automatically, not meaning to be disrespectful, but truthful to who she was now. She started thinking of all the things she could say, but didn't know the right words. Small talk was never something they'd ever indulged in––neither were displays of affection––so it didn't feel right to reach out and embrace. Directness was her best approach. "I'm sure I know why you're here."

"Yes, we're here to take care of the situation," Dorothy Willmington commanded. "Do you have a lawyer? We'll get you a good one. We'll fly one of our friends out if we have to."

"That's not necessary, mother. I have the best local attorney taking the case. Henry Worth. He has an outstanding reputation and the experience in the community to see me through, thank you," Margot answered firmly, but politely.

"Never heard of him," George remarked.

"Well, no, father. Why would you? He's practiced law in Santa Lucia all of his life. He's also a family friend of my business partner's." She stood her ground, knowing it was the only way for her to get through to him.

Her parents glanced around the shop, picking up a trinket or two, and touching a sleeve or a hem. "And what of this partner? It's a woman, from what I understand. Young and not very experienced in business," he commented.

"Not so young. She's my age, with a college education and she grew up in a family with a good head for business. The Huntington-Smythes. They're well known in town, and very successful. I believe they're listed in the *Who's Who* as well," Margot replied.

"Daphne's hard-working, honest and well connected in the community. Her social standing brought us a solid and preferred clientele right from the start of Poppy Cove."

Margot watched as her mother walked around the shop. She saw herself in twenty-five years, not emotionally, but physically. They shared the same build and auburn hair, except her mother's face was more lined and—if one looked closely at her roots, could see the color was no longer natural. She wore a tasteful grey suit in worsted tropical wool, the jacket nipped in at the waist with narrow lapels and a tailored white blouse underneath, and a wide skirt. Her pill box hat had a small netted veil that she had pinned back. She had left her white gloves on while she perused the racks. "These are yours?" Dorothy asked.

"Yes."

"Haven't seen any orders for your supplies to Willmington Textiles," her father commented.

"No," Margot agreed. "I've mainly been dealing with west coast producers. Lower delivery rates." It wasn't necessarily true, but it gave her an excuse her father might believe.

"Prudent," he seemed to approve. "But in the future, I'm sure we could work something out."

Margot said nothing, leaving them to complete their once over. When they were finished, they stood in front of her. "Listen," she said, "I was just about to lock up. I'm sure we need to talk." As much as she didn't want to and had no idea how it would go, she knew they'd come a long way and that had to count for something. "Did you just arrive? How did you get here? Do you have a place to stay?" All kinds of questions were coming to mind, but she stuck to the basics, getting through the time, step by step.

Her parents informed her that they'd flown into Los Angeles earlier that afternoon and had rented a car from the airport. They were staying at one of the private beachfront hotels—the Royal Surf Club—which was the most luxurious small resort in town. "Margaret," her father started sternly, then corrected himself when he read her expression, "Margot, we do need to talk."

She agreed. It was time to put the past to rest in every way. "Let's meet at my house. I'm sure none of us wants to go over things in public. It's a small town and news gets shared around quickly. I'm sure that I can figure out something for dinner."

Dorothy, who never bothered to boil her own water for tea, raised an eyebrow at the idea of her daughter being able to put together a meal fit for their consumption. She was, however, in the same mind that they should conduct their family matters without watchful eyes. Margot got her pocketbook, sweater and gloves together, checked all the lights and left with them, giving her father driving directions to her street. Sitting in the backseat, Margot had the sinking feeling of being back in her childhood all over again.

Once they pulled up outside her little cottage, her mother sniffed, "Is this it?"

"Yes," Margot answered brightly, more chipper than she felt. No, it wasn't a big house, like the one she grew up in, nor the one the Reeds had purchased for her and Nathan, but it was neat and tidy and all hers. Dorothy pursed her lips, not remarking further.

As they got out of the car, they heard, "Oh, you hoo! Margot!" Mrs. O'Leary said as she flagged them down.

As much as Margot was not pleased by the surprise visit of her parents, she did not think they deserved a dose of her nosy neighbor, but she couldn't avoid her now. "Hello, Sharon. We're just heading in for dinner, so if you don't mind…"

"Of course, dear." She stopped right at the house's front walkway. Sparky yapped and walked over to the car, marking his territory on the tires by the curb. Mrs.

O'Leary looked at Margot's parents expectantly. When Margot didn't say anything, she took the liberty of introducing herself, but still did not get out of the way.

"Is there something you need, Mrs. O'Leary?"

"No, not much. Just that—well—we should all feel so much safer now, with the police always coming by. Seems to be a regular occurrence these days, and I don't just mean your Tom making routine visits." Sharon O'Leary laughed heartily, elbowing Margot in the ribs. "Well, I guess I better be going."

Dorothy glared at the woman, disapproving of what she'd said. She switched her gaze to her daughter, giving her a quizzical look. Margot knew there was so much she was going to have to explain. "Let's just go inside, shall we?"

Margot was glad that she'd taken the time the other day to straighten up what the police had rifled through. Her mother would have had a fit if she'd seen the state her house had been left in. Still the same, her mother ran her gloved finger over the top of the living room door frame, unhappily seeing dust. "Don't you have a maid, dear?"

Margot's back was to her mother. She gave a shudder and composed herself before answering. "No, I look after my own place." Margot never saw the need for a maid in her own home. It was easy for her to keep it neat and tidy. So what if she missed the occasional molding or edge? She probably could afford a housekeeper to do a good clean once a week, but it was an unnecessary expense as far as she was concerned.

She walked them through to the kitchen in the back. Being that the house was small, it didn't have a formal dining room. She had her chrome and Formica kitchen table, with a grey top and the chairs in padded turquoise leather. She gestured for her father to sit down and he did, at the head of the table. Her mother sat down opposite him, which put Margot in the middle, as she always had been before, when she sat down. She made a pitcher of martinis, knowing that it was their pre-dinner beverage of choice. No one said a word as she puttered around the kitchen. Margot put down a bowl of salted peanuts in the middle of the table and took her chair.

She took a sip of her drink and started the conversation. "So, how exactly did you find out about Nathan's death?"

George harrumphed, while Dorothy replied, "The local police department, dear. And what a way for us to find out." She crossed her arms on her chest, obviously displeased. "A patrol car, of all things, drove up and parked outside of our house. All the neighbors saw and, of course, had questions."

"It's been very awkward for your mother, very awkward, indeed," George blustered. "I don't mind telling you that we weren't able to show our faces at the club. We don't know if we will ever be, quite frankly."

Margot was not surprised by their reactions. This was pretty much what she expected from them. "Do you even care how I've been over the past years? What's happened to me?"

Dorothy sniffled. "You? Did you give us a second thought? Having a divorced daughter was scandal enough, but for you to turn your back on your family and social stature caused our family further disgrace."

Margot reached out to touch her mother's hand, but she recoiled as Margot came near it.

Dorothy was not finished yet. "And what about us? Did you care about how we felt when you ran away? For you to leave us behind without so much as a letter or phone call—well, that was just cruel."

Margot looked at her mother's face and saw her lips tremble. In all of her own need for escape, she'd never realized that her parents would have been emotionally upset by her leaving. She'd thought about them when she'd left and, over the years, had imagined them mad, but certainly not missing her. In her own mind, there were times when she'd thought they'd have been secretly relieved that they would not have to deal with her and her moods and desires to be creative and independent.

She took a good look at both of her parents, and saw how tired and old they suddenly looked. It was possibly the first time that she'd seen her parents as truly caring about her, that her departure had left an emotional void in their lives. "I'm sorry," Margot murmured. "I didn't think that it would hurt you."

Dorothy began crying in earnest, which Margot had never seen her do before. George got up out of his seat and stood behind his wife, soothing her back. "Give us a moment, would you?" he asked his daughter softly.

Margot started to feel tears well up. "Take all the time you both need, but I'm not going anywhere."

It wasn't a perfect reunion, by any stretch of the imagination, but in the Willmingtons' own way, the three of them had found new ground. The situation was still tense and reserved, but there was an understanding that love and care was now part of their relationship.

As emotions eased, Margot got up and rummaged around in her refrigerator and cupboards, looking for an easy dinner. She ended up making a tossed green salad and western omelettes, not the usual dining fare for her parents, she well knew, but it would suffice, given the circumstances. They continued on with fresh martinis.

"Mmm," Dorothy uttered as she ate her meal with gusto. "This is delicious. Who taught you how to do this?"

Margot was taken aback, not used to hearing praise from her mother, especially when it came to domestic matters. "I did. I had to when I left, to be honest. I also have to confess that I took Bessie's *Fannie Farmer* cookbook when I left." Bessie had been the family cook and kitchen help for many years, before and after Margot had grown up. The cookbook had a special place in her heart, as she remembered sitting at a kitchen stool, watching Bessie cook and helping her when her mother wasn't looking.

"That's where it went to," Dorothy remarked. "That woman turned the house upside down looking for that book. I'll tell her you have it."

"You will? Is Bessie still working for you?" Margot always remembered her as old, even when she was a child. She couldn't imagine what the cook was like now.

Her mother nodded. "Of course, she won't reveal her age to us. Who knows how old she is? She's a little slower, but still can put together a dinner party like no one else."

Margot went out on a limb. "Could you tell her I asked about her? Could you please let her know I'm all right?"

Her father agreed and made eye contact with his wife across the table. "Margar—er, Margot," he said, making an effort to break old habits, "We think you should know, we didn't completely lose track of you."

"Oh? What do you mean?" she questioned.

"After you left, we hired a private investigator. We asked him to find you and let us know if you were all right. We didn't want him to contact you or interfere, but believe it or not, we cared about what happened to you."

Margot gulped guiltily. She had no idea that she'd been followed or found out. She was, in an odd way, comforted to know that they wanted to keep an eye on her. "What did he tell you?"

"Well, he tracked your journey to the west and when it looked like you were permanently staying, he would come by once in a while. He informed us of your business, address, name change, some of your friends, including the police officer who you are currently seeing."

"We'll discuss him further, Margot," Dorothy interrupted.

George concluded, "Once you seemed settled, he stopped coming out, and watched the news wires in case anything ever surfaced that we should know about. We hadn't heard from him in a few months, but he did contact us a day after the police did."

Dorothy added, "We knew we had to come out. Regardless of how it looked, we had to step in. After all, we did bring you into this world and it doesn't matter how grown up you think you are, we'll be responsible for what we brought into this world."

Margot wasn't sure how to take the remark, but let it go. There was only so much nurturing that she could expect from them and now was not the time to flare up or wish for more. She suggested that her parents retire into the living room while she took care of the dishes. They did so, without one offer of helping her. Cleaning up was not their domain.

When Margot was finished, she joined her parents. They sat in the small living room, on opposite ends of the sofa under the picture window, while she sat down in her easy chair. George cleared his throat and announced, "Now, Margot, you need to be honest with us. We're all adults in this room, but we need to know the truth. Did you kill Nathan Reed?"

She understood he had to ask, so she had to answer it yet again. "No. And I hadn't seen him since I left Westport." She told her parents everything she knew about the situation, including information regarding the missing Jeannette. They listened intently, letting her tell the whole story before speaking.

Margot waited while her parents absorbed all that she told them. Her mother spoke first, "Well, I don't like that you had a gun."

Margot didn't know how to reply to her remark and appealed to her father, "Do you know anything about Nathan during the last couple of years? Is there anything that could shed some light on his murder? Even something small might be a clue, it might make a difference and solve the case."

George thought before he responded, but to no avail. "After his father took his retirement package, we haven't seen hide nor hair of Edward and Lucille Reed. A few years ago, someone at the club heard they'd moved to Florida—the Keys, perhaps. As for Nathan, we never saw him around anywhere we've been. Idle talk had placed him in New York City and not doing that well. Certainly not moving in our circles."

"And Jeannette's from New York," Margot stated. "But I really didn't think she was his type, but I guess she could be. She seemed too ambitious and focused to be involved with someone so disinterested in doing an honest day's work."

"Well, you were," her mother said, slyly. "You married him."

Margot's hackles went up. "Now that's not fair. I was never attracted to Nate, especially his lack of ambition. If you remember correctly, you and his parents were the ones who set the whole event up. I only went along with it because I didn't know any better. I certainly know better now!"

George put his hands out, refereeing what could quickly escalate away from the current civility. "We're not here to accuse you of anything, just honestly to help and clear up the situation." He looked at his wife before continuing, "Your mother and I now know that having you marry Reed wasn't a good decision. Edward was convinced his son deserved the best, and as far as we all were concerned, that included you and the business, too. His parents thought that with the right woman and right work examples he would embrace his life successfully. Now we all know that wasn't going to happen." He scratched his scalp and sighed. "For that, we too are sorry, as much as you are for not keeping us in your life."

Margot let the words sink in, then replied in a small voice, "Thank you."

George summarized the situation. "You've got a lawyer you trust, the police are supervising if this Jeannette does show up, and the other leads are being followed. Is there anything more that you need handled? Is there anything we can do?"

Margot was touched by the offer and wondered how she could take them up on it. "There's not much you can do, but I would appreciate you staying in town and seeing me through this."

Her mother reached across the small room and took Margot's hands. "We'd like that very much."

The gesture said it all. Every member of the small family had their hearts in the right place and somehow they all knew it would eventually be okay.

Dorothy pulled back her hands gently, sat up on the sofa again, tugged on her lapel, and crossed her ankles. "Just one more thing."

Margot waited for her request.

"Out of all the society you are associating with now in Santa Lucia, why on earth are you dating a police man?"

Evolution could only move so far, so fast. "Tom Malone is a good man. He's worked his way up through the force and he truly cares for me."

"But a cop, dear?" Dorothy's distain was in full force.

"He's more than that and even if he wasn't, he's a far better man than Nathan ever was. I don't mean to speak ill of the dead, but it's the truth."

"And if he's such an upstanding character, why isn't he pulling strings to make sure your name is clear?" George demanded.

Margot explained what had happened with the police involvement, including Teresa. "Tom couldn't. The Santa Lucia Police Department is very much by the book. They don't work on favors. It's one of the best things about this community. People aren't bought and sold quite as easily as they are in other places." She realized it may have sounded like a dig, but maybe her father needed to hear that. He didn't visibly show a reaction.

"But he's not exactly on the social register, is he?" Dorothy continued.

"I'm really not either in Santa Lucia. Look, when I came here, no one knew me, or my social status. They accepted me just for me, not the family I came from, or which clubs I belonged to."

"But don't you see? You're right back there now. I know all about your fashion shows and charity balls, your Hollywood stars," her mother replied with a know-it-all sneer.

Margot frowned and considered her remarks. In a way, her mother was right. She was involved with the 'in crowd' of the town. The society mavens adored her, but it was still different. Even the top drawer social set in the laid back and generally bucolic town was more accepting and relaxed, not nearly so formal. She couldn't explain what she meant in a way that her mother would understand. The ladies came to her shop and let her know their most intimate secrets as they stood getting measured in their girdles and slips, both by talking and by letting her see them unadorned. Or at least, they had so far. Time will tell how the Poppy Cove customers would react to her current reputation. She didn't want to talk about that aspect with her parents, so she didn't.

It was getting late and they were heading into another possibly volatile conversation. Margot commented, "The two of you should head over to your hotel and get a good night's rest. I'm in the shop tomorrow, but it's Saturday and all around the square outside the store there's an open air market. You could come and browse around. There's a nice tearoom across the way. We can have lunch." Her parents agreed with the plan and left for the night.

CHAPTER SIXTEEN

"Your what?" Daphne almost choked on her muffin. As usual, Lana from the tearoom had brought them over with coffee for Saturday breakfast. Today's were apricot coconut. Lana hadn't stayed, as the weekly farmers' market made the cafe busy.

"That's right. George and Dorothy Willmington have arrived to give their daughter support," Margot stated.

"Unbelievable." Daphne chewed. "You know, I don't think you've ever mentioned their names."

"Probably not."

"How was it?"

"Actually, better than expected. Do you know they've had a private eye keeping tabs on me? They honestly wanted to know I was okay, and didn't try to drag me back home. I had no idea."

"See?" Daphne gave her friend an affectionate squeeze on the shoulders. "They cared and loved you far more than you thought. How wonderful! So, it was nice to see them?"

"Well, I didn't exactly grow up in *Ozzie and Harriet's* household, so it was a little tense, but yeah, it was okay."

"How long are they staying? Can I meet them? Have they met Tom? No, wait, I guess they haven't met him, have they?" Daphne blathered on excitedly. "Have you told them you're going to marry him? Oh, probably not, you haven't told him yet, and you're not that close to your mother, right? Or are you now? I'm so glad they're here!"

Margot looked at her, trying her best to recall all of the questions. "They're staying until the case is solved.

Yes, I'm having lunch with them across the way and I'll bring them by to introduce you. No, they haven't met Tom, but my mother certainly has an opinion about me being involved with a 'lowly policeman,'—her term, not mine—so no, I have not told them I'd like to marry him, and no, we really aren't that much closer. It was fine, but I don't think the reserve will ever be removed. It's just how they are. I do, however, see that they do have some affection and care for me and that's an improvement."

The girls had been standing at the sales desk having their breakfast as they usually did on Saturdays before starting the day. Irene showed up right at nine and the girls tidied up their plates while Irene propped open the door and changed the sign from 'Closed' to 'Open.' Daphne was tending to the bouquets of flowers she'd picked up from one of the vendor's stalls outside to decorate the shop, as they did every Saturday. This time she'd chosen daisies in white, yellow and pink, looking cheery and fresh. Margot brought out the last of the garments that had been pressed and ready for the sales floor last night.

The market out in the square always brought in plenty of customers for the store, both residents and day trippers to the town, even more now that Hollywood had paid attention to their designs. They always had a few movie stars visit—both up and coming and fading—but since the most recent article, the one that unfortunately attracted Nate, more came by. They were a funny lot— some came in dark glasses with scarves on their heads, slinking around in such a way that one couldn't help but notice them, possibly for thinking they were shoplifters. Others came in the store in as much makeup as they wore when filming, demanding all the attention and wreaking havoc, while trying everything on. Then there were the ones like Joyce Jones, pleasant and pretty, both physically and in attitude.

186 *A Nate to Remember*

The morning passed quickly. Margot's lunch with her parents at the tearoom was pleasantly unremarkable. She had made a point of dressing carefully to greet them, wanting to look her best, right down to her undergarments, as just the right support could make an outfit. She must have debated between half and full slip, girdle in extra strength or light support, finally opting for the most control and coverage. She wore a new dress and coat ensemble in a conservative navy crepe that was well tailored but not too revealing. Although her mother had not said anything, Margot was pretty sure she saw the look of approval regarding the jewel neckline and the full long, swing of the coat. Her parents were cordial when she brought them back to meet Daphne, Irene and the rest of their Saturday staff which included Betty and Abigail Browning, who was Margot's doctor's daughter and a good helper. They didn't stay long and were pleased when Margot asked if they'd like to have dinner in one of her favorite restaurants, Antonio's, just down the street. She was hoping they'd find it acceptable. It wasn't fancy, but charming and somewhere she felt at home. It was turning out to be an agreeable day, with little or no mention of Nathan Reed.

There was a mid-afternoon lull after the Avila Square market closed up. Daphne and Margot took the opportunity to sit out by the now vacant fountain in the middle of the square. The April sun was warm and soft, not too strong with just a few clouds to add a pleasant amount of shade.

With all that had gone on for Margot last night, she finally remembered that Daphne had left early yesterday. "Say, where did you go yesterday? Did you have a hot date with Daniel?" she ribbed her friend.

"No." Daphne blushed and did not elaborate at first. "I think I might have found something else out about Nate's murder, though."

"Really? What did you find out?"

"That Adonis had definitely seen Nate leave with those thugs from Bud's last Saturday, and they meant business."

"Wow! Did you tell the police or Henry?"

"No, but I think they found out about it."

"How do you know?"

"I just do."

Margot thought for a moment and looked at her friend and asked her again about yesterday. "Daphne, where exactly did you go?"

"Oh, I just had an appointment," she smoothed an eyebrow, trying to sound casual.

"Where?"

"Um, just somewhere. You don't know where."

Margot sat straighter and registered a look of curiosity. "Daphne Huntington-Smythe, what have you been up to? Have you been investigating on your own? You'd better be careful. If Nate's murder is mob-related, they're serious."

"Oh, I know. Don't worry; I won't do anything dumb—well—not really stupid." She colored. "The less you know about it the better."

The comment didn't make Margot feel any better, but Daphne was not opening up any further and they noticed that the store was getting busy again. They went back to work.

"Excuse moi; I want to try zis on. Someone must 'elp me."

Daphne turned around from assisting Mrs. Falconer with a new cream brocade cocktail dress to see Sophie, live and in the flesh in Poppy Cove. She was tottering on the highest red heels that Daphne had ever seen. They made her ample bottom stick out at a pronounced angle, which tilted her bosom out even further forward than seemed possible. She was clad in a tight, black jersey knit dress that kept slipping off her shoulders, with a big wide red belt, cinching and directing assets both north and south on her frame. Her eyes were lined carefully and fully in black, and her lips were redder than a cherry. As gaudy as it first looked, there would be complete understanding why she'd stop traffic and cause a monastery to go out of business.

"Ooh, zey were right, up at zee school. It is so sweet and leetle. A petite atelier, I loove it!" she gushed in her showy way. With great exuberance, she started going through the racks and piling garments on Daphne's arms.

Daphne gave a nod to Abigail, asking her to start a room for Miss… then she realized that she couldn't recall what her last name was.

"Oh, just Sophie," she smiled at the young girl and carried on her hunt.

Daphne noticed that she was taking garments in the smallest sizes available. She certainly wasn't a size 2 or even 4. At first glance, Daphne would've guessed she was a 10, or possibly even a 12. "Oh, here, let me help you pick them out." Sophie was carrying a pair of new gingham blue short shorts in her hand. Daphne grabbed a 10 and handed them over to her. "These would be better."

"Non," Sophie stated. "Zese ones!" Sticking with the smaller size. "I appreciate your 'elp, but I know my body." She ran her hands down her sides. "I like to feel 'eld, snug in my clothes, oui?"

Daphne shrugged and let her do what she wanted. They could keep a close eye on her to make sure she didn't pop any seams or do any damage to the clothing. Margot had taken over helping Mrs. Falconer, who was deciding between dove grey and soft white kid gloves to go with her new suit. Margot had an amused look on her face as she watched her partner deal with the buxom bombshell.

Sophie toddled off to a changing room, with Abigail waiting in attendance. Daphne sought a reprieve at the sales desk. Irene smirked as she sized up the situation. "She'll liven things up around here."

"Not too much, I hope. She's up at Stearns Academy, teaching art."

"Are you sure that's all she's teaching?" Irene remarked. "Those girls will never be the same after a couple of classes with her."

Daphne shrugged, not wanting to think of what was going on up at the school. The evenings could be awfully long up there on the hill. Sophie may make the nights pass a little more easily for some, and she wasn't sure she liked that.

Irene watched her boss' expression and toyed with her further. "If I were you, I'd be curious if your precious riding instructor had acquired a few new techniques, or had given a few too many 'extracurricular' riding sessions."

"Irene," Margot coolly interrupted. "Please take care of Mrs. Falconer's payment, would you?" Under her breath, she muttered to the girl, "That's enough."

Irene grinned and did what she was told. She knew her comments were cutting, but she found it great fun to tease the innocent Daphne.

Daphne bit her lip, and frown lines appeared on her forehead. "Margot, you don't think Daniel would fall for her, do you?"

"No, don't worry. Irene's just getting your goat, because she knows she can."

Daphne had her own doubts. "Sophie's got a lot of sex appeal. They say some men can't help themselves around women like that. It's a scientific fact; it was in a big article in *Ladies' Home Journal*. There's got to be some truth to it."

Margot rolled her eyes. "Well, maybe some men are animals, but others are a little more gallant than that. Daniel isn't the playboy type, and trust me, I know the symptoms of that."

"Ooh! 'ow am I?" Sophie came out of the changing room in a bright red silk shantung cocktail dress that had a wide off the shoulder collar, forming a deep *V*, both in the back and front. It was very form fitting to the knee, with a back slit. It was an even closer fit, given that she had picked it up off the rack in the size she wanted to be rather than what she actually was. She spilled out of the top. It was amazing that she could actually walk in it. To be fair, she slithered more than strode, but chances are it would get her exactly where she wanted to go.

"Bon! I take it."

Daphne's mouth gaped at the sight. Margot made a suggestion. "Yes, Sophie, you flatter the dress perfectly. But perhaps you'd like a few alterations, just to make it, say more continental?" Margot wasn't sure what that literally meant, but she thought that if Sophie fell for it, she could pretend to change the one she had on and give her a larger size, just changing the the labels. Poppy Cove's reputation as the producer of the garment was important, and she wanted her customers look alluring, not on sale.

"Non! It is good like zis!" Sophie looked at herself in the three-way mirror, catching a glimpse of someone new walking into the store. "Ooh, Danny! You like?" She ran over faster than anyone could imagine she could to the newcomer. She linked her arm with his and kissed him on the cheek.

Daphne audibly gasped when she saw who the woman had sunk her claws into. *Her* Daniel, of all people. And since when was he *Danny?*

Daniel's eyes almost bugged out of his head and he gulped. As he came to his senses, he cleared his throat and extracted Sophie's arm from his. He walked briskly away from her and towards his girlfriend. "Hi, Daphne." It was about all he could get out.

"Hi," she said flatly. She looked down at her modest cotton frock. It was sweet and sunny in a pale pink, with daisies around the hem and collar. She felt like she was twelve.

He kissed her on the forehead. *Forehead?* she thought and responded by giving him one back full on the lips, longer than her mother would have called publicly decent. He was temporarily flummoxed and gave her a goofy smile.

Sophie shrugged nonchalantly and walked back to the change room.

Daphne saw Daniel's gaze as he involuntarily watched Sophie sashay away. He shook his head and took her hand. "Sweetheart, what are you doing tomorrow?"

"Oh, I don't know, I may have plans," she replied, flippantly. She had no other plans, and had counted on spending time with him, but given the appearance and reactions caused by the art tart, she thought she'd better play it cool rather than as clingy as she felt.

"Right, I'll make this quick." He glanced towards the dressing area, making sure Sophie was still occupied. He wanted to leave before she came out again. "Let's make a day of it tomorrow. We can get away, just the two of us. Go on an adventure, just like you've wanted to do. What do you say, Daff?"

She smiled. "Yes, that would be good. What about tonight?"

"Oh, sorry, I can't. I've got an extra riding lesson," Daniel said casually. One of the girls has a show jumping competition coming up and we'll be practicing till dusk. Tomorrow, I'm all yours. I'll swing by your house at nine?"

She nodded, thinking about what Irene had said about extra lessons and such. She didn't like where her mind was going, so she ignored it.

Daniel kissed her again on the cheek. "See you tomorrow," he said and headed out. "Oh, and be sure to pack a bathing suit!"

Sophie came out to complete her purchase. "Now where 'as my Danny gone?" she pouted.

Irene stepped in. "He left. He had to make plans for a big date tomorrow." She glared at Sophie, sizing the woman up. Irene liked to stir the pot, and this time, it was in Sophie's direction. She gave Daphne a wink and a nudge in her side.

"Umph, oh well," Sophie sighed. "Zere are other men, oui?" she asked rhetorically to the group.

"Yes," Daphne confirmed to anyone in earshot, in a voice louder than she intended.

"But not if zee 'andsome ones get murdered." Sophie gave a dramatic shiver and turned to face Margot. "Your ex-'usband, 'e was good-looking, non?" She gave a knowing smile. "More so in person, too."

Margot was startled. "You knew Nathan?"

"Oh, yes, 'e was a man, that one."

"How did you know him?"

"I was in New York," she answered simply.

"I thought you were from Paris?"

"Oui, Paree, but I came to America last year, as artist's model. I stayed in zee village. Ooh, zee clubs—such amusement!" She hugged herself, then grinned slyly at Margot. "Nate, 'e was a devil. No wonder 'e was shot zrough zee 'eart. Broke too many!"

"How well did you know him? Did you see him here?"

"Non, just 'is picture in the paper. I was surprised to see 'im, but 'e always got around, as you say." She picked up her parcel and turned to leave, facing Daphne one last time.

"Did Donny treat you right? 'Ow do you like 'is work? Good 'ands, non?" She laughed and toddled out, leaving more conundrums than solutions.

Irene went to help Abigail straighten out the mess Sophie had left behind, leaving Daphne and Margot on their own.

"Donny? Who's Donny?" Margot asked Daphne.

Daphne changed the subject. "She knew Nate. And had been in New York, and she's French! She could be the killer, or involved, don't you think? She certainly wasn't surprised he was shot."

"It is odd. It could be something." Margot thought about it. It was all too perplexing, co-incidentally, not to be connected. She'd have to talk to Henry about it. She hadn't heard much from him, nor had there been much in the *Times*. The silence was eerie. "I also don't trust that accent. It sounds phony, too pronounced, don't you think?"

"I don't think that's the only fake thing about her," Daphne remarked.

Margot laughed, then steered the conversation back to the other topic Sophie had brought up. "By the way, what was Sophie talking about? Who is this Donny and why did she act like you knew him?"

Daphne tilted her head and shrugged not giving an answer.

Margot pursued further. "Where exactly did you go yesterday? To see this Donny?"

Daphne turned red, then giggled. "Okay, she was referring to Adonis, the artist we met on Sunday. I went to his studio to pose. She was there when I got there."

"You what?"

"You heard me, I went to his studio to model for him."

"You didn't!"

"I did!"

"Were you...?"

Daphne looked around to make sure no one was within earshot before replying. "Naked? Yes!" she answered proudly.

"Sophie didn't pose *with* you, did she?" Margot was panicking, wondering what Daphne was getting herself into.

"No, of course not! What kind of girl do you think I am? Honestly! She left before we got started," Daphne said.

"So seriously, how was posing in the buff?"

"Not too bad," she reflected. "Easier than I thought. He had me in a rather modest position, to be honest. But it still felt daring."

"What's he going to do with the painting? You know your parents would have a fit if he had it in a public exhibition."

Daphne nodded, emphatically. "I'm thinking of buying it when it's done and giving it to Daniel," she confessed.

"Wow! Well, he couldn't miss that invitation, could he?"

Daphne put her hand over her mouth. "Do you think that would be too forward?"

"Well, it's certainly bold," Margot replied. "Look, I'm no expert on relationships. I've got a divorce from a loveless marriage behind me and a man who I've kept in the dark for years. For some godforsaken reason, it looks like he's willing to stand behind me after of all this. I consider myself lucky, not smart, when it comes to how that happened."

Daphne was glad they were still alone. "Speaking of which, you've had experience with men."

"Yes," Margot answered, wondering where the conversation was going. "And so have you. I've always known you to have an active dating life, and you've been with Dan for some time now."

"I have," Daphne confirmed. "But you have a little more than that. I mean, you've been married, so…."

"Oh, you mean *that?*" Margot said louder than Daphne liked.

"Shh! Yes, I mean *that.* I know you said it wasn't the romance of the century with Nate, but he was attractive, and you were supposed to do that after it was legal and all."

Margot felt a little uncomfortable, but she owed it to Daphne to open up. "Of course. As you said, it was the expected thing and I was curious."

"How was it?"

"The first time or in general?"

"Both."

She sighed, thinking how to explain it to her friend. "It gets better. Much better and much nicer with someone you love."

"Do you mean Tom?"

Margot nodded and Daphne self-consciously giggled. "I'm thinking that it's time to let Daniel know I want to."

"You haven't already?" Margot was moderately surprised. She knew they'd been together exclusively for over half a year now; everyone was aware they loved each other—they'd declared it publicly last fall. Daphne would often talk about wanting to marry him, so she'd just assumed. This was the late '50's, after all, and Daphne was a grown woman.

"No." Daphne blushed. "Mother always told me to keep my skirt down and my legs closed until marriage, or at least engagement, but I don't want to wait. I don't think I better with the likes of Sophie, the pole cat, prowling around Dan's cabin at night." The majority of the faculty, Daniel and Sophie included, lived in housing provided by the Academy. "I think I better mark my territory, so to speak."

"Don't rush ahead and do anything you don't want to do," Margot cautioned. "If you love Daniel and are ready, that's one thing, but don't let the likes of Sophie make you feel rushed."

"No, no, I don't. Maybe I'm just saying it wrong." Daphne sighed. "I'm twenty-six years old now. I'm not married, and this is the longest relationship that I've been in. I love Daniel, and trust him, too. I have to admit I'm very attracted to him and spend a lot, probably too much time, wondering what it would be like, especially with him." She took a deep breath. "It's time I behaved like a mature woman, don't you think?"

Margot laughed kindly. "Yes, you may be right. I'd probably feel the same way you would. I don't think you'll go wrong with Dan as your first. He certainly loves you and he's a caring man." She paused. "Better than letting Adonis seduce you!" she joked.

"Oh, my, are you kidding? There's no way I would fall for that! He's really old, and a bit sad. He's definitely one of those starving artist/beatnik types. Do you know he smokes marijuana cigarettes?"

Margot gave a worldly grin and nod of the head, not surprised. "So that's how you found out about Adonis knowing more about Nate being at Bud's last Saturday."

Daphne affirmed the comment and elaborated on the details, including the part about the artist receiving a black eye and that she'd agreed to go back and pose again.

Margot responded in all seriousness. "I wouldn't dare tell you what to do; you know I've done my share of reckless things, but if he's associated with such shady characters, you may want to change your mind. Guys like that are rough and don't care who gets in the way. You could get caught in the crossfire. We still don't know if that's what happened to Jeannette."

"Yeah, I guess. Now we find Sophie's all tied up in this, too. Gosh, I sure hope this gets figured out soon. Maybe I'll just stay away from Adonis until the murder is solved."

"That would be best, I think."

"Are you seeing Tom again soon?"

Margot shook her head. "The police are watching everything too closely right now. We both have orders not to see or communicate with each other, and you know how the telephone wires talk around here. I might as well have a bullhorn with the way Mrs. O'Leary repeats what she hears on our party line. Same with Tom's building. My parents also want to meet him, even though they're not happy he's not of the social or business elite, but we're going to have to wait. I don't want to cause him problems that may affect when he goes back to work. My sneaky visit was risk enough. Thank God Jenkins is on our side."

"You must really miss Tom."

"I do," Margot admitted. "But now that I know he knows all about me and still loves me, it makes it bearable. And I certainly know what my answer is."

"I'll bet you do!"

"By the way, when do you plan to seduce Daniel?"

Daphne smirked, but spoke with complete determination. "Tomorrow. He's planning something for us, but won't he be surprised when he figures out what I have in store for him!"

CHAPTER SEVENTEEN

When Margot arrived for dinner with her parents at Antonio's, there was a hush in the crowded restaurant. Conversations stopped and all eyes were upon her. Thankfully, Antonio Chelli greeted her warmly and openly, leading her to a booth in a quiet, but not isolated spot, where her parents were already waiting. The visit itself was pleasant enough, although it went as expected. They were trying to persuade her to come back to Westport after 'this unpleasant matter' was taken care of. Dorothy and George had spent their afternoon planning and scheming how 'Margaret' would live out the rest of her life, including the possibilities of new husband candidates who'd be big enough to overlook her 'indiscretions and wandering years.' In the past, she might have obeyed them, feeling she had no choice, but now, no matter what kind of trouble she was be in, she had a life that she'd created that she was proud of. She was also strong enough to stand up for herself and let them know, politely but firmly, that under no uncertain terms, she was not going back. Not now, not ever.

Surprisingly, once she stood her ground, they eased up. They still felt free to give advice; her father about the fabrics she could get from his mills; her mother pointing out the run in her stocking even though it was in the back of her leg and happened after she'd left work and could not do anything about it because she didn't have a spare in her purse, as well as asking her if her girdle was too snug, because she was obviously fidgeting and that was very unbecoming.

By the time Margot got home, she was exhausted. She saw her white eyelet pajamas that she'd folded on her bedroom chair that morning. She undressed out of her day clothes, swapping them for the nightwear. She carefully draped the dress suit and unmentionables on the chair, too tired to bother to hang them up. She'd do that in the morning. She washed up quickly and called it a night, thinking of Tom as she drifted off, wondering how he was doing.

****

Daphne woke up early Sunday, thinking about the plans for her day. She was giddily excited. *Today's the day,* she thought. *I will really become a woman.* She knew it made her forward, what she was thinking, but she didn't it consider herself *fast.* After all, they'd been together for some time, and it wasn't like Daniel hadn't tried. She'd gently put off his advances, and he'd respectfully adjusted his behavior. This time, she just wouldn't stop him, but invite him to continue. It should be simple, the most natural thing in the world.

She thought about how it would go. It probably would be best to go along with what he'd planned for the day, he obviously had some kind of fun in mind. He often did. They'd gone for riding and bowling dates, trips to the races and the beach, sailing, not to mention fancy dinners and dancing. She was sure today would be no exception. The only thing is she'd make sure they'd have some time alone at his place, either before or after dinner. As long as she glanced at or caressed him in just the right way, as she'd practiced doing in her mind over and over lately, he'd get the right idea.

She realized she had to pack a rather large bag to carry out her intentions. Unfortunately, Dan was picking her up, so she couldn't just leave it in her car until the time was right. As she lay in her bed, she ticked off on her fingertips everything she needed to have. Her bathing suit and towel, of course. She'd take her new red one-piece, the one with the side gathers that tied at the neck and had white trim. Being that she was the one springing the seduction plans, she realized that she'd have to be the one to take care of 'precautions,' which she'd done and, thus, felt very proud of herself. She'd been able to purchase them all on her own. In an out of the way drug store, mind you, but the pharmacist hadn't even batted an eyelid when she did.

She figured that Daniel must have been planning an outdoors date, hence the request for her to bring a bathing suit, so she'd have to bring her makeup and hair spray, along with her Tabu, the most seductive fragrance she owned. Now what exactly to wear?

Well, she figured to start, her bathing suit and on top of that, a matching red skirt, that had a white waistband and button placket down the front. A white cotton blouse with cap sleeves should suffice over the top. Her red cotton espadrilles would pair well. But she'd need a more alluring dress for later activities. Oh and what about a negligee? Should she bring that as well? When exactly would they get around to *that*—day? Night? She had a filmy white baby doll set she could throw into the bag, just in case. And her white satin mules—yes—those too.

Now back to the dinner dress. She couldn't help but notice how Daniel's eyes had almost come out of their sockets when he saw Sophie in the low *V* of her new dress. She couldn't fill anything out in quite the same way, but she did have a peacock blue shantung dress with the same neckline. The deep, off-the-shoulder collar and slim-fitted skirt would do the trick. She'd have to pack her black patent pumps and matching handbag for that. Oh, and her newest low-cut brassiere and girdle, and stockings, of course. Yes, that should be enough. She hurried to get ready and ran downstairs, not caring if she looked too eager by sitting and waiting for him out by the front door.

****

Margot woke up later than usual Sunday morning. Her sleep was the best she'd had all week. As she came to, she wondered what the day would bring. She usually spent her Sundays with Tom and these days, more often than not, waking up beside him. She rolled over and sighed, hoping that would happen again soon.

She didn't make any plans with her parents. When they parted last night, they were a little rebuffed by her resolve, but it wasn't ugly. They'd just have to get used to 'Margot' if they chose to stay a part of her life. She was actually hoping they would.

She eyed her garments on her chair, got up and started to put them away. Margot opened her lingerie drawer and couldn't believe what she saw. Her ivory half-slip was bunched up and she could see black metal poking out of the pile. She slammed the drawer shut and trembled. She looked over at her bedroom window, seeing that it was about a third of the way open. She couldn't remember if she'd opened it when she came home last night or left it open when she left for work that morning. It was nice out, so either was possible. She didn't see anything knocked over or out of place when she came home, but someone must have come in. When did it happen? She hadn't woken up all night. Then she panicked. Were they still there? She listened and in her fear wasn't sure if she was imagining bangs or thuds, or if it was just her heart. Margot didn't touch anything else, but called Henry immediately. He said he'd be over right away and warned her that he'd have to call the police once he got there. He would take care of it. He told her to sit tight and try to remember all of what she did when she came home and not to touch anything else.

She went out and sat in her living room chair, poised on the edge of her seat, waiting for Henry to arrive. She hadn't changed out of her pajamas, following his orders to not touch anything, not even getting a glass of water. Henry broke all land and sea records getting to her house, but it seemed like an eternity to her. He asked her to go over again her discovery of the gun and what she thought could have happened. It had obviously been returned sometime between 8:30 Saturday morning and 8:30 this morning, when she'd awakened. She'd rummaged in that very drawer before work yesterday, had taken that exact slip out, debating which one to wear and there was no way the gun had been there then.

Henry listened to what she had to say, looked over her house without touching anything. "Are you positive that it's your gun?"

Margot never questioned that. "I think so. It's where I kept it before, but I didn't take it out of the slip. It looks like it, I think. Do you suspect someone placed a different one or a fake one to get me into trouble?"

Henry shrugged. "I just need to cover all angles. Don't say anything to the police when they arrive. I'll handle it. I have to warn you, though, you may be taken in for more questioning, perhaps even charged. Depending on what they find out when they take the gun, if it was the one that was used to kill Reed, it makes it harder to prove your innocence."

She couldn't believe what she was hearing. It was possibly the worst news. She wondered how someone had gotten in with the police watching so carefully. Could they have done this right under all their noses? Would it have been Jeannette?

Henry was on the telephone, reporting the find to the police. Margot thought about Jeannette. In her racing mind, she played out a few ideas. If she recalled correctly, they were of similar build and size. Could Jeannette have come and gone while Margot was at work

or out, and been mistaken for her? She remembered
Sharon O'Leary making some kind of comment earlier in
the week about how Margot had been unfriendly by not
saying hello to her. Could that have been Jeannette,
posing as her and taking the gun?

Henry informed her the police were on their way. She
told him her theory, then gave a full description of the
girl, who she recalled was just an inch or two shorter
than her and a couple of years younger, but from a
distance could easily pass for her. He wrote down some
notes and made positive noises to her idea. He'd look
into it more closely once the police had finished at the
house. She also told him about her conversation with
Sophie yesterday, about how she'd known Nate in New
York, but said she hadn't seen him in Santa Lucia. She
also said that if Sophie was indeed involved with
Nathan's murder, she couldn't be the one mistaken for
Margot. Their builds and mannerisms were far too
different. Henry said he'd speak to Sophie as well.

Detective Riley was the first to knock on the door and
entered with a macabre enthusiasm. He directed a couple
of junior uniforms to dust for fingerprints and stood in
Margot's living room, staring down at her while Henry
told him what she'd discovered and the theory about
Jeannette and her disappearance, as well as the
information regarding Sophie. He sneered at the ideas,
but was willing to look into them, wanting to do a
thorough job with no loopholes that Margot could get
through if she was indeed guilty.

After they'd checked over the house for clues, the
police didn't reveal if they'd found anything substantial
or evidence of a break-in. They asked her where she kept
a spare key, which she admitted to placing under a loose
piece of siding by the door. Riley took the opportunity to
reprimand her that as the girlfriend of a fellow detective,
she should know better than that. She realized that was
one way someone could have come in and not make it

evident. They tagged and removed the gun and the slip surrounding it.

And because Henry had warned her, it came as no surprise that the police asked, or rather demanded that she come to the station. They gave her permission to get dressed while Officer Rose Marie Hartley followed her into the bedroom and discreetly observed that she did not try to destroy or hide anything. Margot put the clothes back on that she still had draped over the chair. The police would not entertain her actions of choosing a new ensemble for going to the station. As she came from her room, she overheard them saying that they would put a rush on the ballistics testing for the murder weapon. Now that Riley had in his possession what had long been considered the 'smoking gun,' he wanted it proved without a doubt.

"I'll let Tom know," Jenkins whispered as he walked by her. "Sorry, Mar."

Two of the officers remained, canvasing the neighborhood, asking if anyone had seen anything in the past day. As the cars pulled away, Mrs. O'Leary was the first they came across. She stood on the sidewalk watching, and stated, "Well, I never!"

Margot left quietly without a word, thankful that they didn't handcuff her and allowed her to be driven by Henry, rather than carted off in a squad car. As he drove her, she asked him to let her parents know what was happening. He promised he would, and that he'd bring them to the station if she desired. She decided not, not until they had some word on what was going on. They'd deal with that when they had to. Henry did his best to reassure her that she was in good hands, and he'd do his very best to prove her innocence, no matter what happened. She silently hoped that would be enough.

Margot was hustled back into the same interrogation room she'd been subjected to the other night. She was not allowed to have her purse or watch. Her jewellery had been removed, as was her belt. She sat there alone, on a cold metal chair, waiting for news. Henry had been out finding any information he could and was also planning to bring her a bite to eat. In the meantime, all she could do was wait. She knew that they were checking out the leads regarding the possibility of Jeannette sneaking into her house. As she toyed with the idea, she wondered that if it was Jeannette, what exactly she had against her or what reason she had to frame her. She couldn't remember ever seeing her before she came in a few weeks ago, looking for work. If she was associated with Nathan, it certainly wasn't when Margot was with him.

Maybe it wasn't her at all. Then who was it? And why did the gun come back? And was it hers and/or the one used? She knew those answers at least would come soon enough. And if it was bad news, how was she going to get out of this one?

While she waited, she took in the room, purely for reasons of distraction. It had a paneled ceiling, with a water stain in the top left corner. There were no windows and it was stifling. Everything was painted a dull, dingy gray, with very little embellishment. There was a chrome wall clock, showing she'd now been sitting in there for an hour. In the center of the room was the metal table she'd sat at before with three more vacant chairs—one positioned beside her and two across the table. There was a small wall speaker and call button and that was about it. She sighed, not knowing what was coming next.

Henry came in, bringing hot coffee and a warm sweet roll. He set them down on the table for her. "Now, we wait." He took off his suit jacket, draped it over the back of his chair, sat down, opened up his file, positioned his pen, and joined her.

****

Daniel and Daphne were whizzing down the ocean side highway in the beautifully blue and sparkling day. The fog had stayed at bay and it was already warm. They had the ragtop down on his Fury, and the wind off the water was refreshing. They laughed and talked, eagerly enjoying their day already. Daphne had relaxed, as Daniel had made it so much fun just to be around him. He did, however, give her quite the look when he lifted her large canvas tote bag into the car, wondering what in the world she was bringing for a day out. He didn't ask, just set it in the car, along with her surfboard that he'd fetched from the garage, securing it beside his in the back seat.

Daphne had seen a basket in the car as well, and when she asked him where they were going, he told her it was a little spot he knew about. It wasn't well known but a real beaut for surfing. They cruised down the coast, and just before they reached the turnoff for Ojai, he hung a right. She saw the new sign 'Emma Wood State Beach.' "Oh, I've been here!" she exclaimed. We used to come here as teenagers before it was a park."

But instead of veering right again into the parking lot, he turned left past the park entrance, and drove the car down a narrow dirt road. He stopped in the middle of nowhere, around the corner and away from the public park. Daphne looked around. The view was breathtaking and away from others. The path had narrowed to a single track and there was low scrub around. Below was a gentle incline to a private beach, amazingly deserted, with a lovely spot to set up a blanket in a little cove. "But I haven't been here," she marveled.

Daniel grinned and started unpacking the car. He lifted her tote, to which she replied, "You can leave that here. I'll just take my towel out, thanks." He gave her a funny look, wondering why she brought it if she wasn't going to use it. Daphne read his expression. "I brought a change of clothes if we went out for dinner," she casually replied. He bought her explanation and shrugged it off, getting the rest of the gear out of the car.

They set up a spot with a blanket and basket on the little beach. "I can't believe we're the only ones here," she said. "You'd think it'd be crowded."

Daniel shrugged. "I used to come here too, years ago. The other side that they made into the state park last year is easier to get to and it's more the happening place to see and be seen, but I thought this might be better for our date," he grinned impishly. There's even a little shack if we get too much sun, or if we want to have a nap." He gestured over his shoulder to a small weathered beach shelter.

His last remark resonated in her ears as she realized what he was implicating. Daphne surmised that he was planning a romantic rendezvous as much as she was. She smiled a 10,000-watt smile back at him, nodding. "On, second thought, would you please get my bag out of the car?" she asked.

****

It was another hour before Detective Riley and Officer Hartley came into the interrogation room. Riley was smug and tight, which gave away his reply before he spoke. He stood across the table from Margot and stated, "Margot Williams, formerly known as Margaret Jane Reed and Margaret Jane Willmington, I am placing you under arrest for the murder of Nathan Charles Reed, in the first degree. You do understand that if you are found guilty, the sentence carries the death penalty in the state of California?"

All of the air was sucked out of the room. Margot was shocked. "W-what? No, wait, I didn't do anything!"

Riley made a motion to grab her arm, when Henry spoke. "Now wait a minute here. With a charge that serious, my client deserves to hear what your findings are. Now sit down, young man, and act like a proper policeman and not a half-cocked hothead." Henry stood up and looked back and forth at both of the officers of the law. Rose Marie was looking down at her feet, feeling awkward at Riley's over-enthusiasm. Riley had his jaw clenched and a vein was pulsing in his neck, visible over his suit collar. He attempted to stare down the older lawyer to no avail. Both Riley and Hartley sat down. "That's better. Start at the beginning and tell us what you found in your reports. No threats or theatrics. We'll jump to the conclusions one at a time, all right? And you'd better apologize to my client. You may think she committed a crime, but that's yet to be proven, and I think we can all agree with her clean record; she demands a better treatment than that."

Margot sat dumbstruck, still reeling from Riley's vicious verbal attack. What she did pick up from what he'd said was that she could go to the gas chamber for this—and it was for something that she did not do.

Riley calmed down, opening up the file folder he'd brought in with him. "Yes, well, sorry, Ms. Williams, as that does turn out to be your legal name. We'll relate the details of the report and the charges, but that doesn't change what they are." He cleared his throat and began reporting their findings, in a more professional manner. "The Smith & Wesson .38 revolver found in your lingerie drawer was indeed yours. The serial number is the same as the one registered and sold to you in New York City. Ballistics testing also proves that it had been recently fired, and the bullet that was found in the deceased came from that exact gun. So this is what we believe happened.

"Nathan Reed had found out you had settled in Santa Lucia and changed your name to Margot Williams. You had developed a highly successful business, garnering national attention. He needed money, and figured you had it to give. He came out here, tracked you down and demanded money from you, maybe as blackmail, or by force. You refused, he wouldn't leave you alone. You had your gun and had enough of him, even worried that he could upset your applecart. You have a good thing going. Nice business, nice boyfriend, nice house, nice life. Then he shows up. It would be simple. No one else knew he was here for you; you could make him a promise, take him out on the wharf and do away with him. That means first degree murder.

"We only have a few questions. Where did you hide the gun originally and why did you 'pretend' to find it now? And what have you done with Jeannette Fox?"

****

Daphne couldn't believe how wonderfully the day was turning out. Daniel wanted *exactly* what she wanted. She remained on the sand and hugged her legs, digging her toes in the sand, trying not to giggle as Dan went to get her bag as she requested. *How could I have thought I was being too forward? It was naturally going to happen anyway. That's what he had in mind for my 'adventure,' too.* Then she thought of what she should do next. Should she change into her dress or the baby dolls, and where? Have him wait outside and get dressed in the shack before inviting him in? No, it was midmorning, for goodness sake, and dressing like that didn't seem right. She must look a fright, all windblown and sandy with faded lipstick. Dab Tabu behind the ears, knees, and elsewhere? And what did he have in mind? Did he have a lead she should let him take? She took a deep breath and let the moment carry her away.

Daniel came back with her bag in one hand and extended his other to her. "Why don't you bring the blanket and come along with me?" At that moment she realized it didn't matter what she put on, Tabu, dress or otherwise. She'd just go wherever he wanted her to go, just as she was.

They said nothing but grinned foolishly as they made their way to the shack door. Daniel kissed her passionately, then turned the door knob and led her in.

Daphne saw stars as she was bopped on the top of her head. Dazed, but not out, she glanced around the room. In her blurred vision, she saw a shape in the corner. Then her sight sharpened and she recognized that it was Jeannette Fox, tied and gagged in the corner, dirty and slumped over. Before she could move, she heard another thud behind her and saw Daniel go down hard, passing out.

"Get over here, girly, and keep quiet while I deal with you." A gruff woman's voice came from behind, and she felt her arms being held back while she struggled.

She started to scream, but the woman put a hand over her mouth, then, as quick as lightning, a gag. She then whipped her around roughly and started tying up her arms and legs. At that point, Daphne saw her attacker. It was Diane from the Poppy Lane Tearoom. Daphne's eyes widened in shock and she started to cry involuntarily.

"Oh, be quiet, I have to think! You and lover boy have ruined my plans." She shoved Daphne in the corner by Jeannette who thankfully came to. She was groggy, but alive. Jeannette closed her eyes in momentary relief, realizing there may be hope, and she wasn't alone. But now what?

Daniel was also captured and tied up. While he was still out cold, Diane dragged him to the opposite side of the cabin. then she paced around the small room. "Now what am I supposed to do with you all?" She stared at them, muttering to herself. "Getting rid of one more of you was enough, but now three?"

She kept pacing and muttering. "If he hadn't shown up on this coast, I could have just gotten rid of her, easy peasy. But no, he had to find her out and go after money, the lazy, stinking deadbeat."

Daphne was bewildered and couldn't follow at first what Diane was saying. *Who? Jeannette? He? Now that must mean Nate.*

"And Ruth, poor sweet Ruth. How could she have gotten herself in such a way? And if only that spoiled rich brat had given her money all those years ago, none of this would have happened. I wouldn't have to be doing this, would I?"

Daphne's confusion grew. Who was Ruth? And what in the world was she going to do now? Daphne heard Daniel groan and start to waken. He had a small trail of blood dripping down the side of his head. Then she saw what Diane had used to conk them on their skulls. There was a rock, bigger than a fist sitting on the table by the door. Diane picked it up, about to strike Daniel again, when the door blew open and a voice came from the door frame. "I wouldn't do that. Put the rock down, Diane." The sun was streaming in, blinding them, but the man sounded familiar. There stood Officer Jenkins, in uniform, pointing a gun steady at Diane, with Tom right behind him, taking control of the scene. "It's over."

CHAPTER EIGHTEEN

Meanwhile, Officer Bruce Jenkins had been going to Tom's, on the sly during his off hours. The two had been going over all the details of the case, looking for any little clue or small thing that Riley had overlooked or had chosen not to see. They both knew that they'd be in trouble if their superiors found out, but if they did get caught, Bruce would just say it was a social call and try to get out of it that way.

The officer had thought about a couple of things Detective Riley had overlooked. He didn't take seriously the claim that Tom had seen something in the bushes outside of Margot's house the previous Friday night. The comment Tom made got lost in the shuffle and was never passed on. The neighbors had been questioned about any comings and goings from Margot's house in the past few weeks. No one remembered anything out of the ordinary, but Sharon O'Leary said that she figured Margot must have been pre-occupied, because one time she didn't return her hello, which she always did. Sharon could not, however, remember precisely when that was.

Jeannette and Margot were of similar build, so it could have easily been Jeannette sneaking around, pretending to be the designer at a distance. Jeannette had been missing for a while, with no leads turning up. Combining that with her curiosity about Margot and coming from New York City, all added up to making her a viable suspect, not a victim. Detective Riley, having the main authority on the case, and chummy with the commissioner, called the shots. Especially now that the chief was left out due to his daughter's possible connection, along with Tom and his supposed involvement.

So when the results came in from Margot's gun, Jenkins knew that Riley was going to throw the book at her. Bruce, however, couldn't believe his theory. There was no way that Margot had done what the detective thought she'd done. She was too refined for that. Even the fact that she chose to leave her life behind and start fresh instead of staying in the same circles and keep running into her ex-husband showed that she'd rather run than fight. There must be something that was overlooked or that they were missing. He didn't care if he was in uniform. He hightailed it to Tom's, telling him the latest discovery.

Being that both Nathan and Jeannette were missing from Mrs. Coleman's Boarding House, the two men went there first. Tom, being now just a citizen and not officially in uniform at that point, waited in the car. Mrs. Coleman was none too pleased to be disturbed on her Sunday morning. She had nothing to discuss, but the elderly Mr. Drake had a thing or two to say.

"That Miss Phillips; she was acting awfully strange this morning." Mr. Drake was sitting outside on the front porch, out of earshot of Mrs. Coleman who would've certainly disapproved of what he'd said.

"Who is that?" Jenkins asked.

"One of the young girls who just moved in. She works at the tearoom, I think. Usually pleasant enough, but she's been acting a little jumpy the last day or so. I've caught her mumbling to herself, and then she tells me to mind my own business. Not very nice if you ask me."

"What was she mumbling about?" Jenkins encouraged.

"Something about having to empty out that shack, getting rid of something. I don't really know, to be honest, but the girl looked like she hadn't slept all night."

Jenkins rapped on the front door, further annoying Mrs. Coleman. He persuaded her to let him in again, and this time into Miss Diane Phillips' room. She protested at first, but he took a risk by showing his badge saying he had a duty to go through her things. Mildred didn't challenge him and relented.

Jenkins did a quick scan of the room, not disturbing much. He did, however, find on her writing desk, a brochure for the brand new 'Emma Wood State Beach' opened up with the map circled. On instinct, he nabbed it and brought it down to Tom.

The two sped their way down the coast. By the time they got to the beach, the main parking lot was full, with plenty of people enjoying the sand and surf, with children running around on the long, broad, open beach, and no real place to hide. Tom got out of the car and ran his hand through his hair, scanning the beach for any odd behavior, anything other than fun in the sun. On the far left of the park, he noticed the trail and signaled to Jenkins. The two walked briskly over and quickly came across the car just down the way. "That looks like Daniel Henshaw's car," Tom spoke out loud. "Why on earth would it be over here?"

They approached the car and looked farther on the secluded beach and saw the deserted picnic scene. Tom continued to scour the area, looking for Dan and possibly Daphne now, as well as Diane and the missing Jeannette.

Jenkins tugged at Tom's sleeve. When he had Tom's attention, he silently pointed to the little wooden shack. There was a silent understanding between them that there must be something going on in there. Unfortunately, they'd taken Tom's private car, not an official police vehicle and had only one way of calling for backup—running back to the park ranger station, at the parking lot on the other side of the slope.

The beach shack had no windows and looked eerily quiet. Even though they only had one pistol between them—Jenkins'—they'd decided to go it alone, figuring they didn't want to lose any time checking it out. They could call for help later if there was anything to report. As they got closer, they could hear some thumping against the walls and a woman talking over the background surf. They approached the only entrance on either side of the door, with Tom signaling Bruce to take the lead, as he was armed.

Diane was taken by surprise and dropped her rock. Jenkins easily wrestled her to the ground and handcuffed her. Once Tom was sure Jenkins had her under control, he checked out the captives. He noticed Jeannette was in the worst shape, regaining consciousness but woozy and weak, appearing to have been held for some time. He got Daphne out of constraints, who then helped release Daniel. The two of them weren't seriously hurt—more shaken up than anything. Dan's cut was superficial, but still needed to be checked out. Daphne ran to the park office to telephone the police and have an ambulance sent, reporting to whom and how just as Tom had told her to do. Diane sat in the corner, now the captive one, throwing a tantrum, and rambling incoherently, not giving them any real information.

While they waited for more help, Daphne and Daniel reported what had happened to them and what they'd overheard, how Diane had said she was going to have to get rid of them all and how she was talking about a Ruth, and how she wanted to get back at a spoiled brat. Diane sat sullenly, not wanting to talk, while Jeannette tried to speak, but had trouble getting her words out.

****

Back at the station, Riley was trying to get Margot to confess, but she still maintained her bewilderment over the gun and continued to confirm her innocence. There was a knock on the door. Hartley stepped outside and came back in shortly. She walked over to Riley and whispered in his ear. His eyes grew wide and the two cops left the room without a word to Margot or her lawyer. Margot and Henry looked at each other, shrugged and waited.

****

At the park, the ambulance attendants deemed Daphne to be fine. Daniel was treated at the cabin, cleaned up and bandaged, while they decided to take Jeannette to the hospital. She was obviously dehydrated and starving, also possibly drugged and roughed up. Fortunately, nothing seemed broken, and she hadn't been shot.

By the time the backup officers had Diane in custody, she realized the gig was up and told her whole story. She had no hope of getting away with anything anymore. Jeannette would tell what she knew by the time she was better, and Diane was too tired to keep it up.

'Ruth' turned out to be the showgirl, 'Phoebe LaRue,' and also Diane's sister. The Phillips girls had grown up in New York City. Diane was five years younger than Ruth, who got a job dancing in a nightclub, where she used the *Phoebe* stage name. Diane was in awe of her glamorous older sister, and often asked her to tell her all about her adventures in the New York nightlife. Phoebe talked about the club owner taking a shining to her, and also a really handsome, slick and rich young man named Nathan. She was so smitten that she carried around a picture of him. Unfortunately, it was photograph with Margaret in it. The way Nathan and Margaret were posed, she couldn't cut his wife out and keep him in the image. Before long, Ruth found herself in the family way, and told Diane she didn't know what to do. Nathan Reed was married and he wasn't going to disrupt the gravy train—in his words—by getting a divorce. He dropped Ruth (Phoebe) and disappeared from the nightclub. Ruth was desperate. The club owner told her it was her own fault and said she was out of a job when her pregnancy started to show. Ruth felt she couldn't tell their parents about the situation. They were strict and had no idea that their daughter was involved in the nightclub scene. She told them she'd been helping out on the night shift at the veteran's shelter, and they chose to believe her. It was easier for them to ignore any clues they might have seen in her behavior than to have to admit to themselves that she was possibly running around town, even though the signs were there—traces of makeup, scents of smoke and liquor, bloodshot eyes.

Heartbroken, scared and desperate, Ruth had decided that since Nathan had ditched her, she'd go right to the source and demand money from his wife. She traced Margaret Reed out in the suburbs and paid her a visit one afternoon, telling her about the baby and exaggerating Nate's affection for her.

Ruth asked Margaret to give her money, or she claimed she would tell her story to the newspapers. Margaret didn't want anything to do with the situation. She tossed Ruth out without giving her a dime.

Ruth came home and worked herself into a lather over the following week. She hyperventilated and started to get cramps. Diane had to tell her parents that Ruth needed medical attention. She ended up in the hospital and miscarried, then died from the complications. Diane felt her sister had died of a broken heart.

Diane moved away from home by the time she was eighteen, determined not to end up like her sister. Truth was, she was not falling far from the tree. She moved to Los Angeles, thinking she could become a movie star, but not ending up with the kinds of roles she could write home about. She waited tables to make ends meet. Then one day on her coffee break, she came across the *Photoplay* magazine that had the photo of Joyce Jones, Daphne Huntington-Smythe and Margot Williams. Diane did a double take and realized it looked just like Margaret Reed, or at least the picture Ruth had of her. Diane had taken a handful of Ruth's possessions when she'd moved out west, including that photo that her sister had kept. She compared the two images when she got back to her apartment and felt it was worth following up her hunch in Santa Lucia.

She kept an eye on Margot for a few days, staying at Mrs. Coleman's Boarding House and getting a job at the Poppy Lane Tearoom across the street from Poppy Cove. She was pretty sure that Margot was Margaret, and one day casually walked up to her house while she knew Margot was away. She found a key near the front door and let herself in, checking out the house. As she entered, she could have sworn she heard a woman calling, "Yoo-hoo!" from outside, but ignored it.

Diane carefully went through Margot's house, and got the confirmation of her hunch when she came across her paperwork in her lingerie drawer, indicating all of her legal names and statuses. Even though she wasn't surprised to find out what Margot had done, Diane still felt shocked and didn't know what to do. She decided to play it cool, keep her head down, stay at her job and watch Margot from a distance.

As she calmed down, she thought maybe she could just talk to her, let her know about Ruth. To be fair, maybe Margot had no idea what had happened to her sister after that day. Then one day, she came home from work and to her surprise, Nathan Reed had checked into Mrs. Coleman's.

He was slick and handsome, just like Ruth had said. He tried to pick her up, and when she mildly rebuffed him, moved on to Jeannette, right under her nose. When Jeannette said no, Nate managed to get involved with Teresa, bringing her to the boarding house during visiting hours.

Nate started asking questions—innocently at first—about Poppy Cove and Margot, to Mrs. Coleman, then concentrating on Jeannette once he found out she was working there. He turned on the charm, inquiring further about the business, but more specifically, regarding Margot and the state of her finances.

Diane watched all of this from a distance, getting to know everyone better. Margot seemed like a good person, but Diane still felt she had to pay for what had happened to Ruth. And to have Nathan there, the real culprit in her sister's demise, well, that was fate and Diane had to play her part in it.

Diane remembered seeing the gun in Margot's drawer and had a plan. She'd steal it, shoot Nathan and frame Margot for it. She grinned, satisfied that her scheme would vindicate her sister and give her peace. She went back to Margot's the following night, the same way she came in before but left through the open bedroom window, as Margot had come home, this time with a man.

Diane kept an eye on Nathan and his activities on the fateful Saturday. She trailed him, along with his date Teresa, to Bud's. She stayed in the front bar, being entertained by the local television and radio personality/lush, Dirk Roberts. She saw Teresa leave with some other man and eventually Nate was escorted out by two thugs. She followed them all back to the boarding house, but stayed hidden in the bushes, observing. Nate go up to his room quietly while they waited for him outside. He then joined them on the porch and they took a package from him. Then they gave him a couple of strong punches for good measure. "Interest," one of them called it.

Diane came out into sight once she was sure the thugs were gone. Nate saw her and made small talk, suggesting they go for a walk to clear their heads since neither of them were sleeping anyway. Diane couldn't believe her luck. She had the gun in her coat pocket, just in case an opportunity arose for her to get justice.

The fog was rolling in and the air was cool. They walked down to the beach, not saying much. Then she slowly started mentioning where she was from, exposing more and more about her sister, until Nate finally clued into what she was telling him.

He casually asked, "Oh, yeah, how is old Phoebe these days?"

Diane's jaw dropped. "She's dead, you creep."

He looked at her blankly and gave a shrug. "Gee, that's too bad." He had no idea yet just how bad.

By this time, they were out on the wharf and completely alone, surrounded by a blanket of thick fog. She took out the gun and pointed it at his chest. She told him the full reason for Ruth's death, all the while maintaining a steady hand on the pistol.

Nate registered a look of shock and began to protest. Diane had never fired a gun before, but it did the job as she followed her rage. He flew back and landed in the water. She quickly pocketed the gun and ran back to the boarding house in a panic.

What she didn't count on was Jeannette Fox seeing her come back. "Where's Nate?" she whispered when she saw Diane come back alone. She'd been sitting in the front parlor.

Diane was startled and felt to see if the gun was still hidden. In her fumbling, she dropped it out of her pocket, then quickly hid it again. She looked at Jeannette and when she saw the look on the girl's face, she knew Jeannette had seen it.

"What did you do to Nathan?" Jeannette gasped. Diane stepped towards her, clamping her hand over the girl's mouth and grabbing Jeannette by the arm with her other one. Without thinking, she took her down the walk and into her car before Jeannette could get away.

Jeannette tried to get out of the car, but Diane took the pistol and conked her on the head, knocking her out.

Diane reached into her other coat pocket and found her car keys. She started driving away, not sure where to go. Then she remembered the deserted shack on the far end of the beach where she'd gone when she'd wanted to be alone and think. She thought it was as good a place as any to keep Jeannette while she figured out what to do next. After she got back to the boarding house, she slipped into Jeannette's room and took her coat and purse to make it look like she'd left on purpose. She stored them in the closet of the tearoom, where Lana assumed they belonged to Diane and never questioned her.

By the next day, Nathan's body had washed up on the beach, and his murder case began. Diane watched it all unfold from the tearoom, pleased that Margot was going to get what she felt she deserved for Ruth and the baby.

Diane still had the gun, but the police were crawling all over everywhere. The longer she played the wide-eyed outsider, the better. Somehow though, she planned to get the gun back to the house. It would be the final nail in Margot's coffin. She'd have to do it carefully, however, and not draw suspicion to herself. She and Margot weren't acquainted well enough for Diane to casually get invited into her house where she could slip the gun back. But she could pretend she was her again and use the key if she was convincing enough. She watched Margot, mimicked her mannerisms and walk, and when Margot went out instead of coming home right after work on Saturday, Diane had her chance.

Then, of course, all hell broke loose for Margot, and all that was left for Diane to do was to get Miss Fox out of the way. She had checked on her Wednesday or Thursday—she couldn't remember which—gave her some food and water, and told her to keep quiet. She re-secured her ties and placed in a new gag and then left her for days in that shack. She wasn't sure what state she'd find her captive in when she returned. Maybe Jeannette would be weak enough that Diane could just toss her in the ocean, out with the tide, or maybe she'd be deceased already. She now realized there were some things she hadn't thought out too clearly.

Diane had parked in the Emma Wood State Beach parking lot early Sunday morning. There were already others enjoying the day, but no one saw her walk in the other direction. She knew things were out of control, but it was all going to be over soon. Then as she was muttering out some random ideas of what to do next with Miss Fox, Daphne and her date had barged into the cabin and ruined it all for her.

Now sitting handcuffed in an interrogation room, she knew there was nothing more to say. Whatever she'd done and whatever book they'd throw at her, she now knew it wouldn't bring back Ruth. "Well, that was a waste," she replied.

EPILOGUE

Saturday, June 14th was a day that would always be remembered among the Poppy Cove crew. Margot Williams had hopefully had her last name change when she became Mrs. Margot Malone. It was a delightful and intimate affair, with just close friends and family, held in the Santa Lucia Public Rose Gardens, across from the ocean side beach.

The bride wore a demure blush silk gown of her own creation. It had cap sleeves in an overlapping petal design, which was mimicked in the floor length skirt with a scoop neck bodice featuring a delicate pearl trim. The maid of honor, Daphne, and bridesmaid Loretta Simpson wore similar designs, but with shorter skirts, finishing at the knee and an unadorned neckline, in a rosier, deeper pink tone. They all wore natty little pink pill box hats, with Margot's including a veil. The groom, Mr. Tom Malone, looked very dapper in his full police dress uniform, along with his best man Daniel Henshaw and Bruce Jenkins as his groomsman. They were very handsome in new slim, black suits and white shirts.

Mr. Anthony and his assistant Todd from the beauty parlor around the corner fussed and fretted all through the reception, until Loretta took Mr. Anthony aside and told him she knew where she could stuff his can of hair spray so that he wouldn't be able to remove it himself. He sat down and pouted in the corner as Todd consoled him with copious amounts of martinis. Lana served refreshments with her new staff member, Teresa Abbott, who' finally settled down and promised her father she would stay out of trouble. Turned out she could make swell jellied salads, too.

The Poppy Cove staff was in full attendance, including Jeannette, who'd made a full recovery from her episode with Diane. Marjorie was pleased as punch and was surrounded by her sewing staff, all proud to have had a small hand in creating the wedding attire. Betty brought her husband Dwight, who polished off at least two sandwiches each time Lana or Teresa circulated through the reception. Irene brought a date—Michael Weathers, of all people.

Poppy Cove's best clientele was there as well. Mrs. Falconer, Mrs. Marshall, Mrs. Morgan, Mrs. Peacock, and also Mrs. Givens—who couldn't get enough of the clothes—along with their husbands. Henry and Claire Worth, Daphne's parents, Patricia and Gerald Huntington-Smythe, as well as the Mayor and Mrs. Stinson were also there. Dorothy and George Willmington, who'd gone back home after Margot was absolved, returned for the event. Margot's father proudly walked her down the aisle, but not before taking Tom aside the day before, telling him to take good care of their girl.

"Well, I knew she was innocent all along," Nancy Lewis sniffed, while her husband Andrew rolled his eyes and Babs stood awkwardly, looking for a way to escape. Nancy latched her arm through her daughter's, keeping her close to her side. She carried on, speaking to Margot's parents between bites of petit-fours. "Oh, yes, I knew she was one of us, our kind, right from the beginning. By the way, did I ever tell you I was related to Danish royalty?" Nancy would drag out the story anytime she had an audience.

The road to the wedding had gone fairly smooth. As soon as the police had a confession from Diane, they released Margot and reinstated Tom. He'd been at the station that day, helping Jenkins bring in Diane, suspension be damned. That evening, Margot went back to her place and finally gave him the full answer to his question and they began to plan the wedding. They told her parents the next morning at brunch, where the Willmingtons met Tom for the first time and begrudgingly admitted that this particular 'beat cop' might, in fact, be good enough for their daughter.

Margot surrendered her gun to the police station, saying that she no longer wanted it or registered as her possession. She had never felt comfortable that she had it, even when she traveled, and never wanted to see it again. It was needed as evidence, but after Diane's trial, it would remain as Santa Lucia Police Department property. As for the relationship between Detectives Malone and Riley, it needed some time and effort, but they learned to work together again. Jack Riley apologized to both his friend Tom and to Margot, saying that maybe he'd been a bit too zealous in his pursuit of justice. They both accepted his apology, but with a guarded, 'we'll see' feeling. So far, Riley had proven to be kinder and more respectful of Margot whenever he saw her.

As the case unfolded, Margot had learned more about Ruth and Diane. Margot had felt bad when she'd heard about poor Ruth, and would have never left the girl in such dire circumstances if she'd known what had happened after Ruth visited her. Margot asked Henry in his legal capacity if he could learn anything more about Ruth's miscarriage and subsequent death. He found out that, according to her medical records, she'd already had a series of bad episodes in the pregnancy before she'd confronted Margot, and in her doctor's medical opinion, there may have been nothing that could have changed the outcome of her situation.

Even after learning the information regarding Ruth and all that Diane had done, Margot still felt bad for the Phillips girls and asked Henry to represent Diane, offering to help financially if needed. He willingly took on the case, and the more that he found out about Diane and her grief, the more that it appeared she might have a case for an instability or insanity plea. In addition, she'd said that she only meant to scare Nate, not kill him. If Henry could build up a convincing case, he believed he could decrease the degree of murder she could be convicted of, possibly eliminating a death sentence verdict. There were so many charges against her, ranging from unlawful entry, possession of a handgun, kidnapping, and, of course, murder—to name a few. Indeed, claiming that she was insane may not have been totally off the mark. Personally, Henry was loving the legal challenge, but he kept that to himself.

At the wedding, Daphne and Margot had a chance for a brief heart to heart following the ceremony in a private powder room. "So you never did tell me. Before the whole incident with Diane, did you have a chance to 'experience the mystery of love' with Daniel?" Margot asked with a grin.

"No! Actually, he was thinking the same thing I was and, well, that's what we were going into the shack for!"

Margot laughed. "Oh dear."

"I know. Anyway, once all was calmed down, the most wonderful thing happened. I didn't want to take away from your thunder, so I was waiting until after your wedding to announce it." Daphne looked around to make sure they were still alone. "Daniel's asked me to marry him! And do you know what I said?"

"I'm going to guess yes?"

"That's right! We haven't set a date yet, but sometime before too long. And, we've decided to wait. Isn't that just too darling? I mean, I know it's a little old-fashioned, but it just seems right. We'll probably get married in the fall, I think I'd lose my mind if I waited too long."

"That's wonderful!" Margot hugged her friend. "By the way, did you ever go back to pose for Adonis?"

"You know, I went back about a couple of weeks after the whole thing with Diane. I had some cuts and bruises from that day and wanted to wait for them to heal. Anyway, when I went back there, the place was empty. He was gone, cleared out lock, stock and barrel, with no forwarding address or phone number. He owed some people money, so I think he just took off as quickly as he arrived."

"So that was enough adventure and daring for you?" Margot asked.

"For now," Daphne replied with a wink.

THE END

*Margot and Daphne's Crooners and Tunes to
Get you in the Mood to Swoon!*

Pat Boone's romantic and mellow voice is easy listening
that's sure to set the right mood for any evening, whether
it's out on the beach or in a cozy cabin.

Paul Anka has the girls in such a swoon that they're all
are ready to change their names. He's a swell singer—
now if he'd only write a song for Barbara Jean!

Jimmie Rodgers has a sweet and easy way of carrying a
tune that makes everyone want to sing along, while
driving down the coast on a clear sunny day. Although
there are sure to be some Santa Lucians we'd rather not
hear.

The Everly Brothers have the tunes to start your day off
right. You'll be smiling from the time your toes hit the
floor.

Miles Davis is a master of jazz that will give you that late
night, last call feeling. Believe me, yours truly knows all
about the last call!

The Champs are sure to have you up on the dance floor
and joining any conga line that's forming, especially
when *Tequila* is playing and flowing!

Johnny Mathis puts anyone who's listening in a romantic
and wistful mood. Don't forget to call your sweetheart
when you hear him singing because "chances are" they'll
be wearing a silly grin too!

Ella Fitzgerald will bring a warm and toasty feeling to any romance when love is on the menu. Especially if the songbird is singing from the songbook of Mr. Irving Berlin.

Frank Sinatra is a crooner to end all crooners! He makes all the girls swoon. Frankie, oh, Frankie, who will you be serenading tonight? They're sure to want to fly away with you.

Elvis Presley—well, guys and gals, all we can say is those hips and those hits just kept coming! Well, now *I'm All Shook Up* and going back to a swell party!

ABOUT THE AUTHORS

 Barbara Jean Coast is the pen name of authors Andrea Taylor and Heather Shkuratoff, both of whom reside in Kelowna, BC, Canada. Barbara Jean, however, is a resident of Santa Lucia, California (eerily similar to Santa Barbara), where she enjoys long lunches, cocktail parties, and fancy dinner dates with attractive and attentive gentlemen. Her interests include Alfred Hitchcock movies, reading Carolyn Keene, music by popular musicians, such Frank Sinatra and Tony Bennett, shopping for new dresses, attending society events and always looking fabulous in kitten heels. A NATE TO REMEMBER is her third novel in the Poppy Cove Mystery series.

 Andrea Taylor always imagined herself being a supersleuth girl detective and writing adventurous stories, full of mystery and intrigue since she was old enough to hold a pencil. She resides in Kelowna, BC, Canada, where she writes under the pen name of Barbara Jean Coast with her co-author friend, Heather Shkuratoff, and travels often to California to further develop the stories and escapades of the Poppy Cove Mystery series. Andrea has also published freelance articles about fashion, current events, and childcare, and is currently blogging on Wordpress about creativity and poetry, as well as researching for her own literary novels.

 As an avid mystery reader, Heather Shkuratoff joined lifelong friend Andrea Taylor to create the Poppy Cove Mystery series, written under the pen name of Barbara Jean Coast. Growing up in a family of talented crafters and sewers, Heather developed her own skills to become a dressmaker and designer, which helps to give rich detail and character to their stories. She lives in Kelowna, BC, Canada, but spends much time in California, researching for the novels and doing her best to live like Barbara Jean.

PRAISE FOR *Death of a Beauty Queen*

"*Death of a Beauty Queen* is a fast-moving book with many interesting characters. The fast action, rich background information and various red herrings make for a compelling read that is difficult to put down."
—Emma Pivato,
author of the Claire Burke Mystery series

"If Austen ever wrote about greed and murder, I imagine it would come out something like Coast's book."
—LuAnn Braley,
Back Porchervations

"Lots of fifties' fashion, lots of flirting, and most importantly of all, a very well-crafted mystery at the heart of it all."
—Kate Eileen Shannon,
Rantin' Ravin' and Reading,
author of the Brigid Kildare Mystery series

"No matter what the year or what the setting, leave it to jealousy, crime and murder to ruin what can be a great time. Author Barbara Jean Coast delivers a story that is entertaining, keeps your attention and leaves you wondering what the ladies will get into next."
—Cyrus Webb,
Conversations LIVE Host,
Conversations Book Club President

CPSIA information can be obtained at www.ICGtesting.com
Printed in the USA
LVOW10s1542200515

439230LV00003B/669/P